Breathless Love

The Bennetts of Langston Falls, Book 3

KG Fletcher

FAIR WARNING: This book contains scenes of detailed intimacy, adult language, and violence. It is intended for readers 18+

Breathless Love

The Bennetts of Langston Falls – Book Three

The characters and events in this book are fictitious. Any similarity to real persons, living or dead, places, or events is coincidental and not intended by the author.

If you purchase this book without a cover you should be aware that this book may have been stolen property and reported as "unsold and destroyed" to the publisher. In such case the author has not received any payment for this "stripped book."

For a complete list of
KG's books visit: **www.kgfletcherauthor.com**

Editor - Vicky Burkholder

Cover art by Once Upon a Cover

This book, or parts thereof, may not be reproduced in any form without permission. The copying, scanning, uploading, and distribution of this book via the internet or via any other means without the permission of the publisher is illegal and punishable by law. Please purchase only authorized electronic or print editions, and do not participate in or encourage piracy of copyrighted materials. Your support of the author's rights is appreciated.

Copyright © 2023 by Kelly Genelle Fletcher

All rights reserved.

ISBN: 978-1-7377472-4-6   ASIN: B0BT57YL4Y

Printed in the United States of America.

Breathless Love

A Small Town Friends to Lovers Romance (The Bennetts of Langston Falls, Book 3)

He's chasing his honky-tonk dreams. She's Nashville songwriter royalty. Will a road trip together set them on a passionate course toward their hearts' desire?

Being a country music star is Hank Bennett's ultimate goal. But after his band breaks up, he's at a crossroads pondering his fate between music and working on the family farm. Lonely, libated, and a little bit lost, he attends the hometown concert of his country music idol, Travis Miller.

But he never expected to cross paths with Travis's gorgeous songwriting sister, Ella Mae.

She's outgoing, easy to talk to, and has several music awards under her belted daisy dukes. There's something magical and mesmerizing about a successful female artist penning chart-topping country love ballads, and he's smitten.

When Ella invites Hank to join them on the road during the last three weeks of the exciting tour, these kindred spirits can't fight their attraction anymore – and his chivalry and wooing antics pay off into a night of unforgettable passion. She's unleashed something inside him, and he's unlocking her desires one by one. But a small town musician wannabe like him has no place in Ella Mae's thrilling tour life when her famous brother becomes jealous of their unmistakable duo.

Will their shared harmony lead Hank toward country music stardom? Or will the dark side of fame steer him off course, leaving him a heartbroken farmer?

For everyone with a dream that seems impossible:
Sometimes opportunity shows up when you're too busy
looking for something else.

Chapter One
Hank Bennett

Hank Bennett was in an inebriated funk.

Slurping the foamy top of yet another cold beer, he staggered away from the concession stand before the liquid overflowed down the sides of his opaque plastic cup. The outdoor concert was in full swing as he perused the sparse crowd milling about the refreshment area, most fans in their seats watching the live show. A wave of applause surged through the air as one song segued into another. This familiar tune was one of Hank's favorites, the country music upbeat and catchy.

Closing his eyes, he hummed along for a few stanzas before his shoulders sagged, and a wave of disappointment washed over him again. Too bad none of his songs would ever receive the kind of accolades and ovation Travis Miller's demanded. The two-time CMA award winner was one of Hank's idols who inspired him to pursue his own dreams of recording and performing country music. Since he was a young boy, he focused on bending his guitar strings and creating original songs for anyone who would listen.

But no one was listening to his songs—not anymore. He was reduced to nothing more than a fan now, his dreams dashed and destroyed before they even had a chance to get off the ground.

The long-time group he fronted, known as The Bonafide Band, broke up last spring, his buddies he'd played with since high school going their separate ways after an extended trip to Nashville. They'd spent a few weeks in the music city recording some of Hank's original songs at a legit sound studio. Hank spent an exorbitant amount of money just to hear his music professionally recorded, his goal of having his own album finally within reach, or so he thought. Producing music was tedious, time-consuming, and expensive, but he loved every second of the experience. His band, not so much. Sure, they thought it was cool to hear themselves on the tracks, and they even got up on a few Nashville honkey-tonk stages at open-mic nights and played for the live crowds while they were in town for their extended stay.

But when it was all said and done, his bass player decided he wanted to settle down and get married to his long-time girlfriend. His lead guitarist headed back to college to finish his degree. And his drummer opted to get out of the south altogether and backpack across Europe. Hank was a lone musician for the first time in his life, and the thought of trying to put together a new band was daunting.

"Hey, cowboy. You wanna buy a t-shirt?"

Hank jerked his head in the direction of the southern female voice, his stumbled movements causing the beer in his cup to slosh onto the front of his black tee.

"Ahh, fuck," he lamented, raising his arms out from his sides.

"Sorry about that. I didn't mean to startle you," the woman giggled. She came from around the counter of a souvenir shack. The pop-up business was conveniently located near the venue's exit, where concertgoers could grab an official keepsake on their way out to the parking lot after the show. Travis Miller's handsome face was everywhere, on shirts and posters, koozies and key chains, the crooner looking like a model out of a *GQ Magazine* with his chiseled face and signature smile.

Hank flicked his free hand before palming the front of his soaked shirt. "I'm the one who's sorry, ma'am," he slurred.

"Sorry about what?" Her hands were planted on her hips as she grinned back at him.

He noticed her toned and tanned bare legs, her daisy dukes frayed around the edges of her ample bootie. She wore flip-flops, and her toenails were painted a bright aqua-blue. As his eyes roamed upward over the rest of her body, his nostrils flared when his tipsy gaze landed on her face. Damn, she was pretty. Dark brown eyes stared, her long lashes flirty and blinking with humor. She had her brunette hair fashioned into two long braids trailing over her shoulders to the middle of her buxom chest, her crop top revealing more tanned skin around her middle.

"What are you sorry for?" she repeated.

"I beg your pardon?" He swayed uneasily, shifting in his cowboy boots on the hard ground. What had they been talking about?

"You said, 'Sorry about that.' Tell me what you're sorry for."

Hank furrowed his brow and took a quick gulp of what was left of his beer, the country music in the air thrumming through his being. "I have no fucking idea," he mumbled, swiping his wet lips with the back of his free hand. And then it suddenly dawned on him.

"Ah-ha!" he exclaimed, raising his index finger into the air. He gallantly took off his cowboy hat and pressed it against his chest. "I remember now. I'm sorry for using profanity in your presence. My daddy always taught me not to curse in front of a lady."

Awkwardly, he dipped his body in an attempt at a chivalrous bow. But his boots slid right out from under him on the hard-packed dirt, and he dropped his hat, falling in slow motion to his denim-covered knees. The plastic cup tumbled from his fingers and spilled.

"Oh, no!" The woman squealed. She raised her hands to cover her mouth as if squelching another giggle as he made a complete fool of himself in front of her.

Sitting back on his haunches, Hank disappointedly watched the last of his beverage seep into the parched ground. Scratching the stubble on his chin, he shrugged. "No use crying over spilled beer." He ran his hands through his sweaty curls before picking up his cowboy hat and settling it back on his head. The humidity in the middle of summer was oppressive in the mountain town, this week in particular one of the hottest on record. Looking up at the pretty woman, sweat trickled down the sides of his face, and his eyelids felt heavy from overindulging.

"You look a little lonely," she commented.

"Nah." He waved her off. "In limbo, maybe. Butt-faced, definitely. Lonely? Never." Hank harrumphed, carefully easing his tired body up off the ground. "You wanna join me for a fresh one?"

Her smile was immediate, the color of her eyes reminding him of melted chocolate. "I'm working right now. But I've got a cooler full of water bottles. Why don't you drink one of those and keep me company while you... cool off a little?"

Sweat trickled down his cheeks, the thought of a cold sip of water tempting. Perhaps she was right? He needed a break from the booze and a moment to cool off. And besides, he was downright parched.

"Thanks. I think I will take you up on that water." He slapped the dirt off his jeans.

"Good." She smiled.

Hank watched her enter the souvenir hut and disappear behind the counter for a second. When she reappeared, she offered him an icy bottle of water over the ledge. "Here you go."

"Thanks." He took the bottle, twisted the top off, and guzzled half the contents before coming up for air. The woman in front of him stared, her eyebrows hitched with curiosity. "What?" he panted, sliding the chilled plastic across his sweaty brow. God, it felt so damn good.

"You're cute, and I'm Ella Mae." She thrust her hand over the counter to shake his.

Hank licked his lips and carefully set the water bottle next to a stack of neatly folded t-shirts for sale. He did a double-take imagining Travis Miller frowning in the image. Goodness, was he that drunk? Reaching for her hand, he awkwardly leaned forward and pressed his cool lips against her skin, his eyes never leaving hers.

"My name is Hank Bennett. And I'm pleased to meet you, Ella Mae."

Her pink mouth lifted into another one of her dazzling smiles. "Did your daddy teach you that trick, too?"

"Nope. That's all me, Ella Mae. It's a Hank Bennett Special." He gave her one of his signature smirks, hoping she was impressed.

"Easy, fella. I think you need to finish your water." She broke their connection and handed off the half-drunk bottle.

Hank winked and took a sip. "So where'd you get the name Ella Mae from? It's... pretty." He watched her demurely tilt her head as if pleased.

"My daddy was a musician and a huge fan of Ella Fitzgerald, and my grandmother's name was Mae. Put the two together, and you get—"

"Ella Mae," Hank spoke with exuberance. "I love it."

"So... you like Travis Miller's music?" She rested her forearms on the counter and leaned forward as the wail of a steel guitar floated through the air.

Hank noticed the front of her crop top gape, where he caught a glimpse of her lacy bra underneath. A rush of heat surged across his cheeks, and he took a hefty gulp of cold water to cool his surging libido. Damn, she was easy on his eyes.

"I do. Travis is the reason I got into music."

"Oh, so you're a musician, too?" She perked up with interest.

"I thought I was." Hank crushed the empty plastic bottle in his hand, the dejected tone of his voice noticeable.

They were interrupted by a pair of concertgoers who eagerly pointed out t-shirts they wanted to buy, Ella Mae going into sales mode. "Hold that thought." She winked.

Hank watched as she convinced the pair to buy more than just tees. By the end of their five-minute shopping spree, they'd bought matching koozies, baseball hats, and a keychain. As Ella Mae rang them up, he strolled around the side of the stand to an area overlooking the amphitheater audience with a fantastic view of the stage. Travis Miller was smack dab in the middle, lit up in the giant orb of a spotlight, his vocals smooth in a rare ballad among another weeping swell of a steel guitar. Sighing, Hank shoved his hands into his jeans pockets and listened.

From the first moment he held a guitar at the tender age of eight, he knew he wanted to play music for a living. For the most part, his large family encouraged him. His three older brothers and baby sister on the family farm showered him with positive reactions to the silly tunes he'd written and played for anyone who would listen over the years. Those immature songs turned into better songs the older he got, and when he put together his band, he was confident he had what it took to make it in the world of country music. Yeah, like every other dumbass with stars in their eyes.

His hometown of Langston Falls, Georgia, welcomed him and his bandmates with open arms into every bar, restaurant, charity event, and festival that came through town, proud to support one of their own. His family's Christmas tree farm and winery also held annual events, and he'd become the main attraction over the last couple of years thanks to his event-planning sister, Becky. But performing for the local fans he grew up with was one thing—going on the road and playing for strangers was quite another altogether.

Sure, he and his band had fun on the road playing all the popular dive bars in and around his home state of Georgia. But the money could have been better, and the cheap hotels and long hours on the road quickly began to wear on everyone.

Folks outside of Langston Falls didn't want to hear his original music. They wanted to listen to covers, the popular music, so they could dance. Hank thought if they could get some original music recorded, they might be able to find a good agent who could find them better gigs. But the competition was fierce, and Hank and his buddies were novices compared to some of the more seasoned bands out on the road. During their brief stint in Nashville, Hank quickly found out his friends weren't as committed as he was, and now he was faced with a decision: should he continue to pursue his dream without them? Or should he give up and work full-time on the family farm?

"Hey, Travis is winding down, and the show will be over soon." Ella Mae came up beside him, twirling one of her braids in her hand. "Are you here with people? With a group of friends, or maybe... a date?"

Hank looked at her and noticed a few freckles smattered across the bridge of her nose. Her large doe eyes did funny things to his insides. "Uh... no. I'm here by myself tonight."

"Great!" She smiled. "I mean..." She laughed and shrugged, not finishing her sentence. The deafening crowd roared as Travis finished his last song, the audience chanting, "one more song" over and over.

"Listen, Hank. I'm gonna be slammed with customers after Travis performs his encore. But when I'm finished, you want to join me for that beer?"

Hank nodded, the thought of spending more time with the cute t-shirt-selling country girl tempting. "Sure. I know of a few bars in Langston Falls."

"We don't have to go anywhere. We can go backstage to the Green Room. They always have a ton of food and drinks for everyone after the performance while the tech crew breaks down the equipment." She made it sound so easy, as if she casually hung out with the famous Travis Miller entourage daily.

"Wow. That's so cool they let you do that."

"Why? Because I'm a lowly t-shirt girl?" There was a definitive challenge in her tone underneath her smile.

Hank shook his head with embarrassment. "No, I didn't mean it that way—"

"I know," she interrupted. "I was just teasing you. I'm not usually the one selling t-shirts. I'm helping out Martina and her husband tonight. They're usually the ones promoting Travis's merchandise, but they had a family wedding in Biloxi. Believe it or not, I'm a musician, too."

Hank's mouth gaped. "You are?" Things were getting interesting. "Do you write? Do you play or sing?"

"Yes, yes, and… yes," she laughed. The happy sound was music to his ears.

"That's amazing. I'd love to hear some of your stuff sometime. Hey, maybe we could collaborate on something, too." He didn't mean to come across so desperate, the exorbitant amount of beers he'd consumed definitely messing with his filters. He cleared his throat to get a grip.

"But you're probably leaving tonight, driving to the next venue for another show, huh?"

"Not necessarily," she said.

"What do you mean?"

Ella Mae turned to see a few customers perusing the shack. "I gotta go tend to business." She tucked a stray hair over her ear and looked right at him, her provocative chocolate gaze causing his toes to curl in his boots. "But after that, I want to introduce you to my brother, Travis."

Before her words registered in his brain, she skipped away as if she'd ding-dong-ditched him. "Wait... *what?*"

"You heard me," she yelled over her shoulder. More patrons filed out of the amphitheater, a line starting to form in front of the shack.

Hank didn't know what to do at that moment. His earlier beer buzz vanished in a flash as a new sensation took over his body. The air was heavy with music and the smell of summer, thick with dreams and possibility. It was sensory overload between the crowd's roaring applause and the pretty smile on Ella Mae's face. Country music superstar Travis Miller was *her brother*?

His mother's voice echoed in his mind, her words often reminding him of the life he'd only dreamt about:

Opportunity is not a lengthy visitor.

Maybe the universe was throwing him a bone, the weird coincidence giving him the nudge he desperately needed. Perhaps his desire to be a musician wasn't over after all? Meeting Travis was a thrilling thought, the country music artist his idol.

But meeting Ella Mae was special, too. Meeting the beautiful female musician was an unexpected twist of fate.

Chapter Two
Ella Mae

Ella Mae was excited for the first time in over two months since they boarded the tour bus in Nashville and headed out on the road for the three-month tour. She loved the gypsy lifestyle, going to sleep every night to the hum of the bus wheels on asphalt and waking up in a new town the following day.

But after a few weeks, traveling took a toll on her and her brother. She missed her giant bed back home on her quiet farm in Franklin, Tennessee. She missed her scrappy dog, Lucky, and her brood of chickens. Her travel routine had turned monotonous, lately setting up shop at each venue and dealing with excited, often drunk fans every night while Martina and her husband were in Biloxi. Her favorite time of day was sound check when she filled in for her brother, Travis, and strummed his guitars and sang in his microphone until the sound was dialed in. She also looked forward to hanging out with him on their tour bus, collaborating on new music but only if he was in the mood.

Travis.

Her big brother was her only family and legal guardian after their parents died in a car crash when she was seventeen. He took care of her, working odd jobs until she graduated high school, the two of them often writing music together to cope with their grief.

Within weeks of receiving her diploma, she challenged Travis to take a chance. They drove all the way to California, where he auditioned and landed a spot competing on a popular television singing show. Even though he was eliminated in the playoffs that season, Nashville came calling. They ended up moving full-time to the music city where Travis signed his first record deal, releasing his debut EP to rave reviews. It didn't take long for his career to skyrocket, Ella Mae right beside him and cheering him on every step of the way.

The brother and sister became a writing duo, collaborating on Travis's signature music. One of Ella's most significant achievements was writing the lyrics to his first hit song, which won him a CMA award. Ella could sing and play guitar too, but she preferred to stay out of the spotlight, being there for her brother whenever he needed her. She would never forget his first extensive tour with an entire entourage playing to sold-out venues and festivals, glad she could still be a part of the music world through their joint creations without facing the fans. She'd much rather stay behind the scenes writing and crafting hit songs, leaving her brother to navigate the fame and notoriety.

Now, Ella Mae was used to the spectacle of Travis's stardom, their roles reversed as she ensured he was taken care of while they were on the road. The entertainment business was shady at times, some of the folks they met or worked with luring her brother into unsavory after hours. The excessive drinking, drugs, and strippers had taken a toll on their bond over the years, and at one point, she almost left him and the music biz altogether.

But Travis being Travis, convinced her to stay because he needed someone to help keep him accountable and stay on the right track. It also helped that she received legit songwriting credits on his albums, the royalties alone helping her purchase her little piece of land and refurbish her house in Tennessee free and clear. So far, so good this tour go-around, the three months of shows in the Southeast going well without any mishaps.

Enter Hank Bennett. He was a game-changer in Ella Mae's eyes. The lanky, handsome musician was just what the doctor ordered. She needed a friend, and a friend who also happened to be a musician was a bonus. Sure, she hung out with Travis's bandmates, their wives or girlfriends, and crew all day long. But these talented players and workers were part of Travis' world, not hers. Meeting a new friend on tour to call her own was a nice change.

Boxing up the last of the shirts, she secured the mobile credit card reader and the cash she'd collected during the show in her bag looped over her head and flicked off the lights. One of the crew would be by soon to haul the boxes to the bus and store them underneath in the cargo hold until the next show.

"Hey," she said to Hank. He was in a daze watching the tech team break down the stage from afar. When he turned to greet her, she inhaled sharply, thrilled he'd waited for her. Damn, he was good-looking. "You ready?"

"Ready to meet Travis Miller? You better believe it."

Ella's heart sank. Maybe Hank was like all the others she'd tried to befriend while on tour, solely focused on meeting her famous brother. She couldn't blame him. Travis was a celebrity, and when most folks found out she was his sister, they turned star-struck and practically begged for an introduction. Silent, she walked ahead of Hank down a long aisle through the empty amphitheater toward the stage, the sound of his boots closely behind.

"Hold on, Ella Mae."

She ignored his plea to slow down and kept a fast pace, suddenly very tired from the long day. A cool shower, soft pajamas, and reading her latest romance book in her hotel room sounded like a nice consolation prize.

"I said, hold on." Hank gripped her by the arm and pulled her to a stop, his gaze tracing her features. "Was it something I said?"

Ella exhaled an exasperated puff of air through her nose. "I know you're more interested in meeting my brother than having a beer with me. I get it, and it's okay."

Hank rubbed his chin and furrowed his brow. "Of course, I'd love to meet your brother. I mean, any musician in his right mind would. But my first priority is hanging out with you. If Travis is too tired or too busy, it's no big deal. I can meet him another time. I want to hang out with *you*."

Ella's demeanor softened. "You sure about that? You sure you want to hang out with a simple t-shirt gal?" She batted her lashes at him with playfulness.

Hank's smile rivaled the full moon hanging above their heads as he looped his strong arm through hers. "Positive."

Crossing the expansive stage littered with cables among the roadies hard at work disassembling the sound equipment and gear, Ella grabbed Hank by the hand and pulled him through a narrow hallway toward the Green Room. The backstage hubbub was in full throttle, the crowd of lively people sipping cocktails and nibbling on snacks hard not to notice. Ella pulled two cold beers out of a galvanized tub full of ice and handed one to Hank.

"Thanks," he grinned.

The two twisted off the caps and clinked their bottles together before taking a swig, the icy beer hitting the spot. Ella noticed her friend and comrade, Willie Branson, and caught his attention. He was the road manager for Travis's tour.

"Willie!" She waved.

The man was a beast, his long flowing beard and matching hair beneath his tattered cowboy hat reminding her of country music sensation Chris Stapleton. Willie was a big 'ole teddy bear, his calm and easy-going nature a bonus on the road when it came to uptight venue personnel and crusty agents. Willie had a way with Travis, too. Ella touted him, the "Travis-Whisperer," because sometimes, when her brother got out of control, Willie was the only one who could bring him down a notch.

"Hey, darlin'! How'd it go tonight?" He gave her one of his signature bear hugs.

"Great. Willie, I'd like to introduce you to my new friend, Hank Bennett."

Hank's eyes went wide, looking up at Willie who towered over him. He shoved his hand out for a shake. "It's nice to meet you, Willie." The man's hand dwarfed Hank's by three sizes.

"Nice to meet you too, Hank. Where ya from?"

"Down the road in Langston Falls. My family owns a Christmas tree farm and winery on the outskirts of town called Bennett Farms."

This was the first time Ella had heard anything about Hank's family, and she was intrigued.

"You know, last time we played here, I took my wife on a tour of the Bennett Farms winery. Y'all sell a red wine called Big Red, right?"

Hank grinned with obvious pride. "We sure do. It's a staple in these parts. Did you like it?"

"Like it? I loved it! I even ordered a case and had it sent back home to Nashville."

Ella eyed Willie with chagrin. "I didn't know you were a connoisseur of wine."

Willie laughed in his throat, the sound heartfelt and guttural. He leaned in and whispered huskily, "Let's keep this information between the three of us, okay?"

"That's awesome." Hank was all at ease, donning a handsome smile during their exchange. Ella liked the way it made her feel.

"Hey, Willie, where's Travis?"

Willie tipped his head toward the hallway. "He's still in his dressing room, probably showering off. This damn humidity is gonna be the death of me. I don't know how Travis does it at these outdoor events. He looked like a drowned rat when he came offstage."

"I'll bet. I want to introduce him to Hank."

Hank immediately waved her off as if embarrassed. "No, that's okay. Let's give the man a break and finish our beers."

"It's fine, Hank. See ya later, Willie."

"See ya, darlin'."

She grabbed Hank's hand again and pulled him through the hallway.

"Seriously, Ella Mae, I don't want to disturb him while he's bathing."

Ella giggled. "You want to meet him or not?"

"I do, but—"

Ella stopped at the end of the hall in front of a closed dressing room door and banged her knuckles on the wood. "Travis? You decent?" She turned the knob and opened the door wide, her eyes landing on her brother.

He sat naked in a chair in front of a large makeup mirror with his back toward them. His eyes met hers in the reflection, and he wickedly grinned as an unfamiliar female face popped up from between his knees. She looked like a deer caught in the headlights.

Ella growled and marched toward the woman in a rage. "*Get out*!" she screamed.

"I'm going, I'm going," she hollered. Her southern accent was thick, and her lipstick was smeared across her mouth. She shoved her exposed tit back into her bra and pulled her lacey shirt into place.

Hank stood rigid against the doorframe, giving the female fan enough room to exit in an aggravated huff.

"See ya around, sweetheart!" Travis waved humorously. He shoved a damp towel over his exposed family jewels and leaned back in his seat without a care in the world.

"Seriously, Travis. How'd she end up in here? Where's security? Where the hell is Mario?"

"Oh, come on Ella-Bo-Bella. A little oral sex never hurt anyone. It relaxes me." His grin was wide, and his pearly whites glinted in the light from the bulbs surrounding the long mirror above a built-in ledge. "I see you made a friend, too." His tone held curiosity as his tired brown eyes ran the length of Hank Bennett's reflection in the doorway.

"As a matter of fact, I did. Travis, this is Hank. Hank, this is my shameful brother, Travis Miller. Please excuse his, uh, lack of clothing and good manners." She wrinkled her nose.

Hank didn't seem to mind Travis's naked disposition and slowly entered the room with wide-eyed wonderment. "It's a real pleasure to meet you, sir." He came up to his chair, stuck his hand out, and waited.

Travis's eyebrows arose, and he looked from Ella to Hank and back again. "Is this guy for real?"

Ella planted one hand on her hip and took a quick sip of beer. "Be cool, Travis," she admonished.

Travis waited for a beat before he stood from his chair, the towel falling from his crotch and exposing his thick cock for all to see.

Ella squealed and shielded her eyes as her brother smiled salaciously and pumped Hank's hand with vigor.

"It's nice to meet you, Romeo."

Chapter Three
Hank

Hank was dumbfounded, pumping Travis Miller's hand up and down in a shake. It didn't matter the man was butt-naked. Standing in the presence of his mega-star idol was a thrilling moment.

"You've got a strong grip there, fella. You work out?" Travis broke their connection and grabbed a pair of blue jeans hanging over a nearby chair.

"I, uh, work on a farm. Lots of manual labor," Hank managed.

Travis buttoned up his fly and picked up his wayward towel, flicking it at his sister. "You can turn around now, Peaches."

Ella Mae squealed at the sting of fabric whipping her bare leg and jerked the towel free from her brother's grip. "Knock it off." These two reminded Hank of his brothers and sister back at Bennett Farms.

Travis laughed, pulling on a tight black tee accentuating his muscular frame. Bending low, he focused on his reflection in the makeup mirror and ran his hands through his damp hair. "What kind of farm work? Crops? Horses?"

Hank couldn't believe he was having a real live conversation with Travis Miller. "Um, yes, sir. My family has a Christmas tree farm and winery in Langston Falls. There's always work that needs to be done in the vineyard and tree fields." He watched Travis sit and pull on his socks and cowboy boots.

"But Hank here is also a musician," Ella Mae chimed in.

Hank's eyes shot to hers, her pretty expression urging him on.

"Is that so?" Travis asked, giving his boot a final tug while giving Hank the once over.

"Um, yes, sir. I just finished recording some original music in Nashville a couple of months ago."

Travis stood and approached Hank, taking the beer out of his hand. His brow furrowed. "Cut the 'sir' bullshit, okay? If you're a musician, we're on the same page, buddy."

Hank swallowed hard. "Yes, sss...." He started to say "sir" but caught himself. "Okay."

"Call me Travis." He took a long pull from Hank's beer bottle before handing it back to him. "Any friend of Ella Mae's is my friend, too."

Hank nodded like a bobblehead doll, thrilled Travis called him buddy and friend. "Absolutely. Whatever you say, Travis."

"Cool. Well, when can I hear some of this music you recorded in Nashville?"

Hank's eyes went wide. Travis Miller wanted to hear his music? What the actual *fuck*?

"There'll be time for that later, Travis," Ella Mae interjected. "You need to get a move on and go greet your guests in the Green Room. They're all waiting for you. And no more beer, mister. I saw what you just did there. You're only one drink away from the devil."

Travis smirked.

"And if I catch you with that trailer trash again, I'm gonna be pissed," she added.

There was a twinkle in Travis's dark eyes as he swung his arm across Ella Mae's shoulder and pulled her in for a side hug. "Aye, Aye, Captain." He planted a kiss on the top of her head before he turned his attention back to Hank. "Nice meetin' you, Romeo. I hope I get to hear some of your music soon."

"I'd, uh, love that." Hank watched his music idol saunter out of the dressing room like a rock god legend. He couldn't help himself and hollered after him, "Thank you for your time!"

With Travis out of the room, Hank turned to look at Ella Mae, his wide-eyed expression morphing into horror. "Did I just say, 'Thank you for your time?'"

Ella giggled and scrunched her nose. "Yup. Don't worry, you didn't come across that geeky—"

"Geeky?" Hank interrupted. He was mortified. "I was a complete nerd, wasn't I? A star-struck dimwit in front of my idol, Travis Miller, who also happens to be your famous brother." Leaning against the wall, he was embarrassed and hung his head, pulling the tip of his cowboy hat lower to hide his reddening face. "Ugh."

"Hey," Ella Mae said. Hank noticed her aqua-painted toenails in her flip-flops sidle up to the tips of his boots. Using her beer bottle, she pushed his hat back up so she could look him in the eye.

"I love it you have real manners. And let me tell you, manners go a long way around here. Travis hates bullshit and fans fawning all over him." She paused and rolled her eyes. "Except for those tacky girls who sneak backstage every so often."

"Yeah, that was awk-weird," he added. "Although, from a guy's standpoint, I have to say it was kind of badass and very rock and roll."

Ella Mae pursed her lips together to thwart off a grin and shook her head. "I don't know why he didn't lock the damn door. I'm so embarrassed you had to walk in on him like that."

"I'm embarrassed you had to see me go full-blown nerd."

The two laughed out loud, the tension in the room easing. The up close version of Ella Mae Miller was stunning, and he had the right mind to get out of there and go somewhere private where they could get to know each other better. He clinked his beer bottle with hers again.

"You wanna get out of here? Or is our encounter coming to an end? You probably have to get on the bus and head out soon, right?"

Ella Mae licked her lips after taking a swig of beer. "Nope. We're staying overnight in a hotel close by before we hit the road first thing in the morning. What did you have in mind?" She leaned closer to him, the long lashes of her doe eyes coyly fluttering.

A surge of warmth pooled in Hank's stomach. This girl was unexpected in the most glorious way.

"If you're hungry, I know of a late-night diner still open. Or—"

"Or?" she interrupted, picking a piece of lint off his t-shirt-covered chest. He inhaled the subtle fragrance of her hair up close. It was sweet, like Tupelo honey.

Lifting one of her long braids that hung over her shoulder, he ran his thumb across the thick plait. "Or we could drive down by the river and... talk?"

Her lips unfurled into a playful smile. "Yes, and yes." She grabbed the beer out of his hand and tossed both bottles in the trash. "I need to let Willie know my plans and drop my bag off at the bus. Let's go."

Linking her fingers through his, she pulled him down the hallway toward the Green Room, her flip-flops slapping the tile floors in quick succession along the way. Hank stayed in the doorframe and watched Ella Mae move through the crowd toward Willie in the corner. They exchanged a few words before she smiled, and the two hugged. Hank quickly scanned the room for Travis and noticed him holding court with a few beauties by the wall with a water bottle in his hands.

"Okay, let me drop this off at the bus, and then we can head out." Ella was breathless, holding on to his bicep and navigating him toward the exit.

Once outside, the summer cicadas were in full symphony mode. The warm air caressed Hank's cheeks as they walked toward an impressive bus parked near the loading dock. He stopped in his tracks.

"What's wrong?" she asked.

Hank swallowed hard, his eyes tracing the giant black Prevost tour bus with classic chrome paneling. "I've never been this close to an actual tour bus before."

Ella's smile widened. "Well, come on then. Let me give you the grand tour." Pulling a key from her pocket, she unlocked the side door and entered, her denim-clad backside swinging with each step into the interior.

Hank was tentative, his heart galloping madly as he took his first step. The inside held high gloss wood and leather finishes with comfortable seating and a lived-in vibe.

"Welcome to our home away from home," Ella Mae announced. Her arms were open wide as she stood in the center of the front lounge.

"Wow," Hank muttered breathlessly, sure his inner music nerd was making another appearance. "What a way to travel."

Ella giggled. "Well, Travis won't hardly get on an airplane unless there's no other choice, so this is how we do it. Our bus driver, Lenny, drives us through the night if we have to get somewhere fast. Travis and I sleep through it all and wake up rested and ready for the day when we arrive at our destination."

Hank nodded, tracking with her.

"So, let me give you the tour." She swung her hand out in a classic Vanna White gesture. "This area here is where Travis plays video games or watches sports. Sometimes it takes him a while to decompress after a show, so you'll find him camped out in the recliner or sitting at that little table where he can see all three TVs."

Looking around, Hank nodded again while scoping out all three televisions.

"We don't really use the kitchen much because we always have catering at the venues he plays." She pulled open a large freezer door from the bottom of a standard-sized refrigerator. "But you better believe we enjoy some late-night snacking. Pizza rolls and ice cream are our go-to's."

Hank laughed, feeling like he was on an episode of *Cribs* peeking into the celebrity's fridge. He followed her through a narrow space where four large bunks were located.

"This here is where we sleep. My bunk is this bottom one to the right, and Travis is across from me." She pulled back a long curtain and revealed a disheveled sleeping area, the cozy bunk sporting a small television in the wall at the end of the bed.

"I keep my personal belongings in the storage compartment underneath and a few things up top in the unoccupied bunk."

Hank was fascinated, taking it all in. "No closet space?"

Ella Mae rolled her eyes, slipped her satchel off her shoulder, and tossed it on the top bunk mattress. "Travis hoards all the closet space with all his stage clothes, hats, and boots. But I don't mind. He's the one performing, and we only go out on the road two or three months at a time, so it's no big deal." She grinned and pulled him toward the back of the bus. "But here's my favorite space."

They entered a large area with plump leather sofa seating in the round. "This is where the music happens," she announced.

Hank took it all in, the mounted guitars on the walls hard not to notice. "What do you mean?"

Ella Mae collapsed onto the leather cushion, looking right at home. "This is where Travis and I spend most of our time traveling on tour when we're not sleeping. This is where we write together."

Goosebumps peppered Hank's skin as he slowly eased himself onto the sofa space across from her. He took his hat off with reverence. "This is where you write songs? With your brother, Travis Miller?"

Ella Mae giggled in response. "Mmmhmm. It's kind of cozy, don't you think?"

"I think," he nodded.

Ella sat up and rested her hands on her knees. "Well then, that's it. That's the tour. You ready to get out of here?" She stood, and Hank followed suit.

"Sure." He took one last look around, trying to memorize it all. They exited the bus, and he watched her lock up.

"Where'd you park?" she asked.

Hank traced the area to get his bearings. "I think I'm over there if that's lot B."

They walked in silence under the tall light poles, most spaces empty since the concert ended. Hank spotted his truck in the distance and pointed toward an area a dozen yards ahead. "It's the silver pickup right over there."

He continued his chivalrous behavior and unlocked the passenger side door for her. "Hold on a second." He tossed a few empty Gatorade bottles into the back and ran his hand across the seat to clean off the dog hair left behind by his brother Jimmy's two labs. "It's nothing fancy, but it'll get us from point A to point B."

The nighttime lighting gave off a soft glow, Ella Mae's feminine features subdued. "I have a pickup truck back home in Franklin. I'm not a fancy girl at all."

Hank's mouth jacked up into a lopsided grin. "Well then, you and I are gonna get along real well." He marveled at her backside as she climbed up into the truck interior. Before he shut the door, her words made him pause.

"I sure hope so, cowboy."

Chapter Four
Hank

An hour later, Hank pushed his plate of half-eaten cherry pie to the side and picked up his coffee cup. His earlier buzz was gone, and he was smitten by his new female companion sitting across from him.

"Well, what'd you think?"

Ella Mae licked whipped cream off her spoon like a lollipop, her pink tongue dangerously tempting. "You were right. This is the best pie I've had in ages. I'll have to remember this place the next time we come through town."

Hank leaned back in the diner booth with satisfaction. "I told ya. I've been coming here for years. This was the place to hang out after a football game back in high school. They used to have one of those old-fashioned jukeboxes right over there in the corner." He pointed to an empty spot near the bathrooms.

Ella looked over her shoulder at the vacant area and smiled. "Tell me what song you played over and over back then. You know, your favorite."

Damn, the girl seemed to already know he was a song junkie, their love of music a bond they shared—and he hadn't even strummed a guitar or hummed an original melody for her yet.

Running his hands through his hair, he dipped his head with amusement. "There was only one song back then. And you're right—I used to play it over and over again on the jukebox, stacking those quarters ready to spend my entire allowance. My daddy introduced me to it when I was a young boy. The song was one of his favorites growing up in the North Georgia Mountains. You probably know it: *Mountain Music* by Alabama?"

Ella Mae slapped her hands on the Formica tabletop, rattling the dishes. "Get out!"

"What?" Hank chuckled, surprised by her immediate positive reaction.

"My dad used to play that song for us, too. It's the perfect blend of Southern rock and bluegrass—classic country. Those harmonies, that fiddle, and those lyrics."

"You got that right. And the electric guitar playing. I used to sit on my bed for hours trying to replicate the exact twang of the instrument on the recording. When I finally figured it out, I was so excited to perform for my family. I stood on the fireplace hearth and played and sang my guts out for all of them."

Ella Mae's eyes twinkled, and the apples of her cheeks turned pink in a broad grin as if she was totally tracking with him.

Hank tapped his boot and started humming the familiar tune. Ella joined him, bobbing her head to the beat, the two leaning into each other and softly singing the chorus in harmony. It was eerie how well their voices blended.

"Oh, man. That's such a great song." She paused and looked right at him. "And you've got a great voice, too."

Hank smirked and picked up his coffee cup, trying to act cool. "I'm just playing around with you."

Ella shook her head. "Well, if that's just playing around, I can't wait to hear the real thing."

They talked about their families over another cup of coffee, Hank learning about Ella's tragedy involving her parents. He seemed to remember reading or seeing an interview with Travis Miller and how he talked about his humble beginnings with only his sister by his side. Hearing her tell the story was sad, the wistfulness in her voice hard not to notice.

"Once upon a time, my daddy was a full-time musician, and my mama was a groupie. I wish they could've seen Travis's rise to fame. They'd be real proud of how far he's come," she said, twirling her empty cup.

"They'd be proud of both of you. I'm sure of it."

The smile she offered him was sincere. "What about you? I heard you tell Willie your family has a winery and tree farm. Sounds like heaven."

Hank nodded. "It's beautiful country, but the work is grueling. I'd rather be playing music."

Ella giggled. "I'll bet. But how cool your family runs something together."

Hank cocked his head. "Well, you and Travis aren't any different. You're a family, and you're running an empire together."

Shrugging, Ella Mae sighed. "I guess you're right. But don't forget, we have an amazing crew and entourage who help us." She looked him right in the eye. "What about your crew? Any brothers and sisters? How about your parents? Are they still together?"

Hank licked his lips, the unforeseen, melancholy moments missing his mother hitting him out of the blue. "My mom died after a long bout of cancer several years ago. It was awful."

The space between Ella's eyebrows creased, her expression full of sympathy as she stretched her hand across the table and laid it over his. "I'm so sorry for your loss, Hank."

He stared at their hands and mumbled, "Thank you." When he looked up at her, she offered him a slight smile as if she understood his pain, and he knew she did. Clearing his throat, he decided to fill her in on the rest of his family.

"My dad, Roy, is the patriarch. He's hard-working and expects a lot out of us. But he's also my biggest supporter when it comes to music."

"Us?" Ella Mae questioned.

Hank chuckled. "Yep. I've got three older brothers and a younger sister."

"Wow!" she laughed. "That's a lot of 'us'!"

"It sure is."

Their waitress dropped off the check, and Hank dug his wallet out of his back pocket. The large wall clock indicated it was nearing midnight. "You still want to take a drive down to the river?" On the surface, he acted very nonchalantly, but inside, he was as nervous as a cat in a room full of rocking chairs. He wasn't ready to say goodbye yet.

"I'd love to," she smiled.

Hank threw money on the table, including a substantial tip, and slipped out of the diner booth. "Let's do it."

There was no one on the road in Langston Falls at this hour of the night. Hank drove down Main Street and pointed out the historical buildings that made up his hometown. Ella Mae seemed interested, commenting on how charming the mountain town appeared in the glow of the lampposts and starry night.

The black asphalt gave way to gravel as Hank navigated his truck down a dark, deserted road under a canopy of thick trees leading to the river. Pulling into a spot he knew well, he turned the vehicle off and rested his arm across the seatback, his fingers dangerously close to Ella's creamy neck.

"So, where are we exactly?" she asked. There wasn't a hint of nervousness in her tone.

"This is one of my favorite fishing spots. I used to come here all the time when I was just a boy. Now, not so much."

"Why not?"

Hank took his hat off and dropped it into the backseat. "Working. Sulking." In the dark, he felt her warm hand touch his thigh.

"I was wondering what was wrong when I first saw you. You looked so sad and lonely."

Hank expelled a puff of air through his nostrils, remembering his earlier demeanor. On a whim, he'd come to the concert alone that night. His only goal was to get shit-faced and sing along with the crowd at the top of his lungs. He hadn't played or sung anything since his oldest brother's May wedding.

Changing the subject, he opened the truck door. "Come on. I want to show you something."

They met in front of the truck, where he thrust his hand out for her to take. Ella Mae held tightly to him as she carefully navigated the uneven terrain in her flip-flops. They walked a few yards toward the sound of water before she gasped.

The full moon illuminated the river's smooth flow directly below a steep embankment, the view of the water perfect.

"What river is this?" she asked. There was a tinge of awe in her voice as the moonbeams cast shimmering diamonds of light on the water's surface.

"This is the Langston River." He stretched his arm out and pointed across the vast waterway as he explained. "It begins on the slopes of the mountains and goes over the falls for which my town is named. Fun fact, Langston Falls has the highest volume of any waterfall on the Northern edge of the Blue Ridge Mountains."

"You don't say?"

"Yep. My dad discovered this special place when he was a boy and passed it on to my siblings and me. It's off the beaten path, so there aren't as many tourists to bother you, especially when it comes to fishing."

The sound of water gliding over river rocks was peaceful as Hank stared at the sparkling shimmers on the surface. The symphony of night creatures creaking and croaking in the summer night added to the sensory experience. He stood there, lost in a relaxed trance, until he felt Ella Mae thread her fingers through his.

"Why were you sad at the concert, Hank?"

Squeezing her hand, he took a deep breath and turned to look at her in the soft, romantic haze of the night. "I'm kind of at a crossroads, Ella Mae. My band broke up after our trip to Nashville last winter. It seems they weren't all on the same page as me and my career," he chuckled. "I've been biding my time working on the farm trying to figure things out."

"Is that why you got drunk tonight? Because it was hard for you to see my brother up there on a stage fulfilling his dream?"

"I don't know," he sighed. Bringing her hand to his mouth, he lightly kissed her skin. "But I do know how awesome it was meeting you tonight."

Her smile was immediate, her dark brown eyes holding orbs of the moon's reflection. "It was nice meeting you, too."

Hank took a tentative step closer to her, closing the gap between them. Between the sound of the river and the thrumming of his heart, a melody seemed to hum between them, and he was more than ready to kiss her.

"What are you doing, Hank?" she said, causing his wayward thoughts to come to a screeching halt.

"I beg your pardon?" Had he crossed a line bringing her out here in the middle of nowhere, giving her hand kisses under the serious moonlight?

She shook her head, and he watched as she gingerly took off her flip-flops and purposefully stood barefoot on the tops of his cowboy boots, the heat from her body noticeable. They were eye to eye, her arms wrapped around his neck. When she melded her luscious lips against his, total bliss threw his body into a free fall.

Pulling back from him, she sighed. "Am I being too forward? Was that okay?"

Hank chuckled again. "Are you kidding me? Your sweet kiss was more than okay—it was heaven."

He pulled her in for a tight hug, his daring fingers slipping lower and palming her denim backside. She didn't seem to mind. He reveled in their closeness, the feel of this soft and feminine creature in his arms stimulating and surprising. If someone would've told him he'd be going to see his favorite country music artist perform that night and come away from the show with a gorgeous songwriter in his arms, he would've chalked it up to a drunken hallucination.

"Hank?" she whispered provocatively near the shell of his ear.

"Hmmm?"

"Sometimes opportunity shows up when you're too busy looking for something else."

Chapter Five
Ella Mae

Hank gently pulled Ella forward by her braids to where he could kiss her again. She moaned in his mouth. "I don't want to say goodbye to you yet. I have so many questions," she mumbled against his lips.

His face was shadowed in the dark, the low rumble of his voice sexy. "Questions?"

"Mmmhmmm. I want to know more about your family and your farm. I want to hear some of your original music, too." A thought crossed her mind. "What if—"

"What if, what?" he interrupted.

Ella bit her lower lip. "What if... you came back to my hotel with me?"

Hank's chest rose in a deep intake of air. "Ella Mae, as tempted as I am, I'm not sure that's such a good idea."

Leaning low so she could step into her wayward flip-flops, she steadied herself against his firm chest. "Why not?" With her footwear back on, she teased him. "You've changed your mind and you don't like me that much?"

Hank seemed taken aback. "God, no! I like you very much. I'd love to spend more time with you."

"Then what's the problem?" She planted her hands on her hips and enjoyed watching him squirm. He really was adorable.

"Hear me out, Ella Mae. I'm the type of guy who likes to... woo a gal."

"Woo?" she laughed.

"Yes, woo." He puckered his lips, accentuating the "oo" at the end of the silly word. "You know, take her out, wine and dine her, that sort of thing. I'm not a player like—"

"Like my brother?" she interjected.

Hank gripped the back of his neck as if embarrassed. "I was going to say, like most guys."

Ella Mae giggled, ready to put him out of his misery. "Relax, Hank. Here's what I'm proposing, okay?" She took a step closer and held one of his hands. "Let's go back to my hotel room. It's got two queen-sized beds. You take one, and I'll take the other. We can lay in comfort and talk until we peter out and fall asleep. That way, we don't have to say goodbye, only... goodnight."

Hank squeezed her hand. "Well, I guess it'll be okay when you say it like that. But what happens in the morning?"

Ella thought for a moment. "We can have breakfast together before the lobby call, and then I guess it will be inevitable. We'll have to say goodbye."

They stood there holding hands, both silent amidst the sound of the flowing river nearby.

"Are you always this confident and practical?" He started to pull her toward the pickup truck.

"I have to be, especially around my brother."

"About that... When he took a sip of my beer in the dressing room, I saw you get on to him. Does Travis have a problem again?" He opened the passenger side door for her, knowing his country music idol had visited a rehab center for alcohol abuse. But that was ages ago.

She released her hand from his and said simply, "You have no idea."

Fifteen minutes later, Ella spotted the tour bus parked on the outskirts of the hotel parking lot, taking up several spaces.

"I need to grab my overnight bag from the bus," she explained.

"Not a problem."

They walked silently side by side, and he stayed outside the bus as she clambered up the stairs and headed for her bunk. Grabbing a familiar bag from the top, she hurried outside and locked the door.

"Here, let me get that for you," Hank offered.

"Thanks."

There wasn't a soul in sight in the lobby, the chain hotel clean and quiet in the late night. Sometimes they stayed in five-star places, but in small mountain towns like this, an ordinary hotel was their only option, especially when they had a day off and weren't pressed for time, having to drive all night to the next location.

Ella Mae walked up to the front desk and palmed the call bell. A few seconds later, a large man wearing an oversized collared shirt with the hotel logo on the chest pocket came shuffling out of the back room.

"May I help you?"

"Yes, you have a key waiting for me. Monica Geller?" She slipped him a twenty dollar bill.

Hank did a double-take and kept his mouth shut.

The hotel clerk typed in the name and immediately nodded. "Yes, I've got you right here, Mrs. Geller. You're all checked in." He was quick and offered her a plastic room key. "You're on the fourth floor, away from the elevators and the ice machine by request. Do you need a second key for Mr. Geller?"

Ella gave Hank the side-eye and stifled a grin. "I don't know. Do you need a key, Mr. Geller?"

Hank played along and shook his head. "Uh, nope. I'm good, Monica."

"Y'all enjoy your stay." The man smiled and handed off the key before disappearing into the back.

Hank mumbled as they walked to the elevator, "What was that all about?"

Ella pressed the button, and the doors opened. "Travis and I use fake names when we check into hotels. This helps keep the fans at bay so we can have some peace and quiet."

"Oh." Hank nodded. "Why Monica Geller? Is she someone you know?"

Ella giggled and leaned against his sturdy frame as fatigue set in. "No, silly. Monica Geller is from the sitcom *Friends*, remember?"

"Oh, yeah. Sure."

She turned and looked up at him in awe. "You've never even seen an episode of *Friends*, have you?"

"I've heard of it," he countered in a high-pitched voice. This made her laugh out loud. "Shhh... it's late, and people are sleeping." They came out of the elevator and walked the expansive length of the hallway to their room at the end, stifling laughter in their tired state.

"Here, allow me." He took the key card from her hands and unlocked the door, palming it wide open for her to enter.

"Thank you." She flicked on the lights and threw her small bag onto the bed nearest the bathroom. "Make yourself at home.

I'm going to take a quick shower. There should be some drinks and snacks in the mini-fridge. It's part of our contract rider."

"Cool." Hank was tentative in his steps and stood by the other bed as if unsure of what to do.

"Hank?"

"Hmmm?" His eyebrows lifted as he looked at her.

"Relax."

He nodded with chagrin, his solid chest rising in a deep intake of air. "Okay."

Ella Mae took her time in the shower, shaving her legs and washing her hair under the decadent spray. Wiping the steam off the large bathroom mirror, she smiled at her reflection, thrilled Hank was just outside the closed door waiting for her. She wondered what he was doing, hoping he'd kicked off his boots and made himself comfortable on the bed next to hers. Pulling on an oversized t-shirt with her brother's colorful branding on the front, she grabbed her hairbrush and exited the bathroom.

The TV wasn't on, but Hank had definitely kicked off his boots. His long, lanky body was pressed into the mattress, and his head was propped on top of two fluffy pillows. His eyes were shut, and his hands clasped across his middle. His lips parted as his breath came out in a raspy snore. She smiled, thinking she'd have to tease him about this in the morning.

Sitting on the edge of her bed to where she could admire Hank, she slowly brushed out her long, wet hair. The room held a male muskiness that aroused a deep primal part of her brain. She studied him silently, trying to memorize every detail: His chiseled jawline smattered with whiskers. The sweep of his dark lashes. Thick curls springing back to life after being smothered by a cowboy hat in the heat of the day. She jumped when he jerked awake and rolled his head to the side to where he looked right at her.

"I must've dozed off," he mumbled. He shifted his body and leaned on one elbow. "You sure smell good. Feel better?"

"Much. Do you want to shower? You're welcome to any of my stuff on the bathroom counter, although some of it is girlie-scented.

Hank chuckled. "I'm fine as long as you don't mind my smelly boots and socks."

She smiled. "I don't mind at all."

The two remained in a staring match until Ella broke the spell. She put her brush down and snuggled under the covers, palming her hands under one cheek.

Hank's dark brows drew together. "You sure you wanna go to bed with wet hair? You might catch a cold."

Smitten by his concern, she reassured him. "I'm fine. I never use a blow dryer."

"You want me to turn out the light?"

Ella Mae's eyelids felt droopy, and her mouth relaxed as a slight smile played on her lips. "Yes, but don't go back to sleep just yet."

"I won't," he replied.

She watched in awe as he reached for the switch on the bedside table, his bicep bulging in the process. She sighed as the darkness enveloped them, the air conditioner humming and rattling under the window.

"Thanks for not saying goodbye to me tonight."

"Thanks for offering me this comfortable bed."

She giggled before her mood turned sober. "Hank?"

"Hmmm?"

"I don't know much about you, but I do know this. Losing our parents bonded us in a way that nothing else could. I mean, I understand how you feel, you know?"

"I do." His voice was hushed and calm.

"My mom and dad died way too soon. So did your mother. We're friends now, so I'm here for you if you're ever sad and want to talk about it."

"I appreciate that. I'm here for you, too, Ella Mae. I understand you've been through some stuff with your brother, Travis. I've been through a lot with my brothers as well." He paused, and she strained to listen to him in the dark. "You and I have much more in common than you know."

"Hmmm," she sighed again, willing her eyes to stay open. "Hold that thought." She yawned and felt her body dissolving into the comfort of the bed. "Goodnight, Hank."

"Goodnight, Monica."

Her lips lifted into a sleepy smile, hearing the crooked grin in his voice.

Chapter Six

Hank

Hank jerked awake and blinked back against the bright morning sun streaming in through the open blinds—and the feel of a soft, feminine woman in his arms. When had Ella Mae snuck into his bed during the night? Not that he was upset about it or anything.

She was tucked into his side, her cheek pressed against his chest. He cocked his head to get a good close-up look at her. Gently, he used his index finger and moved a strand of her hair away from her face, faint traces of sweet honey lingering in the stillness. He relished her closeness and watched her sleep for a moment taking inventory of every delectable feature. The fullness of her ripe cherry lips and the faint traces of freckles dotting her nose. Her long hair trailing over her shoulders. The way she clutched her hands under her chin in a praying position during slumber. He knew they had something unique happening between them. It wasn't just a bond over losing their parents or a burgeoning country music friendship. No. Chemistry was definitely humming beneath the surface, especially after waking up with her in his arms.

Adjusting to the morning brilliance, he shifted her out of his arms and pulled the blanket up to her chin. He was still fully clothed, lying on top of the hotel bed.

"Ella Mae?" he whispered, his voice scratchy with fatigue. When she didn't answer, his lips lifted into a lazy smile, and he swung his legs over the edge of the bed, intent on letting her sleep a little while more while he used the facilities.

Grabbing his boots parked at the end of the bed, he shuffled into the bathroom and took care of business, although it was difficult with his morning disposition. After washing his hands, he splashed water across his face and pressed a towel to his skin. Eyeing a tube of Ella Mae's toothpaste on the counter, he put a little dab on his finger and rubbed the minty gel across his teeth before rinsing and spitting in the sink. Looking at his reflection, he smoothed the wrinkles across his shirt and tried to tame his unruly hair, but it was no use. The stubble on his face was more pronounced, his appearance reminding him of a long day of manual labor on the farm. Sitting on the toilet lid, he pulled on his boots and decided to head downstairs to the lobby restaurant to get them some coffee before their inevitable goodbye.

The bathroom door creaked as he exited, and he was surprised to see Ella Mae up and packing.

"Hey," he greeted. "Did I wake you?"

"No. Good morning," she smiled. With a pile of clothing in her hands, she passed him. "Did you sleep well? I slept like a baby." She patted his shoulder and went into the bathroom, closing the door.

Hank heard the water turn on, wondering what he was supposed to do next. He sat on the mattress and waited. When she came out a few minutes later, she was fully dressed in what looked like overalls that had been cut into shorts. A pink camisole and matching flip-flops completed her look.

"I'm starving. You wanna go downstairs and get some breakfast?" The way she looked at him with her dreamy eyes made him weak in the knees.

"Sure. I'd love to." Standing, he swiped his wallet and cell phone off the nightstand, immediately noticing a few text messages from his family. He frowned when he realized he hadn't checked in with them since he'd left for the concert the night before.

"What is it? Is something wrong?" Ella Mae stood in front of him with a look of concern marring her pretty features.

"It's nothing," Hank said, stuffing his phone into his back pocket. "I need to check in with my family. I should've texted them last night and told them I wouldn't be coming home until this morning. I'll give them a quick call after breakfast."

Ella Mae shook her head. "No. Do it now. They're worried about you."

Hank licked his lips. "You sure?"

She pressed her hand against his forearm. "Yes. You make your call, and I'll go snag us a table."

"Okay." He watched Ella exit the hotel room in a whiff of womanliness, her cut-off denim backside swaying in a sexy rhythm. Damn, those overall shorts left very little to the imagination.

With a few clicks on his home screen, he listened to the ringtone and stood in front of the hotel window with his free hand on his hip, ready for a deserved tongue-lashing.

"Hey, Dad. Sorry, I'm just now calling." He listened to his father tell him how concerned he was when he hadn't made it home.

"I know. But I have a good excuse. I met Travis Miller's sister, Ella Mae, at the show, and she took me backstage afterward to meet him."

His father's tone immediately changed, and they chatted briefly about Hank's encounter with his country music idol, all earlier angst completely vanished.

"I'm going to breakfast, and then I'll be home. Again, I'm sorry for not letting you know sooner." He smiled when his dad told him he understood and loved him. "Love you too, Dad. Bye."

Thankful the conversation was out of the way, Hank descended to the hotel lobby and immediately spotted Ella Mae chatting with her brother, Travis. They were tucked in the corner, Travis's back turned toward him.

Fuck. How was he going to explain things to her brother?

Ella noticed Hank immediately and waved him over, her cheery morning disposition hard not to notice. "Hank, over here!"

Hank took in a deep intake of air and made his way over to the pair. Travis rested his elbow across the seatback of his chair and looked up at him with a hitched eyebrow, the gleam in his eye indicating caution.

"Good morning, Romeo. Fancy meeting you here. How long of a drive was it from the family farm?"

Hank stuttered in his reply. "Oh... I, uh. Well, you see—"

"He's teasing you, Hank," Ella Mae interrupted, rolling her eyes. "I already told Travis you spent the night with me in my room."

Hank felt the back of his neck grow hot, surprised she'd told her brother the truth. "You did?"

Travis picked up his coffee mug and took a sip, all the while his eyes never leaving his. "She sure did. Hope it was a good one."

Hank coughed. "I beg your pardon?"

"A good night's sleep. You look well-rested, buddy." Travis stood and slapped Hank on the back, making him awkwardly stagger. "You want some coffee?"

"Um, sure. Black is fine." Hank watched Travis stroll toward the coffee station, looking every bit like a country music star in his black jeans, white tee, and cowboy boots.

"Have a seat." Ella Mae patted the empty seat next to her.

Easing himself onto the chair, he eyed her with carefulness. "What exactly did you tell your brother?"

Forking a piece of banana from her plate, she put the bite into her mouth and shrugged.

Hank waited for her to chew and noticed how fresh-faced and pretty she looked in the light of day. Her hair was a tumbled mess of natural waves cascading over her shoulders, and her chocolate eyes were bright with energy.

"Is he cool? Or is he about to beat the crap outta me?" Hank pressed, realizing he'd probably beat the shit out of some dude shacking up with his little sister if the tables were turned.

Ella Mae finally swallowed her bite and nodded. "He's totally cool." She patted his thigh, making him flinch. "I'm so glad you stayed with me last night. I haven't slept that well in ages."

Hank found it hard not to smile. "Yeah? Me too. The mattress was comfortable, even fully clothed." He wasn't about to broach the subject of her climbing into bed with him as Travis was already returning to their table.

He offered Hank a mug of coffee. "Here you go, bro."

"Thanks." When Travis didn't sit back down, Hank frowned. "I hope I didn't interrupt anything between you and your sister. I can leave if you'd like."

"Nah, I'm finished with breakfast. I need to get my stuff loaded." Travis turned his attention to Ella Mae. "I'll see you back at the bus in a few, Peaches. Lenny said it's about a six-hour drive to Louisville from here." Travis eyed Hank for a beat before he bid him farewell. "Good to see you again, Romeo. Take it easy."

"You do the same, Travis." He wanted to add, "I love your music," or "I'm your biggest fan," but he didn't think it was the right moment to fan-boy over the man again, especially in front of Ella Mae. He watched his idol saunter toward the bank of elevators and disappear.

"So," Ella Mae started. She crisscrossed her legs on the chair with childlike glee and rested her elbow on the seatback, leaning her pretty head against the palm of her hand.

Hank's lips twitched into a grin. She was up to something. "What's on your mind?"

"I talked it over with Travis."

"Talked what over with Travis?" Hank lifted the mug of coffee to his lips and took a long sip.

"About you joining us on the road for the rest of the tour."

Hank sputtered and choked on the coffee, unsure if he'd heard her correctly. Ella Mae immediately grabbed a few napkins and handed them off while patting his back.

"You okay?"

"Yes," he coughed, pressing a napkin to his lips. "It went down the wrong pipe." Clearing his throat, he looked right at her. "Could you please repeat what you just said?"

Ella Mae pressed her teeth into her lower lip to thwart a smile. "You heard me. I want you to join us on tour."

Hank exhaled long and slow. "I... I don't even know what to say." His mind ran rampant with the possibility. *Holy shit!* Joining Travis Miller on tour was like winning the freaking lottery.

"Say yes," Ella Mae pleaded. She threaded her fingers with his and squeezed. "You said it yourself, you're at a crossroads. Let me show you what life is really like on the road. We only have three weeks left. That would give you plenty of time to experience a real tour firsthand. You could see how you like living out of a suitcase and traveling during all hours of the day. It would do you a world of good and help you decide which road to take. We could even collaborate on some music together, and you could keep me company."

She batted her eyelashes at him, looking so pretty it hurt, her voice turned down a notch. "And if I'm being brutally honest and perhaps a little bit selfish, I must admit, I liked sleeping in your arms, Hank." She stared at him, her pleading tone evident. "Please say yes."

Hank's heart pounded like a bass drum, the thought of being on a real bona fide tour thrilling. Ella Mae was right—this would allow him to figure out his next steps. Maybe he could network with other musicians, write some music with Ella, and observe her brother, Travis, in the spotlight for more than one show. The opportunity she presented was a no-brainer. But what sealed the deal was the thought of her warm body pressed against his again. She was a bright light in his world, her generous heart glowing as he felt himself crashing into her.

"Of course, I'm saying yes. Duh."

Ella Mae flung herself into his arms and hugged him hard. Her breath was hot against the edge of his ear as she whispered, "We're going to have so much fun."

Chapter Seven

Hank

Hank's truck picked up dust along the gravel road leading to Bennett Farms. Eyeing the heavy-gage steel sign spelling out his family's property, he stepped on the gas, anxious to find his father and explain his latest opportunity.

After a sweet goodbye hug and a lingering kiss behind the large Provost bus away from Travis's prying eyes, Hank promised Ella Mae he'd see her soon in Louisville, Kentucky. She told him she'd have a backstage lanyard pass ready for him at will-call and to text her when he arrived at the concert venue.

"This isn't goodbye. This is—"

"See you later?" she interrupted.

"Exactly." He grinned, pressing his lips against her cheek.

Hank touched his mouth, recalling her satiny skin, the sudden turn of events in his life which included a pretty girl and a country music tour like something out of a hit song. She was right. Opportunity had definitely shown up when he was busy wallowing in self-pity and looking for something else. Thank God she was there to set him straight.

Delia and Jaxson came bounding over the green hill in front of the family farmhouse, the yellow and black Labradors panting in the steamy sunshine. Slamming the truck door shut, Hank sheepishly ran his hand through his hair when he noticed his father, Roy, and his older brother, James, come out onto the front porch to greet him.

"Hey, y'all," he waved unconvincingly. Why was he so nervous?

James grinned from ear to ear. "Damn, Hank. Dad told me you got to go backstage and meet Travis Miller last night. How was it?"

Hank looked between his father and brother as he hiked up the porch steps, the excitement building in his core. "Un-fucking-believable."

James slapped him on the back and laughed while Roy shook his head. "Language, Hank."

"Sorry, Dad."

The three men and two dogs entered the house, the welcome air-conditioned space tinged with a meaty fragrance.

"Tell us everything," James implored.

"Yes! I want to hear about it too," his sister, Rebecca, chimed in from the open-air kitchen. She wiped her hands on her apron and came around the large island into the great room.

Hank bided some time and patted Delia's head. "Smells good in here, Becks. What's on the menu for supper tonight?"

Becky sat on the arm of the sofa. "Spaghetti and meatballs. Now come on, Hank, tell us everything!"

"Where's Walt and Teddy?" he asked, knowing he'd have to repeat his story if the whole family wasn't gathered together at the same time.

"They're out in the vineyard. Don't leave us hanging, Hank-ster," James pleaded.

Hank chuckled, shaking his head. "Alright."

He told them how he met Ella Mae at the t-shirt shack and how she invited him backstage after the show. Of course, he left out the part where he witnessed Travis Miller receiving a blowjob from a tenacious fan and how he ended up sleeping with Ella, fully clothed, in the same bed. He fudged the story a bit, alluding to hanging out with the crew all night and having breakfast with Travis and his sister earlier that morning.

"Man, that's awesome. I mean, come on! Who gets to meet their idol in person, right?" The excitement in James' voice was perceptible.

"Ella Mae wasn't all that bad, either," he offered.

Becky gave Hank the side-eye. "So, you like her?"

"Of course. She's a musician and a songwriter, too. She wrote the lyrics to Travis's song that won him his first CMA award."

"Impressive," Roy stated.

"So cool," James chuckled.

Looking around the room at his excited family, Hank hesitated to tell them the best part. Would they give him their blessing, allowing him to take a chance for the next three weeks and live out his dream on the road with a successful country music star? Or would they try to make him stay, insisting they needed his help in the last few arduous months of winery season?

"What's wrong, son," Roy asked. How did his dad always know when there was something on his mind?

Hank filled his lungs with a deep cleansing breath, ready to share his news. "I have a chance, Daddy."

"What are you talking about? With your band? I thought y'all parted ways?"

All eyes fixated on Hank, leaving him shaking in his boots. It was now or never.

"You know, I've always dreamed of making it in country music. After meeting Ella Mae and her brother, Travis...," he paused. "They've invited me to join them on the last three weeks of their tour."

James' eyes practically bugged out of his head. "*Get out*!"

"Oh my God," Becky muttered.

"Say again?" Roy asked.

Hank licked his lips as his heart accelerated. "The Miller's have invited me to join the last three weeks of their tour. I'll see how it's done on the big stages and work alongside the crew. I'll ride in a real tour bus, hang out with my idol, and maybe get the chance to show him some of my songs."

The words coming out of his mouth didn't seem legit, but they were. "I have a chance, and I'm taking it. I've never let go of this dream, even when my band broke up. I've been biding my time trying to figure out my next steps, and *BAM*! Along came Ella Mae Miller and her famous brother. I'd be a fool to let this pass me by."

The silence was deafening as he searched their faces for a glimmer of pride and congratulations. His father shuffled toward him and clamped his strong hand against his shoulder, his voice raspy with emotion.

"I've seen you put in the work. I've heard your talent firsthand." He pressed his lips together and nodded. "A dream won't chase you back, son. It's up to *you* to chase this dream with everything you have."

Hank felt his throat tighten with emotion, his eyes welling with tears. "I can go?"

Roy pursed his lips, the mirth in his expression evident. "Fuck yeah, you can go."

"*Daddy*!" Becky admonished with a stifled giggle.

"What?" He swung his head to look at James and Becky, the humor and pride he emanated apparent. "My boy here is brilliant. He's a grown-ass man with a heck of a lot of talent. He's been offered a gift and needs to take it."

Hank's family surrounded him with laughter and words of congratulations. Relieved, he allowed happy tears to dribble down his face, the trajectory of his life changing in an instant. He was hot on the heels of his neon dreams, knowing his life in country music was what he was born to do.

***

Leave it to his sister, Becky, to help him get packed up while he showered. There was no time like the present. Hank was anxious to get a move on. James found him the best bus route to Louisville, Kentucky, and his dad rallied his brothers Teddy and Walt from the vineyard fields to share the good news and send him off.

Pulling away from the only home he'd ever known, he knew his life was about to change in more ways than one. A pretty country girl was waiting for him across state lines, her generous offer to join the tour something he didn't take lightly. If it hadn't been for Ella Mae Miller, he'd be hungover and melancholy, probably moping around the farm all day with no hope in sight. But now, he had more than hope—he had a chance.

"Be yourself and be good," his father offered after a lingering hug in the parking lot near the bus terminal.

"I will, Daddy. I promise I'll check in with you and let you know how it's going."

Roy chuckled. "Of course, you will." The two meandered across the lot toward the station. "You still have some time before departure. You hungry? You need anything?"

Hank shifted the large duffle bag and guitar case onto the cement sidewalk outside the building. "No, sir. I think I've got everything I need."

Roy reached deep into his pocket and pulled out a worn bandanna, passing it off to him.

"What's this?" Hank could feel an object tucked inside.

"Open it and find out."

Hank peeled back the red layers revealing an ancient pocket watch in his hands. His brow furrowed as he looked up at his father for an explanation.

"That there was Papaw Bennett's. He always had it on him from sunup to sundown. Go ahead. Take a look inside."

Hank angled his cowboy hat back from his forehead and lifted the tiny clasp with his thumb. When he opened the hunter case of the antique watch, he was stunned by the inside cover. Tucked inside was a photograph of his entire family, including his late mother, posed on the front porch of the family farm from many years ago. Once again, his throat tightened with emotion as he looked at his father with gratefulness.

"Your family loves you very much. There's a reason you have so much talent and wanderlust in your blood. You take after your Papaw. He had big dreams, just like you."

"He did?" Hank's voice squeaked.

"Oh, yes. When he took over Bennett Farms from his father, he already had plans to grow hundreds of thousands of Fraser Fir trees, which eventually became the livelihood for many people in our region. But he didn't stop there. When he was in his mid-70s, he began dabbling with growing the first grapevines on the farm. Unfortunately, his lifelong passion for harvesting grapes and opening a winery didn't happen until my daddy was in charge. And now, because of you and your brothers and sister, I like to think Papaw's dream is better than he could have ever imagined."

Hank smiled, fingering the antique watch in his hands. "Yes, it is."

"Papaw passed on his legacy to our family, sharing his love of farming, hard work, and big dreams with those around him." Roy eyed the piece in Hank's hand. "You remind me very much of Papaw, your love of music and the desire to make something out of yourself is admirable."

He covered the watch with his wrinkled hand and held on to Hank tightly. "Bennett Farms will always be here for you. It's your home, no matter what. But you need to make your own way and follow the path God has laid out in front of you. Make us all proud, son. You have what it takes. It's in your blood."

Hank looked into his father's eyes, the hope abundant in his caring gaze. He wasn't about to let his family down.

"I'll cherish this while I'm away. Thank you for trusting me with it."

Roy nodded and squeezed.

An hour later, Hank looked out the bus window and caught one last glimpse of Langston Falls. The summer scenery in Georgia's northeast corner whizzed by him in hues of faded forest green and sky blue, the favorable mountain winds finally blowing his way.

Pulling the watch from his pocket, he flicked open the case again, his eyes tracing the faces of his family in the picture. His father's last words to him echoed in his mind.

"Keep on with your music, son, until the whole world sings along. I believe in you. It's time for you to believe in yourself."

Chapter Eight
Ella Mae

The bus ride to Louisville, Kentucky, was uneventful, the wheels humming against the interstate blacktop leaving Ella Mae in a relaxed state. Travis fixated on the baseball game streaming on the big TV in the lounge as she lay in her bunk, replaying her time with Hank Bennett. She was giddy, for sure, thankful he'd said "yes" to her proposition and anxious to have more one-on-one time with him.

When she'd snuck into his bed the night before, he hadn't flinched, out cold from his night of partying at her brother's concert. And in the morning, they hardly broached the subject of sharing a bed, even though he was fully clothed and nothing steamy happened. Was he uncomfortable by her actions? Had she crossed a line? She knew she'd been bold, but confidence was in her DNA.

Her attraction to Hank was immediate when she first laid eyes on him, looking all pitiful in his inebriated state. His boyish good looks and chivalrous manners were a breath of fresh air in her country music world, and she was bound and determined to get him to rethink quitting his dreams and perhaps take things to the next level—if he'd let her.

But what if she was all wrong and Hank only agreed to join the tour so he could be closer to his idol, Travis? What if his "yes" had nothing to do with her? She'd seen men and, of course, women react to her brother time and time again, her brother's celebrity bringing out the best and the worst in people. It wasn't unusual for the opposite sex to lure her into making an introduction to her famous sibling, leaving her in the dust. But with Hank, it was different. *He* was different.

Smiling, Ella Mae nodded off to the soft rumble of the bus engine, her Hank Bennett fantasy tucked into the deepest, secret parts of her mind. She'd have to play it cool and take things slow if she were to get to know the handsome cowboy better. And she knew she could.

As the bus pulled up to the five-star Hotel Distel in downtown Louisville, Ella gathered her belongings, ready to check in.

"You want to join me for some coffee, Peaches? I could use some caffeine." Travis stretched, gripping the side rails of the bunks in the narrow hallway. His body was lean and muscular from the tens of thousands of steps he made while performing on stages around the world, keeping him healthy and in shape. That, and being sober.

"You go ahead. I want to get unpacked and freshen up before supper. Remember, we're meeting the ASM Global team in the hotel restaurant at seven-thirty. It's fancy, so wear a collared shirt, please.

"Gotcha. I'll be there with bells and collars on." He paused, the smirk on his face hard not to notice.

"What?" she asked.

"What time are you expecting Romeo to arrive?"

Ella felt heat blossom across her cheeks, and she averted his gaze. "I'm not sure. He said he'd be here by the time your show starts tomorrow night at the arena."

"Is he the one?"

Ella jerked her head to look at her brother, her eyes going wide with unease. "What?"

"You heard me. Is Romeo the one?"

Furrowing her brow, she shook her head. "For the record, he has a name, and it's Hank Bennett. And I don't know what you're talking about."

Travis shifted, leaning his body against the wall in front of the bunks with his arms folded across his chest. "Sure you do. I know you like the back of my hand, Peaches. You've never invited anyone to a show, backstage, or let alone on the bus or our hotel rooms over the years. You're always so careful and stand-offish with the fans. What makes this guy so special after meeting him just the one time?"

Ella Mae's chest rose and fell in a deep breath as she stared at her brother. "I... I don't know."

"Well, you have to know something," he chuckled, uncurling his arms. "Listen, I'm not gonna stand in your way. I mean, it's only fair if you want to have a little fun on the road, too—"

"It's not like that, Travis!" she interrupted. "This isn't 'a little fun' as you call it. I'm nothing like you and your shenanigans, okay? Hank is really great."

"Oh, yeah? Then tell me, how is he so great?"

"Well, for one thing, he's respectful and he's a gentleman. And I like talking to him. We have a lot in common besides music. He's... nice."

"He's a nerd in a cowboy hat," Travis laughed.

Ella swatted at his arm. "Stop it. Just because he fanboyed over you doesn't make him a nerd. Give the guy a break, okay? He respects you. And he's at a crossroads trying to figure out if he should give up on his music dreams or keep going. How sad is that? You already know you're the one who inspired him to become a musician in the first place. Don't you remember your fascination with Garth Brooks back in the day?"

Travis rolled his eyes.

"You acted like Hank when you saw Garth in concert on his final tour. I recall you screaming like a little girl when he started singing, *The Thunder Rolls*."

"Oh, yeah?" Travis grinned, his eyes twinkling as if recalling the childhood memory.

"Yeah," she smiled back. He grabbed her by the arm and pulled her into his chest, hugging her hard. "What are you doing?" she whined.

"Giving my little sister a hug. You know I'm only teasing. I'll go along with anything you want to do, even if it means sharing space with a guy you want to get to know better."

"I want him to see what it could be like if he doesn't give up. I want to give him hope."

Travis kissed the top of her head before he let her go. "Ella Mae Peaches Miller, you have a good heart."

Ella gazed at her brother, their bond solid. "So do you."

Travis waved her off and started toward the front of the bus. "I'm looking forward to taking Hank under my wing. You know, hearing some of his original music, having a little jam session from time to time. It'll be... fun."

Ella followed him from behind and stopped next to their driver, Lenny, who remained seated. He was busy looking at a clipboard with the tour itinerary, keeping the large vehicle running until they were ready to exit.

With one eyebrow cocked, she planted her hands on her hips.

"What makes you think he'll be under *your* wing?"

When her brother turned around, the look of chagrin he offered was priceless, his mouth jacking up on one side in a devious grin. "You're all grown up now, aren't you, Peaches?"

Ella Mae lifted her chin with confidence, squelching a grin. "Oh, I'll never grow up." She turned toward their driver. "Will I, Lenny?"

Their portly, middle-aged driver harrumphed and opened the twin glider door outward from the hull of the bus. "I may as well be driving a yellow school bus with the two of you on board. If you ask me, y'all ain't never gonna grow up."

***

The Repeal Steakhouse at the Distil Hotel was packed, patrons noshing on steaks prepared over the flames of oak-aged whiskey barrels. Before coming downstairs to the restaurant from her hotel room on the ninth floor, Ella Mae had read about the dining experience from a brochure. She loved getting to know her surroundings while on tour and learned this particular restaurant was housed in the former site of J.T.S. Brown and Sons' wholesale warehouse and bottling operations. The family lost everything during Prohibition, but soldiered on toward Repeal, hence the name of the eating establishment.

John Fobas, the media manager for ASM Global, went all out, securing Repeal's signature private dining room. The Barrel Room featured whiskey barrel-lined walls and a private bar to complement the occasion away from prying eyes and overzealous fans. John was a leader in the preeminent management company investing and producing live events in stadiums, arenas, convention centers, and theaters worldwide. To finally meet the man and his team was an honor.

The hostess led her toward the back of the restaurant and bid her a good evening. John and his team had already arrived, and so had Travis, much to her surprise.

"Miss Miller, I'm John Fobas. It's a pleasure to finally meet you," John greeted with gusto. The man wore a suit, his black hair slicked back from his handsome face.

"Hello, Mr. Fobas. It's nice to meet you, too."

John lightly touched her arm and gestured toward the bar while holding a glass of brown liquor. "Can I get you something to drink?"

"Sure. What are you having?"

He nodded with glee. "I'm having a bourbon. Old Forester Signature 100 Proof, to be exact. It's the longest-running bourbon brand on the market, and a favorite of the Repeal restaurant, as it was one of the few whiskeys allowed to be sold during Prohibition for medicinal purposes."

"You don't say?" She grinned, intrigued by the knowledge he shared.

"It's pretty basic and a gentle sipper. I'd be happy to get you a glass. Would you like to try it?"

"Don't mind if I do."

"Excuse me, I'll be right back."

Ella watched John approach the bar and place her order. Scanning the room of ASM Global folks milling about, she spotted Travis in the corner holding court with a group of women. Sure enough, he wore a black collared shirt, dark denim jeans, boots, and a huge silver belt buckle. His looks were very reminiscent of country music legend Johnny Cash. When he noticed her from across the room, he winked and held up a green Perrier bottle. She smiled with approval.

For the next thirty minutes, Ella Mae chatted with several people and sipped on bourbon, the flavor less intense than she expected but warm with hints of caramel. Several wait staff offered appetizers off silver trays, the oysters Rockefeller and truffle honey burrata cheese delicious. It wasn't unusual for her and Travis to be wined and dined by venue management while on tour. But it was still something she could never get used to, the over-the-top cocktails and food choices decadent and lavish. Give her skillet fried chicken and collard greens any night of the week, and she'd still be a happy girl.

When it was time to sit down for dinner, John gallantly pulled out a seat next to his at the head of the table. "Thank you," she said. Her brother sat across from her, taking in the exchange.

"My pleasure." John's baritone voice rumbled, his eyes glinting with delight. If she didn't know any better, she'd swear the man was flirting with her.

White and red wines were offered as the salad course was served, the conversation around the table pleasant. As Ella reached for her fork, her phone buzzed with a text message in her small clutch purse parked by her side. Pulling her cell phone out, all the air left her lungs instantly. The text was from Hank Bennett.

Hey Ella Mae. I'm here.

Chapter Nine

Hank

Hank sat in an overstuffed lounge chair in the lobby of the Distel Hotel, anxious to lay eyes on Ella Mae again. Pulling the pocket watch from his jeans pocket, he flicked open the cover and checked the time. He'd made it to Louisville by Greyhound bus in under seven hours, the long stretch of highway giving him time to think about the first words he wanted to say to her. He knew he wanted to thank her right away for giving him this unbelievable opportunity. And he definitely wanted to hug her. Yes, hugging Ella Mae Miller was absolutely in his plans.

When he spotted her walking toward him in the vast lobby wearing a black cocktail dress and heels, he quickly stood and removed his cowboy hat, the words he'd rehearsed earlier vaporized in his throat. She was all shined up like a brand-new copper penny leaving him speechless.

"I didn't think you were coming until tomorrow, before the show." Her voice was tainted with confusion, or maybe it was surprise. At least her engaging smile was intact, her pretty features enhanced with makeup, and her gorgeous hair flowing around her shoulders in big curls.

Hank licked his lips, forcing himself to say something—anything.

"What's the matter?" Her pretty brow furrowed with unease.

"N... nothing. You caught me off guard, is all. You're gorgeous, Ella Mae." His comment induced a beaming smile and a slight blush across her flawless cheeks.

"Thank you, Hank. You're very kind." She clutched her hands in front of her dress and batted her thick eyelashes at him.

Hank realized he must've interrupted something important by how she dressed. "I'm sorry. Did I intrude on your evening? I was planning on coming up tomorrow and meeting you at the arena like we'd planned, but truth be told, I was too damned excited and hopped on the first bus out of Langston Falls."

Ella giggled and nodded. "Of course you did. You're not intruding. I'm just having dinner in the hotel restaurant."

"Oh." Holy hell, did he interrupt her on a date? That would explain her lovely attire and painted lips. "Who are you with?" He didn't mean for his curiosity to get the better of him, the tone of his voice laced with jealousy.

She gave him the side eye and smirked. "I'm with my brother and the ASM Global team."

"The ASM Global team?"

"Yes. They're the management team producing Travis's show tomorrow night at the arena. The record label encourages Travis to accept these sorts of invitations from the big wigs and makes sure to build in extra nights into our itinerary so we can attend. They say it's good for business." She shrugged. "They just served the salad course. It's all good."

"Oh. Well, I don't want to keep you."

Thankful she wasn't on a date with another dude, he parked his hat back on his head and grabbed his duffel bag, slinging it over his shoulder. He wasn't exactly sure where he was supposed to go and felt like an idiot for not giving Ella Mae a heads-up regarding his early arrival. What a way to make a first impression.

"Won't you please join me?"

Hank froze in his stance before he looked down at his attire. "I'm... not really dressed for the occasion." He chastised himself for wearing his loose jeans for travel comfort, and his hair was a complete mess from wearing his beloved cowboy hat all day.

"You look great. You look like you just stepped out of a Nashville billboard advertising country music. Come on." She picked up his guitar case and marched toward the concierge desk. Hank scurried behind her, excited for yet another opportunity with the beautiful songwriter.

"Good evening. How may I help you?" the clerk on duty asked.

"Yes, hi. Could you please have a bellman deliver these items to my room? I'm on the ninth floor, room 914." She showed him her room card and easily took the heavy duffel bag from Hank and set it on the floor next to his instrument.

"Yes, Mrs. Geller. Right away." He waved over a hotel employee and gave the man instructions.

Hank recalled Ella Mae's pseudo name, Monica Geller, from the sitcom *Friends* with a chuckle before realizing she was sending his things to her hotel room. His heart sank, and he tugged on her arm. "I'm sorry for coming a day early. I didn't think about the room situation," he whispered.

Her eyes traced his face before she boldly reached out and touched his scruffy chin. The gesture induced a flash of electricity through his being. "Well, the hotel is completely booked, but don't worry. There's no 'situation.' You can stay with me, like last night." She bopped him on the nose before she turned on her heels. He was dumbfounded, the whoosh of her perfume a scented trail he followed from behind.

Upon entering the fancy private dining room, Hank looked around at all the dressed-up guests and knew immediately he'd made a grave error arriving unannounced. He looked like a homeless man compared to these upper-class folks in the music biz. He lingered in the doorway among the clinking of dishes and conversation.

"I think I should wait for you upstairs in the hotel room."

Before Ella Mae could reply, her brother, Travis, bellowed for all to hear, "Hey, Romeo! Welcome to Louisville!"

***

Hank had never indulged in a finer establishment. He sat right next to Ella Mae, the servers quickly arranging a place setting and squeezing him in next to another female guest. Apologizing profusely for his attire and the interruption, he was met with some very nice introductions from around the table.

Ella Mae explained to everyone how he was joining the last three weeks of the tour as a songwriter, which invoked curious small talk and questions. All the while, Travis looked on with a perpetual grin on his handsome face, taking it all in. Was he glad for the reprieve from being the center of attention? Or was he miffed Hank had intruded, steering the conversation away from the star of the show?

"I'm always intrigued by the creative process," John Fobas stated. "Tell me, Hank. How do you do it?"

"How do I write a song?" he asked for clarification.

"Yes." John forked a bite of salad and gestured toward him. "Are you inspired? Do you have a muse? How does it work for you?"

Hank pressed a linen napkin against his lips, the lingering taste of bold cabernet poured for him, permeating his mouth. "Well, I usually hear a melody first, and I work off that."

"Me too," Travis added from across the table. "If I have a melody, I can show it to little miss lyric right there, and she takes over." He gestured toward his sister with his fork.

Hank eyed Ella Mae sitting next to him and smiled. "Must be nice having a lyricist in the family. Unfortunately, the words in a song are the hardest part for me."

"Well, I'm looking forward to hearing some of your melodies and seeing what we can come up with over the next few weeks together," she offered.

Together.

Was she for real? Or were she and her brother putting on a show? The Millers were CMA award-winning songwriters, and here he was, fresh off the bus, being wined and dined by the bigwigs in country music and talking about the creative process. What the actual *fuck*?

Hank felt the back of his neck explode with heat and reached for his wine glass again, taking a hefty swig.

Ella Mae seemed to sense his nervousness and discretely patted his thigh from underneath the table, her small hand dangerously close to his crotch. Entwining his fingers with hers, he squeezed. He held her gaze for a few seconds, something honest and sincere passing between them.

The conversation turned away from him, thank God, and the main course was served among a smattering of applause as the waiters presented impressive plates of rib eyes, filets, king crab, and asparagus with black truffle béarnaise. Hank was tempted to take out his cell phone and snap a picture of the decadent meal to send to his sister, Becky, but decided he didn't want to look like a freaking tourist.

Well aware of John Fobas's power in the music world, Hank cut into his steak and listened in awe as the man gave the team and the Miller's solid numbers regarding the upcoming sold-out show in downtown Louisville. Hank's eyes nearly bugged out of his head when he learned the amount of work it took to pull off a sold-out concert, especially one of this magnitude. The show last night in the outdoor venue in Langston Falls couldn't hold a candle to what he was about to experience tomorrow night.

More wine was poured, and a delectable dessert of bourbon bread pudding a la mode was served, the salted caramel sauce causing his eyes to roll in ecstasy when he took his first bite. He couldn't wait to tell his sister all about this meal.

Ella Mae seemed humored, watching him indulge. "It's good, huh?"

"Oh my God," Hank mumbled with his mouth full. "The best."

"Aren't you glad you took me up on my invitation?"

Hank stared at her and licked his lips, mesmerized by her dark eyes glistening in the romantic candlelight. He would remember this dinner and her company for the rest of his life. "Absolutely."

As the lavish meal ended and the group dispersed, Hank stood next to Ella and Travis as they said their goodbyes. He felt uncomfortable in his casual clothes, and a shot of jealousy surged as he watched John Fobas wrap his arms around Ella Mae in a lingering hug. She was stiff in the man's arms, her eyes darting to his as if to gauge his reaction.

"Thank you for dinner, John. It was fantastic," she said.

He pulled back and held both of her hands in his own. "I'm so glad you enjoyed it. Let me know the next time you're in town, and we can do it again." The wink he offered her was intentional.

Turning toward Hank, John heartily shook his hand. "It was a pleasure meeting you tonight, Hank. I look forward to hearing some of your new song collaborations with the Millers on the radio."

Hank exhaled a jovial laugh. "From your mouth to God's ears," he said simply. This man really had no idea who he was in the grand scheme of things. And if he knew he'd slept in the same bed with Ella Mae the night before, he might not have lingered in his hug with her.

"I'll see y'all tomorrow night then." John waved.

"See ya, John," Travis replied. As the last of the guests exited the room, he exhaled a whistle. "Whew, I'm glad that's over with. Y'all want to come up to my suite and watch a movie together?"

Ella Mae looked between Travis and Hank. "You need to get a good night's sleep tonight, Travis. And I need to fill Hank in on some things, too. You know, give him the low down on what happens tomorrow."

Travis planted his hands on his hips, the cheeky grin he displayed noticeable. "Sure. Fill him in, Peaches." He slapped Hank on the back and headed out of the room. "Sweet dreams, Romeo."

"Goodnight," Hank said, unsure of Travis's undertone. When he was out of sight, Hank looked at Ella with concern. "Why does your brother keep calling me Romeo?"

Ella Mae rolled her eyes. "He's always been that way. He's the guy who gives out nicknames like people give out candy at Halloween. I can assure you, he's harmless."

"Are you sure he's okay with me being here?"

"Of course. He told me himself he'd go along with anything I wanted. Lord knows I've put up with enough of his crap all these years." She looped her arm through his and led him through the restaurant, still buzzing with wait staff and patrons.

Hank remained silent, making a mental note to dive deeper into her comment later. Walking through the hotel lobby, he noticed Travis surrounded by eager fans vying for his autograph. The country music star seemed in total control, laughing and smiling among the group.

"Does he need any help?" Hank asked, concerned for his safety.

"No. We have a bodyguard on duty."

"Where?" He looked around in amazement, half expecting to see a guy in a suit wearing dark sunglasses with a hands-free device tucked into his ear, keeping a close eye on things.

"See that big guy in the black Polo shirt over there?" She discreetly pointed toward a man standing near the swivel door entrance. The muscular dude was huge, sure to stop an overzealous fan in his or her tracks if needed.

"Yeah?"

"That's Mario. He's awesome. I'll introduce you tomorrow backstage when he's not so focused."

"Cool."

They came to a halt in front of the bank of elevators, and Hank pushed the up button. "Listen, I'll understand if you need to hang out with Travis tonight. My coming here and joining the tour has probably thrown a wrench in your usual schedule. And I'm sorry about the room situation. I'll get my own room the next go around, or I can stay wherever the crew is. I don't want to be any trouble."

The elevator dinged open, and Ella Mae pulled him inside, her arm still looped through his.

"You are not a part of the crew, Hank. You're a songwriter and a musician. And you're staying with me tonight."

With eyebrows raised, Hank stifled a chuckle. She sure put him in his place. Watching the floor numbers illuminate as they ascended to the ninth floor, he cleared his throat. "Yes, ma'am."

Chapter Ten
Ella Mae

Ella tapped her keycard over the automatic lock and waited for a green flash before she pushed the hotel room door open. The lamps were on, and the two luxurious queen beds were already turned down. Chocolate wrapped in gold with little note cards that read "sweet dreams" were noticeable against the fluffy white pillows, and Hank's large duffle bag and guitar case rested on a bench seat at the end of one of the beds.

"Damn," he exhaled, taking it all in. "You've got some fancy digs here tonight. You sure you want me coming in and spoiling the vibe?"

Ella sat on the bed nearest the bathroom and took off her earrings. "If you think this is fancy, wait till you see Travis's suite. He has a full kitchen and a living room."

"Get out," Hank laughed. He took off his hat and ran his hands through his unruly hair. "So tell me where you want me, and I'll do my best to stay out of your way."

Ella patted the empty space next to her on the bed. He sheepishly sat down and waited for her to give him instructions.

"I want you to make yourself at home, okay? It doesn't matter if we're sharing a room for the time being. It also doesn't matter if we're in a fancy hotel, an interstate motel, or on the tour bus. You're part of our team now, so whatever space you're in is just as much yours as it is mine."

Hank seemed to track with her and nodded. "Alright. But you should know, I've never roomed with a girl before. I mean, my sister and I share a bathroom at home, but our rooms are across the hall from each other. I don't want to make you uncomfortable."

"Uncomfortable? How?" she asked. His boyish smile did funny things to her insides as she waited for his response with bated breath.

"I mean... what if I get up in the middle of the night and have to use the bathroom, and I'm in my underwear?"

"Travis gets up all the time in the middle of the night on the bus to use the bathroom, and he wears tighty-whities," she countered with a giggle. "Next."

"Ok-ay. What if I'm... too loud on the phone, or I accidentally leave my stuff all over and infringe on your space? I'm by no means a neat freak."

"Hank, you have one duffle bag. I hardly call that a lot of stuff."

"Good point." He scrubbed his hand across his jaw. "Well, promise me this. If I get on your nerves, or you need some quiet time alone, you just say the word, okay? And I'll be out of your hair."

Ella Mae shook her head. "I've been living and traveling with Travis Miller my entire adult life. If I can put up with him, surely I can do the same with you. Now stop worrying and unpack."

"Unpack? But aren't we leaving after the show tomorrow night?"

Ella stood and opened the empty drawers on the right side of a large dresser. "Take my advice. Every time we stay in a hotel room, unpack your bag. Put your toothbrush in a glass and keep your toiletries on the bathroom vanity. Hang up your shirts to get out the wrinkles."

Hank palmed his chest as if feeling for wrinkles on the tee he was currently wearing.

"Spread out and make yourself comfortable because this place..." She opened her arms open wide. "... this place is your home away from home. Even if we're only in a room for twenty-four hours, set up shop and make it your own."

Hank nodded as if he understood. "Alright, boss. You've got a deal." He stood and approached his duffle bag on the bench seat, unzipping it with fervor.

"And I'm not your boss, Hank. I'm your friend. And..." She waited for a beat. "And I'm so glad you're here."

Hank looked right at her, his features turning softer in the lamplight. He opened his arms wide for a hug. "Come here."

Ella Mae felt a tingle of butterflies in her tummy before she shuffled into his warm embrace. He wrapped his arms around her and spoke softly into her ear.

"We didn't get a chance to hug in the lobby when I first saw you earlier."

"Oh?" She breathed in his spiced scent of cedar and pine, the air around her warm with visceral memories of hiking in the woods on a crisp autumn day.

"Mmmhmmm. I also want to thank you again for this incredible opportunity. I'm not going to let you down."

Ella Mae pulled back from him, her eyes tracing his manly features. "I'm the one who doesn't want to let you down, Hank. I want to show you what it's like to be on a real road tour. I want you to watch Travis and see how he navigates the good and the bad because it's not all the glamorous life like everyone thinks. Sometimes it can be hard—really, really hard. But it can be pretty amazing, too."

Running her palm across his chest, she averted his close-up gaze. "If you still feel like you're at a crossroads after three weeks on the road, I will have failed you. But if after three weeks you feel like you know what you want and can move forward in your life with confidence, well then... I've done my job."

She dared to look right at him, her heels making her taller in front of his cowboy-booted stance. Her heart thundered, the hidden meaning behind her words unintentional. She was attracted to Hank Bennett and wanted to explore more than music with him.

"I'm ready." He broke their connection and resumed unpacking. As he took each piece of clothing out of his bag, she noticed how neatly folded it was.

"I'm curious, Ella Mae. Fill me in on some of the bad stories. What makes it so hard for Travis sometimes? Is it the physical exertion from the show each night? Or maybe he doesn't get along with some of the musicians or crew?"

This was her cue to come clean about her brother. Slipping off her heels, she padded barefoot across the carpet, opened the fully stocked mini-bar, and retrieved two plastic airplane bottles of whiskey. She held the small bottles by the neck in presentation.

"This is what makes it hard for Travis," she said matter-of-factly.

Hank's brow furrowed. "Alcohol?"

"Yes. And drugs, and women. He's been in and out of rehab twice."

"Yeah, I know. As a super-fan, I've been following him since day one."

Ella nodded. "Then you know, the label almost dropped him during his first year after he performed drunk at a show. But he persevered and got sober. And then when they started planning his first tour, he begged me to go on the road with him, you know, to help keep him held accountable."

"So that's why you weren't too pleased when he took a sip of my beer last night."

"That's right. You heard that."

"Yeah, I did." Hank closed the dresser drawers and placed his empty bag under the bench seat. "Please, sit down and tell me more. How long was he in rehab?"

Ella Mae got comfortable on her bed and crisscrossed her legs from underneath her skirt. Unscrewing the top of the plastic whiskey bottle, she took a swig and tossed the other bottle to Hank.

"Is this too much too soon?" he asked, unscrewing his bottle, and taking a sip.

"No," she replied, licking her lips. "It feels good to talk to someone about it. Although, it's kind of ironic we're talking about alcohol addiction while sipping on whiskey, don't you think?" A shot of guilt traveled to her heart.

"Yeah, but we're not the ones with a problem," Hank reassured, tipping back his bottle. "When did things go sideways for Travis?"

Ella pulled on a random string hanging from the edge of her dress. She could tell him part of the story—but not the whole story.

"It started when our parents died. Travis went off the deep end the day the car accident happened. He's a binge drinker and drank every drop of alcohol my parents had in the house because he didn't have the heart to tell me they were dead.

I was only seventeen at the time. When I came home from school, he was passed out drunk, and I couldn't wake him. When I couldn't track down my parents, I got scared and called 9-1-1." Her hands shook as she lifted the airplane bottle to her lips again, the warm whiskey heating her constricted throat. The memory of that awful day hit her right in the heart.

Hank shifted from his bed to hers and put an arm across her shoulder. "I'm so sorry you had to go through that, especially at such a young age."

She nodded and leaned into him, hints of his woodsy aroma infiltrating her senses again. "It was bad enough dealing with the death of my parents, but when Child Protective Services got involved, they made it very clear Travis was going to lose guardian rights to me if it happened again. I could've been placed in foster care. Can you imagine?"

"So, it didn't happen again?"

"Not for a few more years. By then, I was an adult. I thought it was the one time, you know? I thought he was so unbelievably grief-stricken by our parents' deaths that I let it go. But when he won his first CMA award, something snapped inside him, and that's when it happened again."

"What do you mean, something snapped inside him?"

"Hmmm... how do I explain this?" She thought for a moment. "It was like... he'd climbed to the top of Mt. Everest and achieved every goal he ever had for himself as a musician. He reached the very top, you know? And once he reached the top, he felt like he didn't have anywhere else to go. He got nervous and anxious thinking he'd peaked too soon—that he was a one-hit-wonder."

"But he wasn't," Hank comforted, squeezing her shoulder.

"I know. But at the time, Travis didn't know that. He turned to alcohol and drugs to numb his nervousness. He kept it hidden and in check for the most part. And he swore he didn't have a problem. But there were a few times when he totally lost it in public."

"Were you there when it happened publically?"

"Yes." Her voice was but a whisper. "There was nothing I could do. When Travis loses control when he's drunk or high, it's a very unpleasant experience."

They were silent for a few minutes, Hank continuing to hold Ella Mae in his sturdy arms.

"Do you think he's on the verge of a relapse?" he asked.

Ella drained the airplane bottle and swallowed. "I hope not. I mean, so far, so good on this tour. He's been amazing, actually. But I won't hold my breath. Once an addict, always an addict." She angled her neck to look at him. "When your mom died, did you, your dad, or any of your siblings have a tough time and go off the deep end like Travis?"

Hank turned rigid. When he slipped his arm off her shoulders, she internally chastised herself for bringing up such a difficult topic. There was nothing romantic about death.

"I'm sorry, Hank. I didn't mean to pry." She immediately grasped his hand and held on.

"No, it's okay. It's only fair for me to share my story, right?"

"I guess so."

Hank polished off his whiskey and set the empty bottle on the nightstand. "I was almost twenty when she passed away. We were all with her at home when it happened. Well, all of us except for my oldest brother, Teddy—but that's a sob story for another time."

"Go on," she urged.

"When we realized the end was near, my brother, Walt, couldn't take it. He left. My sister, Becky, was a freshman in high school. She and Daddy held onto each other while he stroked mama's face and told her how much we all loved her and that we'd see her again someday. My brother James was the stoic one. I'll never forget the wooden chair he sat on in the corner of the room and how he didn't say one word. He was just... there, in her presence. You know?"

Ella Mae sniffled and wiped away a lone tear escaping the corner of her eye.

"I sat on the bed right next to her. I just... held my mama's hand and concentrated on all the happy memories we had as a family." Hank pressed his lips together, his eyes misting with emotion. "There was no noise when she took her last breath. No... vibration. Just...peace." His sigh was labored with grief, the vibe in the hotel room heavy with emotion.

He broke their connection and stood, jamming his hands into his back jeans pockets. "You mind if I partake of another one of them whiskey bottles?"

Ella Mae nodded. "Help yourself."

Hank continued to talk as he crossed the room to the mini-fridge, his countenance energized recalling a happier memory. "You would've loved my mama. She had the best laugh. Whenever I think about her, that's what I remember the most. Weird, huh? Do you remember your mom's laugh?" He handed her a second miniature bottle of whiskey and sat across from her on the mattress, his lop-sided smile boyish and charming.

Ella held the bottle and closed her eyes, the memory of her mother's laugh coming at her full force. It always made her smile. "I remember her laugh very well."

"Here," Hank said, interrupting her thoughts.

Ella opened her eyes and immediately noticed his arm stretched toward her with an old pocket watch resting in his open palm. She smiled and took it. "What's this?"

Hank sighed. "My daddy gave it to me before I left Langston Falls today. He put a picture of my family inside. It's the last photo of my entire family together before my mom died."

She gently unhinged the clasp and opened the watch revealing the photo. Her eyes traced each face, lingering on Hank's mother. Her heart clenched with empathy. Mrs. Bennett was a gorgeous woman. And Hank had her endearing smile.

Looking up, she studied Hank silently for a moment. His head was bowed as he palmed the plastic whiskey bottle between his hands, his thick hair obscuring his eyes. She cleared her throat and closed the pocket watch. "We must always remember their laughter, Hank. No matter what," she stated.

Hank nodded and swiped the heel of his hand across his cheek. When he lifted his crestfallen brown eyes to hers, something heartfelt and genuine passed between them. He held his whiskey bottle in the air, and she reciprocated.

"Always."

Chapter Eleven

Hank

Hank was genuinely smitten with Ella Mae, the things they had in common mind-blowing. She was a musician and a songwriter. He was a musician and a songwriter. She'd lost her parents. He lost a parent. Her brother went off the deep end. His brother went to prison. His odds of having this much in common with anyone else on the planet were about as slim as winning the Mega Millions Jackpot.

After their emotional whiskey-drinking story hour, Ella Mae excused herself and went into the bathroom to change out of her dress. Feeling loose and buzzing from the alcohol, Hank kicked off his boots and pulled his guitar from the case. With a few turns of the tuning pins, he started strumming a Travis Miller tune, the song one of his favorites. Ella exited the bathroom and immediately started singing the lyrics she'd penned for the award-winning song. He grinned, enamored by her sweet vocals and crystal-clear tone. The girl was not only an accomplished songwriter but an incredibly gifted singer.

"Do the chorus with me," she playfully encouraged.

Hank cleared his throat and continued to strum, his tenor voice rising to meet hers. He knew every tremolo and lick of the song, their vocal aerobics in succinct harmony. As he played the last chord, he let the instrument reverberate for a few seconds before he looked right at her. She seemed pleased.

"Damn, Hank. You're really great!"

He scrunched his nose and shook his head. "Aw, you don't have to say that."

"But it's true." She grabbed the nearest pillow from her bed and placed it in her lap, her oversized pajamas appearing comfortable in her relaxed state. Her face was scrubbed clean of her earlier makeup, and her hair was braided to the side.

"Do you know any other Travis songs?" she asked.

Hank raised his eyebrows. "I know all of them," he said matter-of-factly.

"For real?" She seemed surprised.

"Yup. Name a tune, any one of them. I guarantee you I can play it *and* sing it."

He watched her lick her lips with glee as if she might try to stump him. But there was no way she could. He cut his teeth on Travis Miller's records learning every chord and lyric the man ever recorded.

"How about... *Ride Cowboy Ride?*"

Hank chuckled. Ella Mae dug deep for that one, her song request one only diehard Travis Miller fans might know. When he started finger-picking the intro in the key of D, she squealed with pleasure and clapped her hands. And then he began to sing the first chorus:

He walks in the kitchen from a long dusty ride.

And words can't express what he's feelin' inside.

He's a 9 to 5 cowboy, who don't make enough.

But he can't live without her. She's so easy to love.

As he segued into the second chorus, she took over, her voice sweet like honeysuckle, the poignant lyrics telling a story.

She's had other lovers with more fortune and fame.

But the price was too high on that fast-moving train.

Then she met a young cowboy with nothin' but dreams.

And she's empty without him, apart at the seams.

Hank paused. "You ready for the chorus? I'll take the low notes, you take the melody."

"You got it," she grinned.

He took a deep breath and played the notes leading up to the chorus. Their voices blended in perfect synchronicity.

So ride Cowboy, ride that range.

Ride 'til it's sundown again.

Press hard in the saddle—hold fast the reins,

'Cause, she needs you.

Ride—

Until you get back home.

And she'll be dreamin'—she's ridin' by your side.

Ride Cowboy, ride.

Hank's heart galloped like the horse underneath the cowboy they just sang about in the song. He stopped playing, something magical and serendipitous happening between them. Ella Mae shifted the pillow off her lap and crossed the space between the two beds. He flicked his eyes to meet hers as she pressed her palms on either side of his face.

"You're a very talented musician, Hank Bennett. And don't you ever forget it."

Coming from someone as successful as award-winning songwriter Ella Mae Miller was perhaps the greatest compliment he'd ever received. He mulled over her words like the swirl of new wine in a crystal glass, drinking in the natural sweetness of the moment. And it became even sweeter when she bent low and pressed her lush lips against his, rendering him wordless.

***

It happened again.

Hank awoke with Ella Mae sound asleep in his arms. They hadn't ended the night that way, each of them climbing into separate beds after they sang a few more of Travis's songs and called it a night. When had she slipped under the silky covers and snuggled her warm, feminine body close to his? And for the love of God, why hadn't he made a pass at her when she'd given him every indication she was interested in him?

Call him old-fashioned, but it came down to one word—respect. If he and Ella Mae were going to end up having sex, which was pretty much inevitable by their off-the-charts chemistry, he first wanted to give her the courtesy of a proper date. Sure, her kisses lit his libido on fire, and the make-out session they enjoyed last night after a couple of whiskey shots and country choruses gave him the perfect opportunity to pounce. But he held back. The moment didn't feel right.

He needed—time. Time to woo her and take her out. Time to innocently flirt and go on an actual date. Making love to beautiful Ella was something he wanted to savor when the time was right.

Hank knew the difference between sleeping with a girl and sleeping with someone you love, although he'd never once uttered the words "I love you" to anyone else besides his own family. Granted, he and Ella Mae's relationship was new, and he was still trying to figure out how all of this would work while they were on the road. He also looked forward to watching his idol in real time, excited to experience the behind-the-scenes drama unfold being part of an authentic country music tour among the crew and the fans.

But looking down at Ella's peaceful, slumbering face, he felt something warm in his chest, grateful she was the one who made it all happen for him. The combination of the aroma of her hair and the heat emanating off her skin soothed him. Without thinking, he nuzzled closer to her neck.

"Mmmm." Ella Mae stirred, her eyes fluttering open and landing on his face. Her smile was immediate. "Good morning."

"Morning," he mumbled. He used his index finger and tenderly slid a strand of hair back from her cheek. "Did you sleep well?"

"Like a rock. These past two nights have been my best sleep since we left Nashville." She sat up and looked at him, the gleam in her eyes noticeable. "What about you?"

Hank stretched his hands out in front of him. "Same."

"Good." She bounced off the bed with the energy of a teenage girl about to go on a shopping spree, the void she left in her wake startling.

"Get dressed. Breakfast is in Travis's suite. I'm sure there'll be a giant spread since this is a five-star hotel." She tossed him his cowboy hat and grinned. "You're gonna need your strength. Today's gonna be a long one."

Hank placed his hat on his head and dipped his face in a polite nod. His bare chest cooled from where she'd pressed her warm cheek in romantic slumber against his skin moments ago. "I appreciate the heads up."

Ella Mae hummed as she pulled open a dresser drawer and fumbled for some clothes. Hank licked his lips, aware of how much he enjoyed sharing space with the beguiling woman. She was easy-going and not one to flaunt her or her brother's fame, their cloistered time together wonderful. But the reality hit him in the feels. His world was ordinary, while her world was much bigger and full of things he couldn't even imagine.

He watched her like a voyeur as she shimmied out of her pajama top, the creamy skin of her bare back beckoning him to reach out and touch her. She kept her back to him and swiftly fastened her bra before pulling a pink tank over her head. With bated breath, he watched as she unbraided her glorious mane of hair in front of the dresser mirror, shifting her long locks over her shoulder. Spotting him staring at her reflection, her hands stilled.

"What?" she asked.

"Nothing."

She turned around and rested her hands on her hips. "Like what you see?" She stood there like a goddess, her pink tank hanging over the edges of her pajama bottoms. The girl was sweet and sexy, a natural beauty in the golden light of a new day.

Hank threw back the bedding and stood, still wearing his cowboy hat. His boxers were tented, and his skin was on fire. Standing right in front of her, he trembled when she boldly placed her palms on his bare chest and raked her fingers down his flexed abs. He grabbed her by the wrists and stopped her.

"What's wrong?" The space between her pretty brows wrinkled in a frown.

Hank brought her hands up to his mouth and kissed her skin. "I know we have something buzzing under the surface between us."

"You do?"

Hank let go of her wrists and moved his cowboy hat from his head to hers. "Yes, I do." Tipping her chin with his fingers, he ran the pad of his thumb along her soft jaw. "But I want to do this right. Before I cross a line, I want to take you out on a date."

She studied his face in silence, her pensive expression giving nothing away.

"I like you, Ella Mae. I like you a lot."

"I like you, too, Hank."

He offered her a charming smile. "Then will you do it? Will you go out with me?"

Ella pursed her lips together, her cheeks glowing with a pinkish color. Her voice suddenly amped up with a strong southern accent.

"Why, Hank Bennett, I'd be delighted to go on a date with you."

Chapter Twelve
Ella Mae

Watching Hank take in the thrilling atmosphere of Travis's live show at the arena in front of a sold-out audience of over twenty-two thousand screaming fans was everything Ella could've ever asked for. His boyish innocence and love of music were apparent among the booming slapback of sound and energy in the room, something she was often numb to and took for granted. But for a few hours tonight, she was thrilled to experience the marvel of her brother and their collaborative songs through Hank's eyes. The air was heavy with country music and the swell of the crowd, thick with adrenaline and blinding spotlights. It was a definite rush between the audience's applause and the joyful expression on Hank's handsome face.

When Travis first took the stage, Hank seemed in awe of the spectacle, his excitement infectious. Even though they'd just hung out backstage like old friends, something seemed to switch inside him when his music idol took to the stage. Hank held a goofy grin on his face and shouted over the music, "*This is unbelievable!*" She knew right then giving him this once-in-a-lifetime opportunity had been the right thing to do.

Folks stood on their feet for most of the show, cheering and singing along to every song. Hank mouthed the lyrics, too, his inner fan-boy making several appearances and uniting him with thousands of others in the auditorium. His eyes fixated on her brother, and for a millisecond, she wondered what it might feel like to have that kind of attention on her.

"Come here, beautiful." Hank surprised her and grabbed her by the waist, twirling her in a circle before pulling her flush against his body in a dance pose. The familiar acoustic intro of *Ride Cowboy Ride* floated through the air, the melody ethereal and, dare she say, romantic. Earlier, Ella Mae had plunked and sung the song during the sound check as the technical crew dialed up Travis's instrument and vocal monitor. Her brother must've heard her and added it to his setlist.

"I can't believe he's playing our song," Hank grinned.

Wait a minute, *our song?*

Orbs of stage lighting danced in his eyes, the feel of his hard body pressed against hers making her light-headed and woozy. "He must've heard me playing it during sound check."

Hank nodded. "It's such a great tune."

"It is." She stared up into his face, memorizing his poignant expression.

He pulled her tighter into his arms, his warm breath tickling the edges of her ear. "Our version was better."

Ella closed her eyes and smiled. Their intimate duet *was* better.

After three encores, Travis waved to the delighted audience and strutted off the arena stage like a rock God. Handing his instrument off to a guitar tech, he was greeted by a female crew member offering him a hand towel and a bottle of water. Hank watched in total admiration as Travis guzzled the bottle and wiped his sweaty neck and face.

"You might want to give Travis some space," Ella Mae suggested with gentleness. She didn't want to burst his fan-boy bubble. "He's exhausted from the show."

Hank nodded and took a respectful step back, but Travis noticed him and approached with a beaming smile.

"Well? How'd I do, Romeo? You approve?" He was panting, his shirt completely saturated with sweat pressed against his toned body.

"Oh.My.God." Hank became very energetic. "When you started the first song, I thought my heart would explode. I mean, the music was so loud. What a rush watching the audience lose their minds! Everyone was jumping and singing, some of them screaming their heads off!"

Travis eyed Ella Mae with lifted brows. "I guess that means I did pretty good then, huh?"

She grabbed Hank by his thick bicep. "Easy, fella, you're getting all worked up."

"The show was magnificent." Hank was bright-eyed and enthralled, staring at Travis like a love-sick teenager. "Travis Miller, *you* are magnificent."

"Thanks, man. I'm glad your first show out on the road with us was a success. Now, if you'll excuse me, I need to hit the shower before I head to the meet and greet. See you there?"

Hank blinked back at him with captivation. "Yes, of course. Absolutely."

His blatant nerdiness induced a chuckle from her brother as he slapped Hank on the back. "Be sure to park our protégé close to me, Peaches. I want him to experience the meet and greet up close and personal."

"Will do, Travis. And for the record, Hank is right. Tonight was an amazing show. I'm proud of you."

Travis gave Ella a peck on the cheek. "Thanks. See y'all in a few."

She turned her attention to Hank, who had moseyed out onto the right side of the stage. One hand was on his hip, the other mussing his hair as he seemed to take in the mammoth arena, his denim backside hard not to admire.

"It's been a long day, huh?" she asked, approaching him.

Turning to look at her, his face was flushed and his smile radiant. "I don't want it to end."

Ella Mae nodded. "Well, it's not over yet. Are you sure you're up for the meet and greet? It can get kind of... crazy sometimes."

Crazy was an understatement. Excited fans meeting Travis for the first time were, for the most part, polite. But there were those instances when some fans turned downright wild and out of control, security having to step in. She so hoped tonight wasn't one of those nights.

"I'm up for anything."

Ella Mae brought Hank to the roped-off area where VIP ticket holders were already lined up, waiting for an autograph and their picture taken with Travis. The room buzzed with titillating energy, the lucky fans decked out in their country best.

"There he is!" A pretty young woman squealed, pointing at Travis.

He sauntered into the room with Mario and his manager, Willie, by his side. John Fobas looked on with pride as Travis stood in front of a large backdrop with the colorful ASM Global advertising logo. His pearly whites glinted in the light from his glorious smile as if he were genuinely happy to greet his diehard fans. Things moved quickly, some fans taking selfies with him while others asked him to sign memorabilia. The entire effort was like a well-oiled machine. Mr. Fobas didn't even glance in Ella's direction. He was obviously enthralled by all the beautiful women vying for her brother's attention.

As Travis looked up from signing a bejeweled white cowboy hat belonging to a woman who looked more like a Victoria's

Secret model than a fan, his eyes landed on Hank. "Get on over here and get a better look, Romeo," he hollered.

Hank eyed Ella Mae with hesitation. "Go on," she reassured. "King Travis has summoned you."

Several women eyed Hank with curious pleasure as he walked through the crowd, much to Ella's dismay. Her brother motioned for Hank to stand mere inches from him, the handsome cowboy obliging with a crooked grin and a tip of his hat. Ella stayed by the wayside and folded her arms against her chest. What was her brother up to?

"Y'all, this here is Hank Bennett. He's a rising country music songwriter and a good friend of mine," Travis announced, gently settling the white cowboy hat on the gorgeous woman's head. Hank eyed Travis with surprise as the overly made-up model batted her fake eyelashes at him, encouraging him to join them in a photo.

Ella bristled while squinting at the woman. Everything about her was fake, from her bleach-blonde hair and painted stiletto nails to her injected lips and booty. She was exactly Travis's type, with her boobs spilling right out of her tight shirt. The way she blatantly edged her way between her brother and Hank to pose for a photo with her hands on their butt cheeks had Ella Mae seeing red.

Hank was a gentleman and seemed to take it all in stride, boldly smiling for the camera. After the flash, the woman whispered something into Travis's ear before handing off a business card—or maybe it was a hotel room key card? Ugh.

Ella continued to watch her brother egg Hank on, especially with the female cougars, and young groupies ogling the two handsome men with pleasure. But when Travis signed a woman's chest with a sharpie and started to hand it off to Hank for a turn, she'd had enough.

"*Hank*!" she hollered, startling him.

A look of chagrin came over his face, and he took a step back as if realizing what he was doing. Slapping Travis on the back, he thanked him, and the two men shook hands. Travis offered Ella a thumbs up, he and Willie having a good laugh at his attempts to get Hank to cross over to the dark side. But Hank was better than that, his lapse in judgment apparent as he slipped his arm around her waist, pulling her snuggly into his side.

"What a madhouse," he simply said.

"Yeah, right. You seemed to be enjoying every minute of it with all those female fans," she teased.

"Did not."

"Did too." She intentionally glowered at him while stifling a giggle. Hank could see right through her.

"Come on, don't be mad. Your brother made me do it." He gestured toward Travis, who was still going at it, several lipstick stamps left behind on his cheeks.

"If he asked you to jump off a bridge, would you do it?"

"Probably," he chuckled.

"You're right. You probably would." She playfully punched him in the ribs.

Hank leaned lower, his hot breath caressing the shell of her ear. "But I'd also jump off a bridge if *you* asked."

Ella swallowed hard, the heat from Hank's body starting a fire in her belly. Pulling back from him, she pinned him with a look of longing. "When did you say you wanted to go on that date again?"

One side of Hank's mouth was jacked up into a goofy grin. "Soon, darlin'. Very soon."

Chapter Thirteen
Hank

They quickly fell into a routine, Ella Mae taking the lead and Hank following closely behind. There wasn't much time to figure out the perfect first date. The long hours on the road and a show in a different city every night during their first two weeks together didn't give them much downtime. The tour was tiring yet thrilling. Between the late nights of travel, sound checks, performances, and meet and greets, Hank was experiencing it all.

He got along well with Travis's manager, Willie, and the guys in the band were always cordial and helpful if he had any questions. The crew was accommodating and friendly, showing Hank how to properly roll cables and use glow-in-the-dark tape to spike the different musician areas across each stage.

But it was his interaction with Travis's fans that really got his juices flowing. To see them in real-time displaying overexcitement and enthusiasm regarding the country star and the music he penned with his sister hit him in all the feels. Hank was wound up by the roar of the crowds and the thundering baseline of stimulation. Now he understood the restlessness and coming down factor after a show, observing Travis often amped up and staying awake until the wee hours of the morning.

Besides the actual performances at the various theaters and stadiums, Hank's favorite part of touring was traveling on the tour bus with Ella Mae. They hadn't stayed in a hotel since his first night, the two often sequestering themselves in the back room of the sleek Prevost for privacy. They'd lounge on the curved, plump leather sofa and collaborate on songs and lyrics while sipping cold beers and noshing on pizza rolls after a performance. She was a creative force to be reckoned with, her incredible talent and expertise in arranging lyrics and rhythms a source of unfathomable joy in his world. Well, that—and hundreds of stolen kisses, hand-holding between bunk beds, and whispered words of longing away from her brother's golden ears.

And in twenty-four hours, they'd be pulling into Nashville for two luxurious days off before heading to St. Louis, Ella insisting he stay at her place—as her special guest.

"Hey," Travis greeted, pushing his way through the closed door into the music sanctuary at the back of the bus.

The curtains were spread open across the rectangular windows on either side of the room, revealing the dark mountainous landscape of the Appalachian region among the highway lights as they crossed the Virginia state line. Their show earlier in Cleveland, Ohio, was another success, the tour hightailing it to Norfolk in the late hour for their last show before heading home for a brief respite.

"Hey," Ella Mae replied. She rested her shiny black Takamine guitar on her lap and shifted her open notebook out of the way so Travis could sit down. "What's up? Are we being too loud again?"

Hank licked his lips, palming the side of his worn guitar. He hoped they hadn't disturbed Travis, especially after his grueling, top-notch performance. They'd left him sitting alone in the lounge area up front, eating chips and watching a replay of the Atlanta Braves baseball game.

"No, y'all are good." Travis's eyes locked with Hank's. "In fact, y'all are too good. I've been over-hearing your music all week." He settled himself between Ella and Hank and slapped his thighs. "It's time."

"Time for what?" Ella Mae giggled.

"I want to play, too."

She eyed Hank with a smirk. "Did you hear that, Hank? My brother says he wants to play, too."

"Cool," he grinned. He'd been waiting for this moment. Well, that and another moment with the pretty girl staring at him with pleasure etched across her face. He couldn't wait to finally have her all to himself in the quiet country setting of her homestead in Tennessee.

Travis pulled a Martin guitar off a wall rack, the sunburst design on the walnut wood flawless. "What's the tune you've been dabbling with in the key of D?" he asked, adjusting the tuning pins on the instrument. "I've been hearing y'all play it over and over. It's very moody."

Ella Mae spoke with a hint of pride in her voice. "That's one of Hank's songs. I've been helping him tweak the bridge."

Travis turned to look at Hank, his long fingers ready to play the first chord. "Well, I haven't got all night. Play me through it, Romeo."

Hank pulled a quick air intake through his nose before he nodded with pleasure and counted off the beat. "And a one, and a two, and a ...."

Hank was thrust into a dream world for the next several minutes as the three of them strummed his song. It was one he'd performed at the Harvest Hoedown last fall, dedicated to his big brother, Teddy. Hank was in awe, watching his idol's hands pick and strum the guitar effortlessly to the hauntingly beautiful melody. His warbled voice filled the small space as he sang in harmony with Ella Mae, his creation about a gentle man who taught him life lessons, something he was proud of. For his brother to remain steadfast through his darkest hours was an amazing testament to his faith and strength, something he aspired to have, and the inspiration behind the music.

Travis added a few signature licks as he listened intently to them serenade him, in tune with the feel and rhythm. The vulnerability and transparency Hank evoked were as honest as he was ever going to get, the unexpected pang of homesickness while singing about his big brother pinging his heart.

Hank strummed the last chord and let it reverberate, allowing the original song to end in a soft undertone before he looked up and nodded at Travis. The man set his guitar by the wayside and clapped his hands. Unsure of what was happening, Hank's eyes widened, and he looked directly at Ella for answers. The smile on her face was infectious as she winked back at him and stood.

"I'm gonna go grab a bottle of water. Do you boys want anything?" She laid her guitar across her vacated seat, her lengthy hair spilling over her shoulders across her flannel pajamas.

"I'm good," Travis replied.

"Thanks, but I'm okay." Hank offered her a tentative smile.

She ruffled his unruly curls with playfulness and exited the back room, her slippers shuffling along the wood floors as she closed them inside. The air buzzed with uncertainty and confidence, the thrum of the bus tires humming beneath them. Hank was unsure how to ask his music idol for his honest opinion of his original song.

"You have it," Travis suddenly announced.

"Have what?"

"You have the 'it' factor."

"The 'it' factor?" Hank questioned. "You mean talent, right?" His heart rate sped up a few ticks as he hung on to every positive word coming out of Travis Miller's mouth. To hear what this man had to say was a dream come true.

Travis leaned back against the leather sofa and tiredly interlocked his fingers behind his head. "Talent is overrated. But having something to say and a way to say it is a whole different ballgame."

Hank scratched his head. "I'm not following you."

Travis shifted, leaning his forearms against his thighs and tenting his hands in front of his face. "You, my friend, have something to say through your music. And if you don't get out there and say it, you'll never know. *And...* it'll piss me off if you don't try, and then I'll have to hunt you down so I can kick your ass." He chuckled, his piercing dark eyes fixated on Hank's face.

Hank laughed out loud. He was in total awe of this meaningful conversation, glad he hadn't imbibed more than a few beers after the show so he could take it all in with focus. Earlier on tour, when he'd first played his original song for Ella Mae, she'd told him he was something special, too. But he chalked up her positivity to her politeness. To have Travis Miller give him his stamp of approval was a game-changer.

"There's a reason you, me, and my sister have been given this gift of storytelling through music," Travis continued. "You need to use your talent and share your story. Giving up and working on the family farm is not an option, bro. You'd be doing the world a huge disservice."

Visions of Bennett Farms filtered through Hank's mind, the rolling vineyards and evergreen blanket of trees across two-hundred acres of family land conjuring up all sorts of visceral memories. He pressed his eyes shut, the big red barn an optical illusion filling his senses. He could almost taste the sweetness of his favorite wine, smell the strong olfactory of pine through his nostrils, and feel the sticky sap on his fingers. Unconsciously, he swiped his hands across his sweatpants, feeling the ghost of pinesap residue from countless grueling hours in the fields.

He exhaled a loud sigh and opened his eyes wide, all traces of his family farm evaporated. "I don't know what I need to do. You're the reason I got into country music in the first place. And somehow, here I am... traveling on a freaking tour bus. And my idol, Travis Miller, just played my damn song."

Travis studied him for a moment, the smirk on his face droopy with fatigue. "Why is it when you get famous people call you by your first and last name? Travis. Miller." He shook his head. "I've never understood that."

"Well, what do you want me to call you?" Hank asked, bemused by Travis's laid-back sense of humor.

"Call me... the star-whisperer." He unexpectedly made a jazz hand move with his fingers spread in a circular motion in front of his face making Hank chuckle with unease. He then stood and palmed Hank's shoulder. "Because you, my friend, were born to be a star."

Hank's mouth gaped as he watched Travis exit the room. Was this a joke? He mulled over the country music sensation's words and shook his head. Was he born to be... *a star*? No fucking way. The man had to be high on something, or maybe he was throwing him a bone, being nice because he knew he was at a crossroads.

For as long as he could remember, he visualized his career being the frontman of his own country music band. Over the years, he depended on his boys back home to carry him through a performance, their combined talents pleasing the local fans. Did he have it in him to perform as a solo act with only hired guns to back him up? Did he really have the potential to be what Travis indicated? Did he have what it took to be—*a star*?

"Hey, you okay?" Ella Mae asked. Hank hadn't even noticed her return, the concerned look on her face evident.

"Yeah. Sure." He ran his hands through his hair.

She scowled and sat right next to him. "No, you're not. Did Travis say something to upset you?"

"No. It's nothing like that."

"Because if he did, I'll go out there right now and give him a piece of my m—"

Hank grabbed her by the cheeks, slamming his lips against hers in a deep kiss. When they came up for air, Ella Mae blinked back at him in surprise.

"What was that for?" she asked breathily.

Hank scrolled her pretty features before leaning his forehead against hers. "That's the beginning of about a billion thank you kisses I have lined up for you."

"Oh?" Her smile was slight as she entwined her fingers with his.

"Yes." He pulled her forward into a hug and kissed the side of her head. "You've breathed new life into me by inviting me to come on tour with you and your brother. I'm never gonna forget any of it. No way."

"I guess some one-on-one time with Travis inspired you, huh?"

"You could say that." He broke their connection and tucked her hair over her ear, their gaze intensifying.

"But it's you who's inspired me even more with your loving kindness and incredible talent. You're my muse, Ella Mae. Being this close to you all these days and nights has caused ...," he paused, trying to find the right words. "... has *increased* a level of inspiration and passion inside me. It's uncanny, and I don't want it to end."

Her big brown eyes muddled, and she leaned against his shoulder. "It doesn't have to end, Hank. This is only the beginning."

Chapter Fourteen
Ella Mae

The show in Norfolk went off without a hitch, Lenny driving them through the night to get Travis and Ella safely home in Nashville for a few blissful days off. It was nearly noon when the big rig pulled into the Music City, the mid-day sky a perfect cornflower blue among puffy white clouds.

Travis was dropped off first, his weary countenance concerning as he stated he would sleep the entire two days and nights off. The man had knocked the socks off his fans, giving them everything he had over the last few weeks. He deserved some much-needed rest. His Nashville home was located downtown in a renovated historic building, her brother preferring the close proximity to the recording studios and his manager. Her place was located in Franklin, Tennessee, a mere thirty minutes south of the city.

As Hank chatted animatedly with their bus driver up front the closer they got to her home, Ella gathered her bags and gave her bunk the once-over. Pulling back the curtain of her brother's bunk, she frowned when she noticed one of his leather bags left behind on the mattress. She knew he was dog-tired, but for him to leave a bag behind, especially one that always seemed in his grip, wasn't like him.

With a quick pull, she unzipped the case. She rummaged through it, scrunching her nose at the sight of what appeared to be a few dirty tees and a couple of spiral notebooks filled with notes and lyric fragments—until her fingers brushed up against several crushed and empty water bottles at the bottom. Pulling one out, she scowled. Why would Travis keep empty water bottles in his tote when they had a recycle bin on the bus?

She took the empty bottles out of the bag to dispose of and paused, a flicker of a warning messing with her mind. Was her brother hiding something from her? No way. He'd been so good during this tour. She would've noticed if something was amiss. But peering into the bag again, she realized something was off with this weird empty water bottle scenario.

Angling her head to ensure Hank was still conversing with Lenny up front, she leaned into the bunk and twisted the cap off one of the bottles, offering a quick prayer up to the heavens. Holding the plastic up to her nose, she breathed in deeply, the distinct smell of alcohol immediate.

Her shoulders sagged as she grit her teeth. "Son of a bitch," she growled.

Frantic, she pilfered through the bag again and counted fifteen crushed water bottles. *What the hell?*

"The countryside is so pretty out here. Reminds me of Langston Falls," Hank announced, coming up beside her.

She quickly stuffed the bottles into Travis's bag and zipped it up, leaving the evidence positioned on the mattress as if it were a pipe bomb about to go off.

Hank pressed his hands against the thin walls between the bunks, his boyish smile melting her heart. "Maybe you can come and visit me when the tour is over? I could show you where I wrote my very first song in the hayloft of our historic red barn."

Ella Mae shuffled toward him and wrapped her arms around his middle, her mind reeling with the proof her brother was drinking again. Pressed against the hard planes of his broad chest, he must've sensed something was wrong.

"Hey. Are you okay?"

She nodded against his shirt and sighed. "I'm fine. Just... tired."

He continued to hold her as the bus leaned into a wide turn and the big wheels went from smooth asphalt to the private graveled road leading to her home. They were almost there.

Hank stroked the back of her long hair. "A few days at home and some rest will do you good. I'll even cook a meal or two if you let me."

She nodded again, thankful for his kindness, the smile he always seemed to induce from her lips a welcome reprieve from her angst. Selfishly, she decided right then and there she wasn't going to let her brother's fall off the wagon come between her and a few blissful days off with her handsome cowboy. She'd confront Travis on the other side.

"Come on," she said, dragging him toward the front lounge area where they could look out the large windows.

Her property was an expansive paradise of trees and summer-faded grasses leading up to a restored farmhouse, the black-painted wood fence line whizzing by in a cloud of dust kicked up by the tour bus's large wheels.

Hank whistled as the home came into view. "Wow. How many acres do you have?"

"Thirty," she replied with pride in her voice. "The house was built in the late 1800s and underwent several terrible renovations. I got it for a steal because it was in such disrepair. But I had to have it. Wait till I show you some of the original woodwork, wide-plank floors, mantels, and hardware. I even have a couple of sliding pocket doors we were able to salvage in the reno."

"What's that building over there?" he asked, pointing out the window.

Ella beamed with pleasure. "That's the original log house built on the property before the farmhouse was constructed. It's also been renovated into guest quarters."

"Cool," Hank grinned. "My brother James still lives in the renovated carriage house on our farm. There's lots of history with these kinds of homesteads. This is another item to add to our list of things we have in common."

Ella smiled. "You got that right."

A few minutes later, with their luggage and guitar cases unloaded on the ancient cobblestone walkway in front of her house, they waved Lenny off and watched the tour bus head back down the long stretch of road toward the highway. She was about to bust at the seams with excitement, anxious to show Hank her home, all thoughts of Travis and his secret pushed to the wayside.

Walking up the broad stairs of her wrap-around front porch peppered with multi-colored Adirondack chairs, she paused to unlock the front door. The sound of several artistic wind chimes pinged the air with calming, melodic white noise. Hank walked the expansive porch to the side of the house and looked out over a faded pasture, the summer wind fluttering the edges of his hair hanging over his ears. Holding the screen door open with her butt, she turned the key into the refurbished front door, the hinges groaning with age.

"You coming?" she asked, pausing in the threshold.

Hank looked over his shoulder at her, the grin on his face infectious. "Yup." His cowboy boots clomped across the weathered boards. "You want me to grab our stuff?"

She shook her head. "No. Let me show you around first."

The screen door closed with a thwack behind them, the clean and quiet interior of her home a welcome sight. Hank stopped in the foyer and admired the high ceilings and antique light fixture.

"Wow!"

"I know, right? That's how I felt the first time I toured this place, only I had to watch my step because the floors were warped and caving in some places from water damage. But that's all been fixed." She flung her right arm out to the side. "This was once the formal living room, but now it's more of a practice space or a cozy spot to plunk out a few songs if I'm in the mood." She watched Hank enter the music room and run his hand across the polished mahogany of a baby grand piano in the center.

"Do you play piano, too?" he asked.

"I do."

His expression morphed into pure surprise. "Damn, girl. You're amazing."

Ella pointed to her left, where the original paneled woodwork of a cozy library was laid out before them. She had a desk expertly placed in front of the bay windows with a fantastic view of her front porch and yard, the window seating peppered with colorful throw pillows and a thick quilt.

"This is the library slash office."

Hank looked around as if impressed. She showed him a half-bath on the main level, the modernized kitchen complete with a farmhouse sink, and another room she dubbed "the family room" with a restored wood-burning fireplace.

"You did all this yourself?" he asked in apparent awe.

"No, silly. I had a contractor and workers. It took them over a year before I could finally move in and call it my own."

As they ambled upstairs, she explained how she'd had solar panels installed on the red metal roof for lower-cost utilities and how rain barrels were situated on all four corners of her home to catch the precipitation for recycling in her flower and vegetable gardens. She showed him two guest rooms with a connecting bathroom and her convenient upstairs laundry room and stopped outside her closed bedroom door.

Gripping the antique knob, she looked right at him with boldness. "This is where you'll sleep for the next two nights—with me."

The heat in Hank's eyes was evident as he moved closer and moved her hair over her shoulder. "What about our date?"

She averted his gaze and sighed, disappointed he was still adamant about a first date before they took things to the next level. "Well, if you'd rather stay in the log cabin out back—"

He cut her off, leaning low and pressing his lips to hers in a deep kiss. When he pulled back, he traced his thumb across her lower lip, his voice low with intention. "I'd love to sleep with you for the next few nights. I mean, we've done it before."

"Exactly." She smiled and started to open the door again, but he stopped her.

"Wait."

"What is it?"

"I want to make you dinner tonight, something special for you on your first night home in a while. Can I borrow your truck and get some supplies? You can point me in the right direction of town. Consider this phase one of our first official date. Deal?"

Her mouth morphed into an ear-splitting grin, the butterflies in her tummy fluttering with possibility. "You've got yourself a deal, cowboy."

Ella Mae showed Hank the rest of her property and handed her truck keys off so he could head into town for a grocery run. Even though her assistant, Michelle, had been over earlier and stocked her refrigerator with her favorites, Hank insisted he wanted to cook something special. What he had in mind, she had no idea.

Waving him off in a cloud of pickup dust, her thoughts reverted to her brother, Travis. The summer heat in the late day was oppressive, and she swiped her hand across her sweaty brow as she trudged up the porch stairs and plopped onto a cushioned chair. Perhaps she should show him some sisterly love and check up on him? Pulling her cell phone from her back pocket, she hit a few buttons and heard the ringing sound. When Travis picked up, his voice sounded upbeat and peppy.

"Hey, Peaches. Miss me already?"

Ella Mae snort-laughed and rolled her eyes. "Hardly." She heard music in the background. "What are you doing?"

"Relaxing. Making a little supper before the Braves game starts on TV. What are y'all up to?"

Ella licked her lips, unsure if she should broach the subject of the empty water bottles she found in his bag. "Did you, uh, forget something on the tour bus?" She held her breath.

Travis was silent for a beat before he spoke with precision. "Nothing I'll need while I'm at home for a few days. Why?" He suddenly cursed under his breath. "Did I leave my fucking wallet on the lounge chair again?"

"No," she soothed. "But you did leave a bag on your mattress. You know? The brown leather one you keep your notebooks in? I hope you didn't need any of those while we're off because I left it on the bus."

More silence.

"Ummm, yeah. I won't be needing it. The cleaning crew can, uh, shove it in the closet, I suppose."

Ella Mae pursed her lips to the side. "I suppose." She cleared her throat. "You have anything you want to tell me, Travis? I might be out of pocket for the next couple of days entertaining Hank. Anything I need to know?" The air surrounding her seemed to still as she waited for her brother to reply.

"Nothing on the itinerary as far as I know. You and Hank have a good time, you hear? He's a good fella. I approve."

Ella swallowed her disappointment, knowing Travis was dodging her questions. "Thanks, Travis. Get some rest."

"I will. And Peaches?"

"Yes?"

"I love you."

Ella sighed. "I love you, too."

Chapter Fifteen
Hank

Hank parked Ella Mae's truck under a shade tree in the grocery store parking lot and pulled his phone out of his jeans pocket. He quickly dialed up his sister back home in Langston Falls.

"Hank!" she greeted with excitement. "How are you?"

"Hey, Becks. I'm fine," he laughed, thankful for her familiar voice. "How's dad and the rest of the boys?"

"Dad's great. Everyone is great. Tell me about you. Dad loves the text group you created so we could all hear about your travels. How was the show in Norfolk?"

"The show was amazing, gah! I wish you could've seen the fan's reactions to Travis. It was... incredible."

"I knew it would be. Where are y'all headed now?"

Hank pressed his cowboy hat lower on his head. "Well, we have a couple of days off, so we're in Nashville."

"Ooo! That sounds like fun. Where are y'all staying? At another fancy hotel?"

Hank chuckled with chagrin. "Nope. Ella Mae and her brother both have homes here. I'm staying with Ella on her farm in Franklin. You should see it, Becks. Her place reminds me so much of Bennett Farms."

"Wow. So you're staying with Ella Mae—just the two of you? I take it y'all are getting along real well then, huh?"

Hank nodded and looked out the windshield. He noticed an elderly couple pushing a cart toward their car loaded with grocery bags. "We are, Becky. Ella Mae... she's brilliant. She's been helping me with a few of my songs. You won't even recognize them now. They're so much better."

"I'm so happy for you, Hank. Truly, I am. Are you with her now?"

"No. That's why I'm calling."

"Oh? What's wrong?"

Hank laughed and exited the vehicle. "Nothing's wrong. In fact, my life couldn't be any more right at the moment." He nodded at the elderly couple and offered to take the empty shopping cart off their hands.

"Hank? You there?"

"Yeah. Sorry about that. I'm at the local grocery store. I called because I need your help and expertise. I want to make Ella

Mae dinner tonight. You know... something special for our first official date."

Hank could hear the pleased tone in his sister's voice. "Well, you certainly called the right person for the job."

"I was hoping you'd say that."

An hour later, with several grocery bags on the passenger seat, Hank parked Ella's truck and was greeted by a barking dog. Ella Mae was right behind the animal, her infectious grin wide and beautiful. She'd changed into a flowing maxi dress in a bright shade of green, and her hair was piled on top of her head in a messy bun. Cowboy boots donned her feet, and she held a big blue bucket in one hand as she approached the truck.

"You need any help?"

"Nope. I got it. Who's this handsome fella?" The scrappy animal looked up at him with a panting muzzle and sidled right next to Ella's legs as if protecting her.

"This is my dog, Lucky. You just missed my neighbor, Chuck. He brought him over. Chuck takes care of Lucky on his farm while I'm on the road."

Hank kneeled and stroked the dog's head. "Hey, boy. How's it going?" Lucky gave Hank a few curious sniffs before he licked his hand.

Ella Mae giggled. "He likes you."

"I like him." He ruffled the dog's fur with playfulness, his voice exaggerated with a silly tone. "Who's a good boy? Who's a Lucky boy?" Lucky turned frisky and scampered off like a greyhound before quickly changing direction and running full speed past the two of them with the energy of a puppy.

"He's got the zoomies. He's so happy to be home."

Hank laughed at the dog's antics. "He's happy to see his pretty mama. What's in the bucket?"

"Oh, it's empty. I just fed my chickens. Chuck takes care of them, too, while I'm gone. I'll introduce you later."

"To Chuck or the chickens?"

"My chickens, silly. They're a part of my family, too. You'll meet Chuck when he picks up Lucky before we leave for St. Louis in a couple of days." She looked past him toward the truck. "I can help you take in the groceries. What are you cooking for me anyway?"

Hank placed his palms on her shoulders and turned her around, urging her toward the house. "I got this. It's a surprise. I don't need you snooping in the bags before I'm ready."

"Oh, a surprise, huh? I love surprises." She coyly looked over her shoulder at him, batting her lashes. "Me and Lucky will be hanging out on the front porch. If you need me in the kitchen for anything, just holler."

"Will do."

Hank scurried inside with his arms loaded with grocery bags. He carefully laid everything out and took inventory. Opening and closing a few drawers and cabinets, he found the pots, pans, and utensils he needed to get dinner started. His sister talked him through an easy meaty spaghetti meal, complete with garlic bread, a healthy salad, wine, and a store-bought triple-chocolate cake. Leave it to Becky to know the way to a woman's heart and stomach.

With the Italian sausage browning in a cast-iron skillet, he quickly chopped garlic and onion to add to the mixture. Searching the drawers a second time, he couldn't find a can opener for his tomatoes and paste. Cracking open the kitchen side door leading out onto the wrap-around porch, he hollered, "Hey, Ella Mae? You got a can opener?"

Lucky's head peered around the corner, his dark ears perked with interest. He heard Ella reply, "Top drawer by the sink. Look near the back."

"Top drawer near the sink," Hank repeated. He pulled the handle and pushed a few things out of the way. Sure enough, he found an old-school hand-held can opener and got to work.

"Did you find it?"

Hank jerked his head to find Ella Mae standing in the doorway, her feet now bare and tendrils of loose hair falling out of her messy bun. Streams of early evening sunlight surrounded her in a glorious orb, making her appear ethereal, like a beautiful goddess.

"I did," he grinned, holding up the stainless steel opener. "Can I interest you in a little charcuterie and wine while I cook?" He motioned to the kitchen table, where he'd laid out a few expensive blocks of cheese, some red grapes, and an assortment of crackers.

Her grin said it all. "I'm impressed. Of course, I'd love a glass of wine if you have one with me."

Hank was quick on his feet and pulled out a kitchen chair for her, his chivalrous behavior amped up a notch. He was taking this first date seriously.

"Thank you."

"You're welcome."

Lucky stretched near Ella's legs and settled onto the cool floor. Hank poured wine into colorful cobalt blue tumblers he'd found behind the pretty glassed-in cabinet in the kitchen corner and handed her one. "Cheers, Ella Mae."

"What are we toasting to?"

Hank didn't hesitate. "Cheers to my lovely muse and her beautiful home." His eyes fixated on hers as their glasses touched. Bringing the wine up to his mouth, he took a sip while watching her face blush with subtle color. "You like it?"

"Yes. What is it?"

Hank pointed to the bottle on the table next to the charcuterie board. "It's called, 'Big Red.' It's the one Willie said he bought a case of, remember? It's a popular blend from my family's winery in Langston Falls. I couldn't believe it when I saw it on the shelf in the grocery store."

Ella Mae picked up the bottle and ran her fingers across the red and green label. "This is your family's wine?"

"Yup." Pride filled his being. "You sure you like it?"

"Very much." She eagerly took another sip, as did he.

"This wine was made from grapes grown on the hillside right outside my childhood home in Georgia. The sweet taste reminds me of the fond memories of the past and..." He paused.

"And?"

Hank smiled with chagrin, hoping he wasn't completely geeking out in front of her. "And... the promise of an even better future."

His quixotic words seemed to strike a chord, her cheeks blushing with color. "You're such a romantic, Hank. That's one of the things I like most about you." She took a lingering sip. "This wine is a great choice, and it sure smells good in here. What are you making for dinner?"

Hank set his wine glass on the counter and opened the various tomato cans, dumping them into the meat mixture in the skillet. "I'm making my sister's easy spaghetti recipe. I hope you like Italian sausage."

"Mmmm, of course," she replied. "So your sister's a good cook?"

Hank stirred in the tomatoes. "Becky's an amazing cook. She makes all the daily meals for our family and the farm hands. She even has her own YouTube channel where she blogs about it. It's called, *The Farmer's Daughter*."

Ella Mae gasped. "That's your sister?"

Hank's smile was wide as he turned to look at her. "Yes. You've heard of her?"

"Heard of her? I'm a *huge* fan. I listen to her podcast on the bus all the time. I even made her pecan brittle last Christmas. You know, the easy recipe using club crackers?"

"Oh, yeah. It's a family favorite. I could eat an entire batch if she'd let me." Hank placed a lid on the skillet and turned down the heat. "This needs to simmer for a few. Shall we take our appetizers and wine outside and sit on the porch?"

"Let's."

The two of them gathered the wine and the charcuterie board, with Lucky bringing up the rear. Ceiling fans gave off a slight breeze as they sat in the shade and looked out across the expanse of land, reminding Hank of home.

"This is awesome, Ella Mae. Thanks for inviting me to stay with you."

She demurely looked at him and offered her free hand resting on the arm of the Adirondack chair. Entwining his fingers with hers, the two smiled at each other.

He knew right then this was shaping up to be the most remarkable first date of his life.

Chapter Sixteen
Ella Mae

Ella plunked the last chorus of the famous bar room song on the piano, her and Hank tipsily singing at the top of their lungs about friends in low places. Lucky howled, causing them to burst into a fit of laughter.

"Awe, come on, Lucky! It wasn't that bad," Hank chuckled, swiping a finger underneath his eyes.

Ella Mae shook her head, her cheeks aching from smiling and laughing hard all evening. "He always does that when the music or singing gets too loud. I think he's trying to add his own doggie harmony."

Hank ruffled the fur on Lucky's head. "Well, he's a good dog. He's definitely lucky to have you for his mama." Stepping into the curve of the piano, he poured the remnants of the second bottle of Bennett Farms wine into Ella's glass. "You want me to open another bottle? Or are you ready for dessert?"

Ella pressed her teeth into her lower lip and averted her gaze. She'd been having so much fun during the evening being wined and dined by the handsome cowboy, she'd almost forgotten about dessert. The sunset was long gone, the dark night closing them safely inside their happy musical bubble. This was really happening.

"Um... I think I've had enough wine. Serve me any more of it, and I'm likely to make a fool of myself. If you don't mind, please, I'd like some dessert now," she boldly announced.

Hank's eyes glistened with pleasure, and she thought he might offer his hand and lead her to the bedroom upstairs. She was more than ready to be wooed into the next inevitable phase of their relationship. Instead, he took off toward the kitchen.

Scowling, she rested her hands on her thighs, disappointed she'd read him wrong. "Hank?"

There was no reply, only the sounds of drawers being opened and closed among a rattle of dishes coming from the kitchen. She started to second guess her bold request for some dessert, not thinking he'd literally go into the kitchen and gather a sweet treat. Frustrated, she picked up her wine glass and took a hefty swig. Maybe it was better this way, especially after all the delicious wine they'd consumed.

Lucky panted before settling near an air conditioning vent on the floor. Footsteps across the wooden floors became louder as Hank returned to the music room. When he reappeared, she noticed a fork and a plate loaded with a thick slice of chocolate cake in his hands, the youthful grin on his face ridiculous. This induced a silly giggle from her lips.

"What have you got there, cowboy?"

"Dessert," he replied matter-of-factly.

"I can see that." Disappointment flushed her expression for a second time. This wasn't the kind of dessert she had in mind.

Hank sat beside her on the piano bench and loaded the fork with a generous bite. "Open up your pretty mouth for me, darlin'."

Ella stared at his full lips, the rumble of his sexy voice calling her darlin' vibrating her core. Desire washed over her so powerfully she swayed in her seat—or maybe it was the wine. Slowly, she parted her lips and opened them wide. Hank gently fed her the decadent bite of cake and seemed to wait for her reaction.

"Mmmm," she mumbled, intentionally licking her lips. Hank seemed to home in on her mouth as his eyebrow hitched with what appeared to be fascination. "Now it's your turn."

Taking the plate from his hands, she scooped up a large bite and held it in front of his mouth. "Open wide."

Hank leaned in with his mouth agape, his lips closing over the forkful of chocolate. His Adam's apple bobbed in his throat as he swallowed. "Mmmm, it's delicious. But I know something that's one hundred times better."

He took the dessert from her and set it on the closed lid of the piano, but not before raking his index finger across the thick frosting.

"What are you doing?" Her voice was laced with curiosity.

Hank kept quiet and touched the chocolate tip of his finger to her lips. She licked the frosting and then took it a step further, wrapping her entire mouth around his finger. His eyes went wide, and he exhaled a slow, hot breath as she sucked the chocolate right off.

Pulling his finger out of her mouth, he shook his head. "Do you have any idea what you do to me?"

Ella eyed his bulging groin, her wine-soaked gumption on full display when she dared to place her hand on his thick, warm denim. Her touch caused him to flinch, but she was undeterred. Moving closer, she nipped at his ear, her chocolaty breath full of lust.

"This has been the best first date of my life," she whispered.

"Really?" He seemed surprised.

Peppering his scruffy cheek with featherlike kisses, she paused in front of his mouth, daring him to finally cross a line. "Yes. And now you can officially check our first date off your list so we can move on."

"Move on to what?"

"Really, Hank? You have to ask?"

His piercing gaze scrolled her features as if trying to make up his mind. Well, she was more than willing to make it up for him. Standing, she pulled him to his feet and led him toward the staircase. He followed her from behind, not saying a word, his fingers steadily gripping hers. When they were on the other side of her bedroom door, she let go and flicked on a bedside lamp.

"Are you sure about this, Ella Mae?" He stood there like a chiseled Michelangelo statue staring right at her. God, those eyes. His mouth. His chest and broad shoulders. Those hands that effortlessly created beautiful music on his guitar—the same hands she desperately wanted touching her body.

Standing in front of the bed, she provocatively lowered the strap of her maxi dress, her eyes never leaving his. "Yes."

Hank remained quiet and watchful, but he didn't stop her. The dress slipped from her figure and pooled at her feet, leaving her standing there in her underwear and bra. He was clumsy in his motions, ripping off his boots, pulling his tee up and over his head, and flinging it to the side, his glorious chest on full display. Within moments, her back hit the soft mattress and his weight pressed into hers. His lips slowly made a trail down her neck, his fingers tracing her curves. Straddling her waist, he leaned in and placed his hands on either side of her head, his face hovering above hers. Ripples of pleasure shot straight to her core when his digits dragged across her cheek.

He devoured her mouth with a searing-hot kiss, igniting every nerve ending in her body. She reached between them and slid her hand over his bulging cock, desperate to feel him inside her.

"I want you, Hank," she whispered. "I've never wanted anyone so badly."

"I want you, too, Ella Mae."

He sat on the edge of the bed and shucked off his jeans, revealing his commando composition underneath. Heat pooled at her center as her gaze drifted from the smooth, hard muscles of his naked body down to his cock, her brow furrowing for a beat when she noticed a jagged scar dangerously close to his groin.

"What happened?"

Hank ran a hand across the evidence of his injury and shrugged. "Chainsaw accident a few years ago. I was careless and almost hit my femoral artery."

"Oh my God," she muttered breathlessly.

"I'm okay, Ella Mae." His dark eyes held hers in a gaze full of lust. "But I won't be if you don't get naked right now."

"I thought you'd never ask." She grinned and unhooked her bra, flinging the garment toward the pile of clothes on the floor. Her nipples pebbled underneath his touch before he looped his fingers through her lace panties, pulling them down her legs and exposing her.

She yelped at the first sweep of his tongue through her wet folds. His mouth was hot, his tongue coaxing and exploring. And then he eased a finger inside her, the scent of desire permeating the air.

"You're so beautiful, Ella Mae," he mumbled against her thigh. "I have protection. Are you ready for me? Or do you need more of this?"

Ella shook her head and swept his unruly hair back from his face. "I'm ready for you, Hank." She waited for him to sheath himself with a condom, her heart racing at full speed. This was really happening.

Her gasp was audible as he plunged into her so deep it hurt, yet she wished she could take him deeper. Wishing she could stop time and stay wrapped up in this man, their bodies amped up with fervor as they raced toward the finish line. Wishing she had met him earlier. Wishing he would always be on tour with her and her brother. She wanted to savor this moment and make it last, but her primal need for him shocked her.

Ella inhaled deeply, drunk on the wine, the sex, the scent of Hank's skin, and how he filled her completely. The masculine weight of his hips between her thighs had her seeing stars, and she urged him faster. Running her hands across his back and over his perfectly round, muscular ass, she moaned. And then he crushed his lips against hers again, the passion between them exploding.

His fingers threaded through her hair as he pummeled her wet core pulsing against his thick shaft. She surrendered completely, unashamed of the way she wanted him. And Hank seemed to want her just as badly. She felt it in the aggressive way he moved inside her, heard it in his scratched voice whispering her name against her ear, and knew it from the way his lips continued to lick and nip her skin. Arching her back, she rocked her hips and begged him not to stop, crying out with wild abandon. They flew higher and higher together until they careened over the edge, their worlds exploding into shared erotic pleasure.

Afterward, they lay beside each other, their bodies tangled among the twisted sheets. They were hot and sweaty, breathless from their incredible first time together.

"Oh.My.God," Ella pronounced in a gasp of air.

Hank turned to look at her. "I know, right?" He continued to pant. "You're incredible. That was the best sex I've ever had in my entire life."

Ella raised her eyebrows and agreed wholeheartedly. "For me, too. It was like... harmony, you know? Like... when you're writing a song, searching for those perfect notes, and when you finally land on them, *bam*! Our bodies were like that, Hank. We were in perfectly synched harmony."

Hank nodded with gusto as he sat up and unrolled the condom off his dick, wrapping it in a tissue he pulled from a box from the nightstand. "Why does that make perfect sense to me?"

Ella leaned back on her elbows. "Because you're a talented musician, and you understand me more than any other man I've ever been with?" Something shifted between them while they were having sex. They weren't just friends anymore—Hank Bennett was officially her lover.

His features softened in the bedroom lighting as he lay back on the bed. Dragging a finger down her cheek, he traced her lips. "I do understand you. And I want us to explore more. More music. More togetherness. More passion."

"More," she whispered in agreement.

Changing their position to under the covers, he spooned her from behind, his fingers curling around her hip and stroking her soft mound. A single touch from his hand induced another electric current of pleasure as she writhed closer to him.

His thick digits slid slowly inside her as his whispered, erotic exhale skirted across her ear.

"More."

Chapter Seventeen

Hank

Every body part of Hank's was loose and relaxed as he sat on the front porch and watched Ella Mae scatter chicken feed among her feathered brood released from their coop. With her sweet scent of honey and flowers, the beautiful woman smiling at him from across the yard made the air around him feel warmer with visceral memories of wine and magnolias on warm summer nights back home. He would never forget their first night of passion together—ever.

Out of breath, Ella Mae clomped up the steps in her cowboy boots, her shorts revealing her long, tan legs underneath. She wore a plain white tee shirt with sleeves rolled up to her shoulders and an oversized straw hat to protect her face from the blazing sun. Plopping in a seat next to his, she pulled off her hat and swept her hair back from her face.

"It's gonna be another scorcher." She picked up her iced coffee between them and took a lingering sip. "What do you want to do today?"

Hank took in her beauty like a prized Rembrandt painting, his eyes scrolling her pretty features. He was tempted to carry her back upstairs where he could examine her up close and personal for the entire afternoon. But there'd be time for that later. A full day stretched out before them with nothing on the itinerary. It was a gift from the heavens. He lazily leaned his head back and watched the chickens hunt and peck for food in the grassy yard.

"Have you ever wanted to just get in your truck and drive until the map turns blue?"

"Hmmm," she hummed. Ice cubes clinked in her Mason jar glass as she set it back down. "That sounds like the beginnings of a song idea. East coast or west coast?" she asked.

"Doesn't matter."

"I prefer the Atlantic Ocean... or the Langston River."

Hank turned his head to look at her again, the smile on her face engaging. "The Langston River is a beautiful body of water, although it's freezing year-round. If you're up for it, I'd like to take you there again."

"I'd like that very much."

The porch fans pulsed a slow breeze above their heads as the colorful wind chimes pinged and dinged every so often among the faint summer breeze. The chickens clucked and pecked the ground, their colorful feathers standing out against the green backdrop of grass. Hank had never been so relaxed in his entire life. He felt like he'd died and gone to country heaven.

"Speaking of songs, and since we don't have anywhere to be, can you tell me a little more about your song we've been working on? You know, the one we played on the bus with Travis?"

"*Brotherly Love?*"

"Yes."

Hank scrubbed his hand across his stubbly jaw. "Well, as you know by the lyrics, I wrote about my oldest brother, Teddy."

"I know. But you've never told me the story behind the music. What happened to him?"

Hank sighed. "I don't usually talk about Teddy to anyone but family." He glanced at Ella Mae, who appeared crestfallen. "But I've never felt closer to anyone like I felt with you last night, so I guess that's under the same umbrella as family, huh?"

Her dazzling smile lit up his insides. It was easy talking with Ella Mae. She was a great listener, allowing him to stumble over his words as he tried to express the pain his entire family went through when Teddy was incarcerated for a crime he didn't commit.

"Five years in prison?" Her tone held bewilderment when he finished, the excessive term hard for anyone to wrap their head around.

"Yup. It was totally unfair. The entire town knew it, too. But there was nothing any of us could do. Teddy sacrificed his life so Robyn wouldn't have a record. Those were the hardest five years of our lives."

Ella Mae rested her chin in her hand, her elbow leaned on the arm of the Adirondack chair. "And you were so young. Gosh, Teddy sounds like a very selfless man. I can't wait to meet him."

Hank allowed a half smile to don his lips. "You're gonna love him. He's gentle and caring. He's strong and has more faith than anyone I know." Shifting in his seat, he blinked at Ella. "Robyn's a lawyer now because of my brother's sacrifice, and she and Teddy got married last May."

"That's right. You mentioned your brother's wedding was the last time you played live. And by the way, your comment made me very sad."

Hank stared across the land, the memory of that day forever etched in his mind. He already knew back then he was at a crossroads, the unknown future toying with his reverie. But he'd kept it together for his family's sake, never showing his angst or complaining about it.

Just like his brother, Teddy, he knew he had to stay positive like their late mother always taught them. He had to keep breathing, sleep when he was tired, and get through each day the best he could without grumbling. And now here he was in Franklin, Tennessee, in the company of a beautiful woman, creating musical harmony together.

"Well, I'm not sad anymore." He reached across the space between them and took her hand. It felt natural being with her. "I haven't been this happy in a long time."

"I'm happy, too." She squeezed his fingers, but her smile faded as she looked away.

Hank scowled. "Why do I get the feeling that's not one hundred percent true?"

Ella Mae pursed her lips and let go of Hank's hand. Shaking her head, she seemed to struggle with her words. "I, um, didn't want to bring this up and ruin our day."

"Bring what up?"

Standing, Ella shuffled to the porch railing and gripped the ledge, her long hair floating in the breeze. Hank came up beside her and hooked his arm around her waist, inhaling the strong scent of honey.

"Tell me."

When Ella looked up at him, her big doe eyes were muddled with tears. His heart broke knowing she'd been carrying some sort of burden. Her hesitation in sharing it with him only added to his concern.

"Darlin', you can tell me anything. I'm here for you, I promise." He cupped her cheek, unaccustomed to her vulnerability.

Her weak smile was fractured with uncertainty, her voice laced with an angry sadness. "I'm pretty sure Travis is drinking again."

Hank shook his head. "That's not possible. We've been with him every single day for the last two weeks. I've never seen him drink alcohol except for a sip from my beer bottle when we first met."

Ella Mae huffed, walked over to the front porch stairs, and sat down with an aggravated thump. Hank followed and sat next to her, careful to give her space.

"Travis is sneaky. Always has been. He left his leather bag in his bunk, and of course, I was nosey and opened it to make sure it wasn't something he might need during our time off." She looked right at Hank, her brow furrowed with doubt. "There were over a dozen crushed-up water bottles in the bottom of the bag. I opened one and smelled it. He's been hiding vodka, Hank. Probably drinking it right in front of us this whole time, acting like it was only water. I'm so fucking mad at him."

Hank mulled over this new information, concerned for Travis and his addiction. "Did you call him out on it?"

"I tried. But he wouldn't admit to anything. Although he did say he approved of you and wanted us to have a good time on our days off."

Hank cleared his throat. "Well, I'm glad he approves."

Ella Mae rolled her lower lip between her fingers. "What am I gonna do, Hank? These few days off could be a catastrophe for Travis and the tour if he goes on a wild drinking binge without me around to stop him."

"Did he tell you if he had any plans?"

"No. When we spoke yesterday, he said he was making supper and about to watch the baseball game. He also indicated he wanted to sleep a lot. I mean, of course he's exhausted." She shook her head again and continued.

"You know that feeling you get in your gut when something's off? That's how I've felt since I found those water bottles. He can't screw this up, Hank. He can't. We only have a few more shows. He's gotta make it till the end of the tour. Why is he so selfish? Why would he drink when he knows damn well he has a problem? I mean, how many times does one need to go to rehab? Why can't he beat this thing? I can't go through this again. I can't!"

By this time, Ella Mae was distraught, her voice strangled with fear causing Lucky to whine and lick at her flushed cheeks.

"Sweet girl, you're jumping to conclusions. He didn't seem out of control to me. In fact, his last show in Norfolk was the best concert I've ever seen in my entire life." He hugged her close, rocking her in his arms as she comforted her dog. "Maybe he had a little slip-up, but he still seemed in control. Would it make you feel better if we went into town and checked in on him?"

Ella Mae sat up and swiped her hand under her nose. "I've thought about it. But selfishly, I wanted to spend all my free time with you."

Hank grinned, smoothing her hair back from her face. "We'll still be together. We can do a quick drive-by and then play tourist. I could show you my unbelievable dance moves at one of the honky-tonks where my band played last winter." This induced a giggle from her, the pleasant sound music to his ears. He was glad he was there to comfort her, glad she'd opened up to him.

Standing, Hank held out his hand to help her up from the stoop. "Whaddya say? You up for a little Sunday drive into town?"

"It's Tuesday," she corrected.

"Sunday—Tuesday. They're all the same when I'm with you."

Ella Mae gripped his hand, and he pulled her up into a standing position. The look of love and gratitude on her face was hard not to notice. "Sounds like the beginnings of another hit country song to me."

Chapter Eighteen
Ella Mae

Downtown Nashville teemed with tourists out and about on the sunny day taking in the flashy honky-tonk signs, the Johnny Cash Museum, and marveling at the historic Ryman Auditorium. Ella found an open spot on a side street and parked her truck. She'd changed into a pair of jean shorts and a loose-fitting blouse, her signature cowboy boots ready to hit the pavement and catch her brother in his devious act.

"Hold on, Ella Mae." Hank grabbed her by the arm. "You sure you know what you're gonna say?"

"Yes. We're going to march up to his place on the second floor unannounced, and I'm going to ask him point-blank about the water bottles. Hopefully, we won't walk in on him throwing back tequila or shot-gunning hard seltzers in the middle of a binge."

The two continued along the broken sidewalks toward the back end of a historical building. Ella explained her brother's private residence on lower Broadway was one of three single-level condos in the renovated structure, all owned by famous country musicians. Pulling Hank by the hand, she led him to a large, wrought iron gate with a keypad and punched in a code. Crossing the empty parking lot, they continued up some stairs and into a dark hallway with exposed brick, old hardwood floors, and an elevator. She pressed the button as the two eyed each other, her nerves frantic with what she supposed they could walk into. Travis would either be completely fine, or he'd be shit-faced. Hell hath no fury if it was the latter.

Sticking a key into the elevator console, the cab slowly climbed to Travis's private entrance on the second floor.

"Have you ever surprised your brother before? You know, showing up unannounced?"

Ella Mae stared at the numbered lights above the door as they ticked, her eyes wide with trepidation. "Many times."

The elevator opened into a small entryway revealing the giant great room of Travis's home. The entire place held exposed brick walls and had twelve-foot floor-to-ceiling windows revealing the downtown area below. A big screen television was on a sports channel, the sound muted. And laying across the L-shaped, over-stuffed sofa was her brother, sound asleep—or maybe he was passed out drunk?

Ella placed her index finger across her lips and looked at Hank. He nodded in response, staying behind in the shadows of the hallway. Careful, she tiptoed toward her brother, conspicuously eyeing the items scattered across his coffee table. It looked like he'd had breakfast delivered, the Styrofoam container practically licked clean and the faint scent of bacon lingering in the air. A large paper coffee cup was within arm's reach, and Ella wondered if he'd added a shot or two of whiskey to it.

Settling her body near his feet, she pressed her hand against his ankle, and he stirred.

"Peaches?" Travis mumbled in a scratched tone. He rubbed his eyes and sat up. "Wh... what are you doing here? What's wrong?"

Her heart hammered. It was now or never. "I was worried about you."

"Worried? Why?" Swinging his legs over the sofa, he ran his hands through his disheveled hair when he noticed Hank in the wings. "Hey, Romeo. How are ya?" Her brother's tone changed instantly as if he were putting on a show.

"I'm great, Travis. I love your place. It's so cool you're in the heart of Nashville."

Ella tilted her head and looked at Hank. The man was sweet as pie, never causing a stir, his manners always in check. He ambled into the great room, acting like nothing was amiss.

"It is cool being here when I'm not on the road. I have a beach house on the West Coast, too." Travis stood and gathered his breakfast trash. He seemed totally coherent.

"Oh yeah? What beach?" Hank asked.

"Malibu. I can't stand the cold winters here in Tennessee." He started toward the open-air kitchen. "I love it here when it's not freezing. This place is three blocks from the Riverfront, across the street from the Johnny Cash Museum, and one block from the Ryman. You could definitely say I'm living in the heart of the city." After dumping his trash into a garbage can, he leaned across the marble island and played host. "Can I get y'all anything? I've got some club soda and bottled water. Sorry I don't have much of a choice."

Ella Mae pinned her brother with a piercing stare. Bottled water, her foot. But he did seem fine, and she could see no traces of him partying or boozing it up.

"Hank, go check out the view from Travis's bedroom. You can see part of the Batman building downtown."

"The Batman building? Cool." Hank shuffled out of the room, leaving Ella and her brother alone.

She hurried over to the island, her words coming out in a rushed whisper. "I know you've been hiding vodka in water bottles. I saw them in your bag on the bus, Travis. Don't lie to me."

Travis shook his head and kept his cool. "Those must've been from ages ago. I swear, Peaches, I haven't had a drop since the tour started. I swear to God."

Ella scowled, unsure if her brother was telling the truth. She wanted to believe him. She wanted to so badly. But it was hard after all the other times he'd blatantly lied to her to keep his addiction a secret.

"Go ahead, look around. I promise you won't find any alcohol or drugs in here." His pupils looked normal as he stared back at her, daring her to snoop around his private residence.

Guilt filled her completely, and her shoulders drooped. Hanging her head, she muttered, "I'm sorry, Travis. When I found those hidden bottles in your bag, I thought—"

"I know what you thought," he interrupted. "You were convinced I'd fallen off the wagon and was trying to keep it from you." By this time, her brother had come around the island and held her by both shoulders. "Look at me, Ella-Bo-Bella."

Staring up into her brother's handsome face, his words came out carefully with slow intention. "I promise you, I'm sober. I've got nothing to hide from you, okay?"

Ella swallowed hard, still unsure if he was telling her the truth. "Okay—"

"Man, you were right," Hank interjected. "The design of the high-rise looks exactly like Batman's mask." He was fully animated, his face lit up with pure joy.

Travis let go of Ella and walked toward Hank, slapping him on the shoulder. "It's the AT&T building, but the Batman building sounds way cooler, don't you think?'

"Totally," Hank chuckled.

The threesome lingered for a few more minutes before Ella Mae and Hank said their goodbyes, leaving Travis alone to continue his rest and watch sports on TV. Hank weaved his fingers between hers and squeezed as they made their way outside.

"I thought he looked fine."

"Me, too," she agreed.

Hank pulled her to a stop. "So you wanna go play tourist now?" The way he looked at her with his boyish grin and tousled hair left her pining.

"Sure. But later, I've got other plans," she grinned.

***

They spent the afternoon wandering the streets of downtown Nashville, the bright sun interspersed with neon lights and carnival-like sounds of country twang filtering out the front doors of every bar and restaurant on Broadway. They had a blast at the Ernest Tubbs Record Store, where they searched for iconic treasure among the wooden bins of plastic-covered CDs and albums, humming along to songs being played over the store speakers.

They played a game to see who could stump who first, singing a verse or two of a hit song and then holding up the record album for confirmation. Hank was not shy, belting out a Merle Haggard chorus or shaking his booty while crooning a famous Elvis line. She reciprocated with her smooth rendition of Patsy Cline and stumped him with a 1970s classic.

"That's not Loretta Lynn?" he asked.

"No, silly. *Don't Make My Brown Eyes Blue* is Crystal Gayle's song, not Loretta Lynn's. But you were in the ballpark. Loretta and Crystal are related. They're sisters."

"Get out!" Hank was surprised as if this was news to him.

"Yes, they're famous siblings, both having a thriving career in the country music biz."

Hank looped his arm through hers as they walked out of the record store, their next stop finding a place to eat. "Well, I'll be."

They meandered through the crowds and came up to an old, renovated building turned into a restaurant. Hank pulled the big door handle and allowed Ella to enter first. The indoor space was vast, with red and white checkerboard print prevalent in the indoor dining area. Because it was still early before the dinner rush, it took them only a short time to order food and drinks from the bar on the first floor. Hank offered to carry her glass of wine up the stairs to the third-floor rooftop seating area, where they found a table for two without any problem.

"I love this scenic view of the city," Ella Mae sighed. She took a sip of wine and watched Hank slurp the foamy top of his beer. "That's the Cumberland River, and you can see the Batman building over your shoulder." Hank swiveled his body and looked up at the familiar skyscraper, the grin on his face infectious. The earlier humidity had dissipated, and a slight breeze played with the edges of Ella's long hair. "It's a beautiful city, don't you think?"

"It is." His smile was warm. "I'm glad to be here... with you, Ella Mae." His dark eyes were intense.

Heat peppered her cheeks, delighted by his remark. "I'm glad you're here with me, too."

A waitress delivered their food in red plastic baskets overflowing with sweet potato fries and hot chicken sandwiches topped with American cheese and pickles. Ella didn't realize how hungry she was until her taste buds exploded after her first bite.

"You like it?" she asked Hank with her mouth full.

"Damn, that's some good eatin'," he replied, wiping his mouth with a paper napkin.

A trio of musicians played classic bluegrass in the corner, and they tapped their feet and politely clapped after each song. It was so comfortable being with Hank. She'd never had this much fun with a man.

They lingered after their delicious meal and enjoyed another round of drinks as twilight descended. Hank insisted he sign off on the check and offered his hand to help her out of her seat. He dropped a twenty in the trio's tip jar, much to her chagrin. They strolled toward the area of her parked pickup truck, navigating around the lines at Tootsies, Layla's, and Tequila Cowboy. Music hung thick in the air like perfume, the distinct styles echoing into the night.

Ella pulled Hank around a corner where the sights and sounds faded. She stopped at an open park bench along the sidewalk and waved her hand for him to sit. She sighed happily when they were both situated and snuggled into his body, admiring the Ryman from across the street. The century-old building with stained-glass windows was highlighted with dramatic up-lighting in the fading light of day, the brick structure regal and essential in her country music world.

"Don't you think it's cool the Ryman was once a beautiful church?" she asked.

Hank slung his arm across her shoulders and pulled her closer. "I do. Man, what I wouldn't give to be able to play there one day."

"Travis has played there at least a dozen times. It's surreal every time it happens."

"He's a lucky man." He turned and pinned her with a look she knew full well—one part pride, the other part yearning, the wish in his voice apparent. "And how cool is it for you to hear your own songs sung and played in such an iconic place?"

"Very cool," she whispered.

They sat in silence for a few more minutes before an idea unfurled in Ella's mind.

"Come on." She stood and offered Hank her hand.

Wrapping his fingers around hers, he chuckled. "Where are we off to now?"

"I feel like rendering a few—with you."

"Oh, no. Please don't take me back to one of those crowded honky-tonks. I'd rather go back to your place where we'd have more privacy."

"Don't worry. It's not a honky-tonk. It's more of a...," she pondered to find the right words. "It's more of a listening room where talking is strictly discouraged. It's a place where they encourage the audience to focus on the music and connect with the song's emotion and its creator."

Hank stopped in his tracks. Even though his face was shadowed in the early evening, Ella could tell he knew exactly what place she was talking about.

"You're taking me to the Bluebird, aren't you?"

Ella Mae pressed her teeth into her lower lip. God, he was so cute when he was excited.

"Yup. And if you ask me, it's the only songwriter's mecca in these parts."

In a grand gesture, Hank swept Ella off her feet and swung her around with wild abandon making her screech with pleasure. And then he pummeled her mouth with a hard kiss, leaving her breathless for more.

Chapter Nineteen

Hank

Ella Mae pulled into an unassuming strip mall parking lot where the Bluebird Café was located and found a spot close to the entrance. Hank was surprised the famous club was situated in a common area and not downtown, where the tourists flocked. Jogging to the door sheltered by a navy-blue awning with the white, cursive lettering of the Bluebird logo, his palm sweat with nerves as he held tightly to her hand.

"I can't believe I'm here," he whispered in disbelief.

Ella Mae looked at him and smiled. "Believe it, Hank. This place is iconic. And management loves it when published songwriters stop by from time to time. They're gonna love you, too."

"Wait a minute... me? But I'm not published."

"Doesn't matter. You're with me. You need to try *Brotherly Love* out on a live crowd tonight. And if we're gonna test the other new song we've been working on, I'm gonna need a male vocalist to sing it. Unless, of course, you want me to pass it on to Travis and have him come out here instead—"

He grabbed her by the shoulders outside the door and pulled her in for another searing kiss, shutting her down. When they came up for air, his enamored gaze scrolled her beauty. "If I forget to thank you later, you need to know this is one of the greatest moments of my entire life."

Her eyes twinkled. "I'm glad I could be a small part of this important moment, cowboy."

As they crossed the threshold of the famous listening room, a big man wearing a distressed trucker's hat seemed to recognize Ella Mae immediately.

"Do my eyes deceive me?" the man chuckled, coming around a small host station and giving her the once over.

"No sir, it's me, in the flesh." Ella opened her arms wide and greeted him with a big bear hug.

"It sure is good to see you again. How long has it been?"

Ella Mae patted his back and shook her head. "I can't remember. Before Christmas of last year, maybe?"

The man whistled. "Way too long if you ask me."

They disengaged, and she pulled Hank into the conversation. "George, I'd like you to meet my new writing partner, Hank

Bennett. Hank, this here is George Allen. He manages the Bluebird."

Hank did a double-take when she used the word "writing partner" before shoving his hand in a shake. "Nice to meet you, Mr. Allen."

"Please, Hank. Everyone around here calls me George."

"Oh, okay... George."

"What time do the open-mic folks go on?" Ella Mae asked.

George looked at his cell phone and shook his head. "Well, I was planning on having them start at seven-thirty, but now that you've shown up, my plans might have changed."

"Don't do that, George," she pleaded. "These songwriters have been waiting a long time for their chance at the Bluebird. Why don't you have them go on as planned, and Hank and I will close out the evening?"

George took off his hat and ran his hands through his hair. "Tonight could go long. You sure you don't mind waiting around? I'd hate for you to get bored and leave without performing a few."

"We don't mind at all. I've been dying for Hank to see what all the buzz is about this place."

"Ah, a first-timer. Cool," he grinned. There was a wide gap in between his top front teeth. "I'll let Jeanette know you're here, and she'll set you up at a table in the back, away from prying eyes. Anything y'all want tonight is on the house."

"You're the best, George," Ella gushed. "You should know we don't have our guitars with us as this was a spur-of-the-moment visit. We had a day off from the tour and went to Nashville for dinner. I was telling Hank about this place and had a hankering to try something new on a live audience. It's a song we've been collaborating on."

George nodded excitedly. "Excellent. And no worries. We got plenty of guitars in the back. I'll make sure the tech crew knows and has a couple of pretty ones ready for you." He left the two of them in search of a guitar tech.

The intimate performance setup "in-the-round" looked intimidating to Hank, and he wondered how many songwriters knocked someone's drink off a table if he or she made a wrong move while performing with an instrument in hand. Ella seemed to sense his concern.

"You nervous?" she asked, looping her arm through his.

"Little bit." He cleared his throat, trying to keep his cool. His family back home was going to be over the moon when they found out he performed at the iconic Bluebird.

"Hey, y'all. I'm Jeanette, and I'll be taking care of you tonight. I've got your table all ready for you." She tilted her head toward the back of the room, causing her dark ponytail to bounce. Dressed casually in faded jeans, a Bluebird Café t-shirt, and cowboy boots, she led them to an intimate table for two lit up by a single candle.

Handing off a cardstock menu to both of them, she gushed. "George told me you're playing after the open mic folks. I just have to say I'm a huge fan of your music, Miss Miller. I think it's great how you've shown the big wigs in country music that female songwriters are a force to be reckoned with." Her dark eyes glistened with gumption in the mood lighting.

Ella was a consummate professional. "Thanks, Jeanette. We girls definitely need to stick together."

Jeanette giggled. "You got that right. Now, what can I get for y'all?"

Ella Mae ordered sparkling water and Hank followed suit. There was no way he'd risk getting tipsy before performing in this famous space. Knowing folks would lose their minds when they found out the songwriter behind Travis Miller's hit music was gracing the stage, he needed to keep his druthers about him.

"I love this room," Ella sighed.

"Oh? What makes you love it?" He eyed the front of the menu with curiosity. "Other than the fact it's a famous performance space for songwriters like yourself and also a venue where chart-topping artists got their footing in the industry?"

Ella Mae sat back with ease and looked him right in the eye. "You just read that off the menu, didn't you?"

"Maybe I did," he teased.

"Well, I love the vulnerable environment. I mean, take a good look around. It's brilliant. This arrangement gives the audience an up-close and personal view of the musicians while they perform. There aren't many places like it in the world."

"Yeah, about that. Isn't it... awkward? I mean, the audience is practically sitting in the performer's lap."

"That's what makes it unique. You'll see," she soothed.

For the next hour and a half, Hank and Ella Mae watched the fledgling songwriters take the stage and perform. Some were obviously nervous and fudged their songs, their warbled voices and botched playing noticeable, while others were flawless, their tunes sounding like something already on mainstream radio. Hank was mesmerized, taking it all in, his nerves ramping up when George finally took the stage to introduce them.

"Let's give another round of applause to our performers tonight!"

The entire room erupted with polite clapping as George waved them over to join him in the center of the room. "I've saved the best for last. Y'all are in for a real treat tonight. Here at the Bluebird, it isn't unusual for a special guest to show up and grace us with their talent. And tonight, this guest is a real humdinger. Back from her recent CMA award for the hit song she wrote for her brother, Travis Miller, the Bluebird is proud to introduce to you one of ASCAP's Country Songwriters of the Year, *Miss Ella Mae Miller*!"

The mere mention of Travis's name induced a few screeches from the crowd, several females excitedly looking around to see if Travis himself was present. Hank took the lack of his intro all in stride as he looped a guitar strap over his body and followed Ella's lead. The audience went nuts as the house lights surrounding the performance area dimmed. Hank didn't miss a beat, immediately strumming Travis's biggest award-winning hit on the borrowed instrument. The crowd noise dissipated as a perpetual grin donned his face. He'd just died and gone to country music heaven.

Ella Mae nodded at him, indicating she wanted him to sing lead. His jaw clenched as he concentrated on an intricate riff going into the first verse, his reverberating singing voice through the house speakers catching him off guard. He tapped his boot while sitting on a chair, his legs spread wide open with the guitar's body resting on his thigh. The lyrics came easy to him, his vocals sounding eerily similar to Travis's deep voice. And why wouldn't it? He'd cut his teeth on Travis Miller songs and knew the ins and outs of all the words and phrases on every one of his albums.

During their performance, Hank couldn't take his eyes off Ella Mae. They were having fun, their vibe reminding him of playing in the center of someone's living room or in the back of the tour bus having a jam session. She added harmonies to his lead, her voice pure and sure, their amazing sound tumbling throughout the room like two lovers under the sheets. It was thrilling and, dare he say, sensual the way they pulsed and sang in tandem to the country rhythm within close proximity of each other.

Performing live on a stage with Ella Mae Miller was not what he expected. George was right—he was in the presence of a real humdinger. Why she wasn't on the road performing her own hits as a solo artist or sharing the stage with her brother on his sold-out tour was beyond him.

The entire room erupted in a frenzy of applause when the song ended. Ella Mae waited for a beat before she spoke into the microphone.

"Thank you so much. And thanks to George and the wonderful crew here at the Bluebird. I love stopping by when I can. The Bluebird feels like home to me." She looked right at Hank and smiled. "And I bet y'all are wondering who this handsome fella sitting next to me is. It gives me great pleasure to introduce y'all to Mr. Hank Bennett!"

A few female hoots and hollers echoed in the space, along with a smattering of energetic applause.

"Hank has been on tour with Travis and me, and we've been working on a few new songs, including one of his originals. Keep an eye out for this handsome cowboy. I predict he will be the next big singing songwriter in country music."

Hank gasped, her stellar introduction making him turn rigid in his seat.

"This next tune is one we've been working on recently. It's a Hank Bennett original called... *Brotherly Love*."

Her bedroom eyes stared back at him with longing—or was it pride? He didn't care. His heart beat in triple-time with adoration. He was one lucky bastard.

This was the most important night of his life, and he sang his song with Ella Mae accompanying him with perfect harmony like they'd been singing intimately together for ages. Hank lost himself in the melody and lyrics, his performance natural and as honest as he could get. He told his story through music and noticed right away the mesmerized faces of the audience up close, tears streaming down more than one person's face. He could see the emotions his song conveyed and the profound effect it had on people.

Ella Mae was right—the vulnerable vantage point of where he sat in the middle of the audience was totally unique. The entire performance was surreal and captivating. He never wanted to forget this moment, like the flash of a shooting star or the last real hug from his precious mother. It was pure magic.

When the song ended, the entire room, including Ella Mae, stood on their feet in a roaring ovation. A wave of heat flushed his neck, and he thought he might burst into tears. And then she moved toward him, cupping his chin as her guitar hung from her body.

"Remember this," she nodded before kissing him on the lips.

His breathing turned erratic as he memorized the feel of her lush mouth while the crowd pulsed to the rhythm of his heart. Pulling back from him, she stood upright and joined the audience, clapping her hands again.

They performed several more familiar Travis Miller songs together without banter. The audience recognized the radio hits and joyfully sang along. Ella's songwriting success was unfathomable, and Hank offered a silent prayer of gratitude to the heavens. This was something beautiful and profound that would haunt him in unexpected places for the rest of his adult life.

When she started the new song they'd written together, his chest felt too small for his heart, and he struggled to breathe, his voice catching in his throat more than once. This feeling was sacred, and he was incredibly thankful to share this first-time performance with Ella Mae.

Hank allowed the swoony feeling to come over him again, a distinct hum reverberating through his body. He focused on Ella with the precision of a sharpshooter, and heat began to pool at his center. Her talent. Her eyes. Her mouth. Her hands strumming the acoustic instrument. His senses pushed at the seams, their contents threatening to spill.

Closing his eyes for a beat, he willed himself to remain calm and cool, daring to imagine he was deeply rooted in her famous music world while performing for the fans, the song they created together a "surefire hit," as his daddy would often say. They sang of dogwood blossoms and the earth dressed in green, their song entitled, *Beautiful South* conjuring up all kinds of visceral memories of Bennett Farms.

As his eyes flicked to hers, the sight of her deep happiness mid-song was almost too much to handle. Ella Mae was the most selfless woman he'd ever met, welcoming him into her life without any expectations. But what did he have to offer her in return?

And that's when it hit him. He had something pure and simple to offer Ella Mae Miller. It wasn't flashy or award-nominated, expensive, or trendy. It had nothing to do with bold red wines marked by the family label or even the most perfect Christmas tree grown on his ancestral land. Nope. He had something in mind he'd never offered any other female before.

Hank could offer Ella Mae—his love.

Chapter Twenty
Ella Mae

The ride home from Nashville took forever, the truck cab buzzing with a noticeable sexual undercurrent. Hank thanked Ella a million times, giddy from his performance at the Bluebird. She was glad she could do that for him—proud of how captivated the audience was by his original music and youthful charm.

The truck headlights illuminated the porch of her house as Lucky barked a welcome and trotted down the front steps to greet them.

"Hey, boy. How are you doing?" She ruffled Lucky's fur and was quick with her key in the door lock.

"Can I do anything? Help you in any way?" Hank asked, bringing up the rear. His hot fingers grazed the small of her back.

If she was being totally honest, there was only one thing on Ella Mae's mind—sex. But first, she needed to feed her dog.

"Let me get Lucky taken care of in the kitchen. I'll be out in a minute."

"Okay."

Clumsy in her actions, she dropped everything she was holding on the kitchen table and heard her truck keys slip and hit the wood floor. She didn't bother picking them up, intent on mixing her dog's supper in record time.

"Bon appetite," she mumbled, setting the dog bowl on the floor and scratching Lucky behind the ears one last time.

Eager, she pranced through the small hallway connecting the kitchen to the living room and was startled when Hank spun her around, backing her into the wall. He caged her with his arms and consumed her mouth with a mind-blowing kiss that ignited every nerve ending in her body. She was unashamed in how she so desperately wanted him, their earlier vocal intercourse at the Bluebird an aphrodisiac prepping her for more to come. She reached low between them and slid her hand over his denim-covered hardness, frantic to feel him inside her again.

"Bedroom," she whispered hoarsely.

Hank growled and nipped at the delicate skin below her ear. "I'm going to devour you."

Ella gripped his hand and pulled him upstairs, anxious to get him in her bed. Her back hit the soft mattress within moments, and his weight pressed into hers. Their lips crashed together, the kiss passionate and full of lust. She ran her hands down his back and over his muscular ass, lost in obsession. He pulled off her boots, and in one fell swoop, he removed her shorts and panties, her gaping center throbbing with desire. When he leaned low and flicked his tongue across her wet folds, her vision blurred as she struggled for her next breath. He traced her seam straight up her middle, pausing to pay attention to her swollen nub.

"Oh, God," she gasped, tangling her fingers into his hair. She gave in to the immediate rush, spiraling higher and higher by the coaxing of his tongue and fingers until she careened off the edge. Her entire universe exploded in a crash of kaleidoscope color and ended in a high-pitched scream of release.

When her ragged breathing finally stabilized, she opened her eyes. Hank sat on the edge of the bed and pulled off his boots and t-shirt. She let her gaze drift over his broad shoulders and strong back. The man was rugged and brawny, a farmer's son. He unbuckled his belt and let his jeans fall to the floor. Heat flooded her already saturated core when she realized he'd gone commando all day again, the jagged scar on his upper thigh a part of his history. Everything about him exuded masculinity, from his burly arms and chest to the scruff on his chin and thick, rock-hard cock between his legs.

Heat flared in Hank's eyes when he noticed her visible desire. "Are you ready for me, darlin'?"

Ella Mae took in a staggered breath as a naked Hank stealthily moved toward her like a mountain lion ready to consume his prey. With his spiced scent of cedar and pine, the handsome man she'd met outside the t-shirt shack made the air around her feel warmer with intuitive memories of crackling wood fires on a cool autumn day. Forever, the smell of this man would live in her memory.

The tips of his calloused fingers dragged across her cheek before he helped her out of her shirt and bra. He massaged her fleshy mounds, nipping and kissing her chest. And then he leaned back and efficiently sheathed his cock with a condom before he plunged into her.

Her primal need to be closer to him was shocking, and she cried out with wild abandon. She dug her nails into his back. She bit his shoulder and yanked his hair. She rocked her hips, begging him not to stop. She wanted this man with every fiber of her being. And he seemed to want her just as badly. She could tell by the forceful way he moved above her. The way he swore under his breath the closer he came to climax.

"Don't stop," she pleaded. "Go harder. Go faster, Hank." She wasn't shy about letting him know what she liked or how she liked it. And he reciprocated, speeding up and relentlessly pounding her with power. Their heated skin slapped together, the pain intense and hurting so good.

Hank gripped her ass and drove into her like he owned her. She held on for dear life, the rush of pleasure as she careened off the edge of desire and into total bliss sucking the breath right out of her lungs. Her voice was silent as his movements stilled in an orgasm of his own, his muscles straining above her. The out-of-body experience annihilated every cell in her being, leaving her floating in ecstasy.

Collapsing next to her, Hank lay on his side, sweaty and panting, their limbs tangled together atop the mangled sheets. He pushed damp strands of his hair back from his face. "Best. Day. Of. My. Life," he managed in between staggered breaths.

Ella nodded in agreement. "I agree. You need to be celebrated."

"What?" His lopsided grin was infectious.

"You heard me," she giggled. "You need to be celebrated."

"Why?"

"Because you're talented. And handsome." She lifted her head off the pillow and leaned against her palm. Staring back at him she said, "You're a gifted songwriter, Hank. It's been my pleasure working with you. And damn, our new song went over so well. But I knew it would."

"You think?" He mimicked her position, his dark eyes locked in on hers. "You think it could be a hit? Like one of your Travis songs?" His sensitive, artistic nature needed stoking.

She nodded. "Absolutely."

"Well, it wasn't just me out there in the round tonight. You need to be celebrated, too. You're the most talented woman I've ever known."

His words meant the world to her. But tonight was not about her—it was about Hank Bennett, talented songwriter and performer, corporeal lover, and sensual partner in crime.

"No way, cowboy. Tonight is all about you. You deserve it."

Before he could say another word, she grabbed a tissue from the nightstand and disposed of the used condom. He watched her every move, his boyish grin doing funny things to her insides. With boldness, she straddled him and pulled her long hair over one shoulder. Resting her palms on his chest, she leaned lower and pressed her lips to his, feeling his thickness rise between her legs.

His mouth was hot, his tongue exploring and coaxing. She kissed him again and again, reveling in the scrape of his stubble against her face as heat poured into her from the pressure of his mouth. She let her fingers trace his full lower lip as desire washed over her so powerfully she swayed on top of him. His eyes held hers captive, and he drew her closer. She took a deep breath, his scent flooding through her. God, why did he have to smell so damn good? She couldn't help herself and gave into temptation, snaking a hand between them.

"Ella Mae, I need to get another condom," he warned.

"No," she exhaled in a shallow breath. "I want to feel you. All of you. Don't worry, I'm on the pill."

Hank licked his lips as if making a decision. Gripping his width, he aimed his cock at her center, easily slipping into her deep heat. She started to pulse, their shared rhythm of heat and friction sensuous.

"Fuck, that feels so good. You're a goddess on top of me like this," he whispered lustfully, squeezing her breasts. His voice was raw with arousal.

"I'm in mid-celebration," she giggled, riding him like a stallion.

Their bodies became one, the euphoria of finally experiencing a deep connection with Hank, a gift. All the days before she met him had felt like she was searching through huge audience crowds—for what, she wasn't sure. But now, with this intoxicating man deep inside, she felt certain she'd found him and held a fierce reverence for someone who shared her passions.

Anchored against his center, their kisses turned desperate as if they couldn't get enough. She needed him. And then it hit her in an instant. She realized she wanted Hank by her side for a lot longer than a couple of weeks on tour. She wanted him to be with her—forever.

"*Yes*! Come with me," she screamed, leaping over the edge of desire and begging him to join her.

He was unraveling her, slowly but surely. She could feel it happening as if she were gently unsnapping her skinny jeans that fit too tight. She could breathe when he was near, yet he absolutely made her breathless. The air was heavy with panting and the smell of desire, thick with uncertainty and ecstasy, tension and euphoria. She was on sensory overload and about to combust, the following sentence out of her mouth surprising them both.

"Stay with me, Hank. Stay with me in Nashville after the tour."

Hank lifted blazing brown eyes to meet hers head on.

"What?" he panted as if trying to hold back for a beat.

"You heard me. I want you to *stay*."

Ella squeezed his balls, causing him to cry out in pain—or maybe it was pleasure? The explosion of bright light glowing from behind her eyelids rivaled the arena spotlights aimed at her brother on stage. A surge of heat poured into her between Hank's stiff legs, his arms pulling her forward into a fierce embrace. Collapsing on top of him, her eyes trailed up and over his heaving chest before they found dark pools staring back at her. She shifted off him and snuggled into his side, feeling his lips press against her head.

The only sounds in the room were of their heavy breathing slowly dissipating. She didn't dare say anything, hoping he was mulling over her invitation to stay. If he agreed to join her in Nashville after the last two shows of Travis's tour, they could do a total deep dive and write more songs together. She could introduce him to all the session players she knew, and they could record a demo together. Heck, she'd even play and sing backup for him if he decided to do a showcase for some of the bigwigs at the record label.

"What's going on in that pretty little head of yours?" Hank's voice was scratchy and low.

"Nothing," she squeaked. Had he not heard her request mid-thrust?

The feel of his fingers stroking her hair caused her eyelids to grow heavy. She was exhausted from the full, emotional day. Worn out from overthinking her ridiculous request.

"Did you mean it? Or was that the sex talking?" he asked.

"The sex talking?" Wide awake again, she sat up and blinked back at him, her bare bosom on full display. "I don't say things without thinking them through, Hank. For the record, I think you and I make a great team."

"Is that all?"

She looked away, struggling for her next words, careful in her response. But the words wouldn't come. Funny. She was an award-winning songwriter and lyricist, and this was the first time she was ever at a loss for words.

"Hey," Hank said, holding her chin between his fingers so she'd look at him. "I heard you loud and clear, darlin'. I just want you to be sure you know what you're asking."

"I am," she whispered, struggling to hear him over her thundering heart.

"I think we make a great team too. I also think you're an incredible lover, and I'm... I'm falling for you."

Her breathing stopped, her eyes misting with relief.

"I don't want to leave you, Ella Mae."

He sat up and held her face between his hands.

"I want to stay."

Chapter Twenty-One

Hank

The faint sound of someone knocking and Lucky's incessant barking woke Hank from a deep sleep. The morning sun streamed through the windows as he quietly slipped into his discarded jeans, careful not to jar the mattress. Pausing by the bedside, he looked down at a peaceful Ella Mae sleeping and traced her cheek with his fingertips. Her lips parted, and her breath came out in a raspy snuffle, making him grin. She was out cold, and he didn't have the heart to wake her.

Closing the bedroom door with a quiet click, he padded barefoot down the ancient wooden stairs and saw the shadow of a big man on the doorstep. Lucky wagged his tail and barked as if the pooch knew precisely who was on the other side.

"Willie?"

Hank stepped out onto the front porch and closed the door behind him. Travis Miller's larger-than-life tour manager,

Willie Branson, took a step back and removed his tattered cowboy hat, revealing his long flowing hair that matched his beard. The beastly man appeared smaller to Hank. His shoulders slumped slightly, and his expression held sadness from behind droopy eyes.

"Is everything alright?"

"No, son. I need to speak to Ella Mae right away."

Hank knew instantly something was wrong with her brother, Travis, and Willie was once again pulling double duty. When Hank first met Ella, she touted Willie, the "Travis-Whisperer," because when her brother got out of control, Willie was the only one who could bring him down a notch. Hank couldn't imagine what the man had endured during those unfortunate occasions.

"I'll go get her. Come on inside and make yourself at home."

"Thanks."

Hank high-tailed it to the bedroom and cautiously approached Ella Mae's bed. Tilting his head, his eyes outlined her slumbering figure and paused to take in her beautiful, serene expression. He hated to wake her but knew he didn't have a choice.

"Mmmm," she moaned. A slow smile uncurled from her full lips as she blinked awake. "Good morning."

"Morning." Hank lingered in the quiet moment, brushing her hair back from her cheek, his expression lacking.

Her brow furrowed, and she sat up. "What's wrong? Are you okay?"

Hank inhaled a deep breath through his nose. "Willie's here."

He'd barely gotten the words out of his mouth before she sprang into action, leaping naked from the bed and grabbing a robe off the hook on the back of the door. Hank was quick on her tail as they scrambled down the stairs to the living room, where Willie paced next to the baby grand piano.

Tying the robe snug at her waist, Ella Mae kept her distance from Willie as if waiting for him to tell her something tragic and awful. Willie shuffled his weight from one foot to the other and placed his worn hat back on his head, not even offering her a greeting.

"Bus is on its way. We'll be leaving within the hour. Hopefully, this will buy us some time."

Willie walked out of the house, the screen door slapping behind him. Ella Mae folded her arms against her chest and shook her head.

"What just happened?" Hank asked, careful as he approached her.

"It's Travis. He's... drunk or high on drugs. Or maybe today is our lucky day, and he's on both." When she looked up at him, her eyes were wide and sad, the earlier love light extinguished.

"You don't mean that," he replied, concerned by her condescending tone.

"You're right. I don't." A strangled cry erupted from her mouth, and she held her arms open wide. "Hold me, Hank."

He was quick and enfolded her in his arms, allowing her to cry against his bare chest. "Shhh...," he soothed. "You're not alone, darlin'. I'm right here, and I'm not going anywhere." He felt her nod as he stroked the back of her hair.

In the beginning, Ella had told Hank that she wanted to show him the ins and outs of an actual road tour. She wanted him to observe Travis and how he navigated the good and the bad. She even admitted life on the road wasn't all glamorous and that sometimes it could be very hard. She was right. This was hard. This was real life. And he had no idea what he'd gotten himself into.

***

Ella Mae had showered, packed, and locked up the farmhouse within the hour. Even her neighbor, Chuck, had come by to pick up Lucky and feed her chickens before they hopped on the tour bus and left the farm in a puff of road dust. Hank sat up front near Lenny as he drove, worried about what was happening. It was one thing to witness sibling banter, but observing a sibling intervention was a different ballgame.

Ella Mae sat in her brother's captain's chair with her knees drawn up to her chest. Her hair was still wet, and there wasn't a stitch of makeup on her pretty face. Hank licked his lips, trying desperately to remain unruffled.

They were meeting Willie and Travis at the concert venue in St. Louis, Missouri, a six-hour bus drive from Tennessee. From what Hank could decipher, Travis had been on an all-night binge alone in his condo. One of the neighbors was awakened by a loud crash and called the cops. Apparently, Travis had taken a baseball bat to his flat-screen television in a rage over a Braves baseball game and continued his destructive behavior smashing anything and everything in his path. Empty bottles of booze were strewn throughout his destroyed home, and a small amount of marijuana was confiscated, a misdemeanor in the state of Tennessee.

Carted to the local police station, Travis was bailed out after Willie was notified. The only rainbow in this latest storm of events was the fact it happened in the wee hours of the morning before the tourists were out and the paparazzi caught wind.

"Can I get you anything? Maybe, make some coffee or something?" Hank offered.

Ella Mae shook her head. "No thanks. Go ahead and make whatever you want for yourself. I'm good."

Hank narrowed his eyes at her. "But are you?"

He shifted seats to be closer to her. "I know what it's like to feel helpless when a family member messes up. There's nothing we can do but watch from the sidelines. It's painful and infuriating." He reached out and held her hand. "Are you sure you're comfortable with me hanging around during all of this?"

She inhaled an audible breath and looked right at him. "Do you wanna leave?"

"No, of course not. That's not what I'm saying. I don't want you to feel obligated to me when your brother is having a hard time. You're his only family. He needs you."

She nodded as if mulling over his response. "Let's wait and see what we're up against in St. Louis. If Travis is as bad as Willie says, I may have to leave the arena and take him back to the rehab center in California on the next flight out."

Hank raised his eyebrows and hoped to God that wasn't the case.

By the time the bus pulled up to the eighteen thousand-seat arena in downtown St. Louis, it was almost suppertime. Traffic on the freeway was abysmal and added an extra hour to the trip. Willie was right there waiting for them with backstage lanyards and showed them through the maze of underground hallways to the dressing room where Travis was recovering. Upon entering the large room, Hank was taken aback, thinking Ella Mae's brother looked perfectly fine.

"*Peaches*!" he shouted in a slur of words when he spotted his sister in the reflection of the giant lit-up mirror.

Instead of chastising him or going into an angry rant, Ella Mae calmly walked up to Travis and wrapped her arms around his middle, laying her head against his chest. Travis laughed at first, rocking her back and forth in a slow dance of sorts. But his light-heartedness was short-lived. He stopped, and they stood motionless, holding onto each other, their sibling love fully displayed. And then Travis's body suddenly shook with deep sobs of guilt, his moaning and bawling hard to listen to.

"I'm sorry... I'm so... sorry," he wept.

Hank felt his eyes well with tears witnessing the brother and sister reunion. He was reminded of his own brother, Teddy when he was hauled away from the Langston Falls courtroom in handcuffs after the unfortunate verdict was read after his trial. His entire family didn't even get to hug Teddy goodbye, the pivotal moment in his family's history forever singed in his memory.

Slipping out of the dressing room unnoticed, Hank waited in the hallway alone. He wanted to be there for Ella Mae and her brother, but he also wanted to give them space to figure out their next steps. Travis had two sold-out shows left. Could he perform tonight in this condition? Hank wasn't sure. Earlier on the bus, Ella Mae assured him Travis would come through like he always did.

But goddamnit, what a stressful situation. What did his band think of all this? Or the tech team? What about all the fans who paid good money to see their favorite country music artist perform sober and in good form? Did Travis ever think about all these people he could potentially hurt by his actions? The thought infuriated him.

Taking advantage of the quiet moment, he pulled the watch his dad had gifted him from his jeans pocket and opened the antique lid, staring at the photo tucked inside. The sudden urge to hear his father's voice had him replacing the watch in his hand with his cell phone.

"Hank! How are you, son? Did you make it to St. Louis?"

The sound of his father's voice induced another rush of emotions. Clearing his throat, Hank tried to keep it together. "We did. Getting ready for another sold-out show tonight."

"Wow, that's great. Just great. I'm so glad you're gettin' to do all of this."

Hank kept the conversation light-hearted and told his dad all about Ella Mae's farm, her dog, and playing at the Bluebird the night before. He intentionally left out the part about her brother's current inebriated condition.

"I would've loved to have been there. What an incredible moment for you."

"I know, right?" Hank chewed on his lower lip, unsure what to say next. "You know, dad… I may hang out a little while longer in Nashville after the last show tomorrow night. Hope that's okay?"

Roy Bennett's deep and robust laugh echoed through the phone. "No worries, son. I already figured as much. Take all the time you need."

Hank nodded, thankful for his father's support. "Thanks, Dad. You're the best."

"I love you, Hank. Soak it all in."

"I will. Love you, too."

Hank hung up and leaned his head against the wall, causing his cowboy hat to hang low over his eyes. The reality of his and Ella Mae's current situation swept through him like a tidal wave. What if he couldn't stay behind in Nashville because she had to leave for California to take her brother back to rehab? He'd definitely miss her. Being around her these past three weeks opened him up, laying him bare to the possibility he'd found his person. Someone he wanted to be with all the time. But maybe that wasn't possible—at least for now.

A gusty sigh escaped him as he decided to wait it out. This was, no doubt, a turning point for both of them. And if he would've known these were to be their last few hours together, he would have made the moments last a little longer.

Chapter Twenty-Two

Ella Mae

Ella Mae nervously hung out in the wings while watching Travis's band get into position across the darkened stage for the show's start. She'd left her brother in Willie's capable hands, the tour manager practically dressing Travis himself while giving him a pep talk. She'd all but forgotten John Fobas, the media manager for ASM Global, was on site, the gigantic performance space one his company invested in. Of course, Mr. Fobas would have to be there for this show. What were the odds?

"Hey," Hank said, pressing his hand across the small of her back. "Any word?"

Ella closed her eyes and tried to memorize the feel of his touch against the black dress she'd changed into. Oh, how she wished she could take him by the hand and high-tail it out of there, away from the chaos and angst, to a place where they could linger in a deep and meaningful kiss without a care in the world.

"Willie's taking care of him like he always does," she answered in a monotone voice, not moving from her stance. Her arms were crossed tightly against her chest, her feet rigid in her polished boots.

"How are you holding up?"

"I'm fine." She felt his lips press against her cheek, her breath hitching with longing.

"Will you be okay while I go change real quick?"

"Sure."

Hank didn't say another word and left her alone, disappearing behind the side curtains. That's when she saw her brother appear from across the stage, clinging to Willie. The tech crew went to work wiring him up with his in-ear monitor, and stood nearby with his guitar. Squinting in the dim light, she noticed Willie hand something off to her brother before offering him a water bottle. She was floored when Travis threw back what looked like a pill of some kind and washed it down.

"What the hell?" she mumbled under her breath. Jerking her body into motion, she went behind the big screen backdrop to get to the other side of the stage without being seen by the audience, her booted steps swift and her emotions simmering beneath the surface.

"*Miss Miller!*"

Ella Mae stopped in her tracks, aware of John Fobas calling after her. Plastering an exaggerated smile on her face, she turned around.

"Mr. Fobas, good to see you again."

The handsome man was dressed in his signature suit, his black hair slicked back from his face. "Good to see you, too. I tried to speak with Travis before the show, but I was told he was indisposed." John laughed. "I certainly didn't want to embarrass him behind the scenes before he's introduced to the crowd."

Ella swallowed hard. "Nothing embarrasses my brother. Nothing at all." That was the understatement of the year. Maybe if Travis *was* embarrassed by his drunken behavior and humiliated in front of thousands of fans, he might change his ways? Or maybe not.

"I look forward to joining you at the after-party. We have a lot to celebrate," John flirted.

Turning on the charm, Ella Mae nodded, batting her eyelashes at the man. "We sure do. Now, if you'll excuse me, I have to remind my brother of something before he starts. Enjoy the show."

"I will."

Once on the other side, Ella Mae slowed down and took in the scene in front of her. Travis hopped up and down, shaking his arms as if preparing for a marathon. Willie stood nearby with a water bottle in his hand, ready to pass off if Travis needed a quick sip before he took to the stage. There was a little more color in her brother's face, and he seemed to be holding it together under the circumstances.

Coming up alongside Willie, Ella gripped his thick arm. "I saw you give Travis a pill. What was it?"

Willie's bushy eyebrows rose as he looked down at her. "Uh, nothing. Just a little ibuprofen for his headache."

"Huh," she exhaled, not buying it. Taking a few steps toward Travis, she tapped in on the shoulder.

"*Peaches*!" he happily exclaimed. Hoisting her off her feet, he clumsily swung her around in a woozy circle before setting her down. She grabbed him by the cheeks making his lips pucker.

"What did Willie just give you, huh? Tell me. What kind of pill was it?"

Travis's head bobbled as he looked between Willie and Ella, the goofy look on his face an indication he was feeling no pain. "Nothing. Just a little upper. You know, to get the juices flowing—"

"*What?*" Enraged, Ella Mae bullied her way toward Willie and flattened her palms against his chest, pushing him with all her might. The mountain of a man barely moved. "What the *fuck*, Willie? What are you trying to do to him?"

"Now calm down, darlin'. It's the only way he can get through this show after a bender."

"No... *no*! If he can't get through the show without pills or alcohol, then we need to cancel."

By this time, the booming voice of an announcer came over the speakers, thanking local sponsors. Frantic, she knew she only had a matter of seconds, and grabbed her brother by the arm pulling him away from the ignited stage full of blinding lights.

"*And now, please give a warm St. Louis welcome to... Travis Miller!*"

"Please, Travis. Don't go out there. I'm begging you! You're not in the right mind to perform in front of a large crowd tonight."

Travis stared down at her, his hooded expression soft and mellow. "Don't worry, Peaches. I got this."

"Let him go, darlin'. He'll be fine. He always is." Willie physically moved her away from her brother, and she watched in horror as a guitar tech slung an acoustic over his shoulders. Travis strutted confidently into the light in front of the masses, the thunderous roar from the audience deafening.

Recoiling from Willie's grip, she growled, "If this turns out badly, it's all on you." She snatched the water bottle out of his hand and twisted the cap off in a fury, tipping the liquid to her lips. Her gag reflex engaged immediately at the taste of pure vodka.

Coughing and wheezing, she flung the bottle against the wall in a dramatic crashing wave of liquid. "You fucking *traitor*!" she screamed.

The need to get out of there was very real. Running through the maze of backstage hallways, she passed several crew members and security, her lungs threatening to split wide open. When she reached the loading dock, she collapsed against the side of the cinderblock walls. The giant garage-like door was still raised, and she noticed the Prevost tour bus glimmering in the moonlight like a shiny new toy. Laying her cheek against the cold, painted surface of the wall, she pressed the heel of her hand against her forehead and sobbed.

She cried just as hard as when Travis first messed up when she was still a teen and learned her parents were dead. But the crazy thing was, now she felt even sadder because she'd been betrayed by not only her brother but also by Willie and probably the entire team. Unlike the tears she cried when she was still in high school, these weren't fueled by grief. No. These tears were full of anger and shame without empathy to water them down.

"*Ella Mae!*" Hank's voice echoed throughout the hallway.

Had he witnessed what happened before Travis took the stage? She pulled herself together, and a moment later, she heard the sound of his cowboy boots against the cement floors and then felt his hand on her shoulder. He was out of breath and panting.

"What's wrong? Why did you run off like that? And why are you crying? Did something happen?"

Sliding down the wall, he sat beside her, gathering her in his arms and holding her close. This induced another bout of tears as she drank in his familiar scent of masculinity, gripping his shiny button-up shirt with all her might.

"They've... been lying... to me," she stuttered in-between hiccup sobs.

"Who's been lying to you? Travis?"

"Y-yes. Travis and Willie. And probably... the entire band and crew." Pulling back from him, her vision was clouded, taking in his handsome features up close. "Willie gave Travis drugs before he went on stage. And there was vodka in his water bottle."

Hank's brow furrowed deeply, his concern evident. "Come on." He stood with decision and helped her to her feet.

"Where are we going?"

Leading her back the way she came, Hank held tightly to her hand, the sound of music growing louder and louder with each step. "You need to be there for him if he falls apart."

Ella pulled him to a stop. "I can't. I... I can't go through this again. Not in front of this many people."

Hank gently coaxed her forward. "Yes, you can. And I'll be right there with you to help."

Passing security, they flashed their lanyards and headed to the side of the stage opposite Willie, who stood there like Big Foot, watching Travis's every move. He was in the middle of one of his signature ballads, the weeping wail of a steel guitar piercing the air with sound during a musical interlude. Hank wrapped his arms around Ella from behind and swayed to the song's romantic rhythm.

"See? Look at him. He's doing fine. It's like he's on auto-pilot or something."

"Or something," she mumbled. Pressed against his chest, she could feel Hank's heartbeat. For a millisecond, she relaxed—until Travis started singing. He was pitchy, his slurred words noticeable as he clumsily sat on the edge of the stage, his booted feet precariously dangling as he attempted to serenade the attentive audience.

John Fobas approached the two of them, the look on his face none too pleased. "What's going on with your brother out there tonight? Is he... drunk?"

Ella Mae stepped out of Hank's embrace, the moment of reckoning falling on her shoulders. "Yes, Mr. Fobas. He is. Do you want me to stop the show?"

John took a step back and puffed out his chest, his accusing tone riddled with disrespect. "Are you kidding me?" He pointed aggressively at her. "Do you understand the gravity of this situation—the liability to my company if something happens to Travis or someone in the audience?"

"Watch your tone, Mr. Fobas," Hank chimed in, physically lowering his finger out of her face. He stood tall and tipped his hat back with bravado.

Ella's eyes flicked to her handsome cowboy, thankful he stuck up for her. But she'd, unfortunately, been in this position before and knew how to handle herself. Still, having Hank by her side helped her muster the strength to get through the rest of the show.

"Nothing is going to happen, John. Do you hear the crowd? They're singing along to every word. They have no idea he's off-key, and they'll cue Travis if he forgets the words. I'm sorry this happened. If anyone complains, they'll get a refund."

She knew full well how expensive it was to cancel a show outright last minute. It happened one time before on Travis's first tour, although the audience was much smaller. Financially, the reverberations were significant with a venue already rented, advertising paid for, tickets sold, local vendors hired, ticket-takers, staffers, and security already on site. Insurance could cover some of the costs, but she knew John Fobas, the promoter, and Travis, the entertainer, could also work out a financial arrangement if the show could be rescheduled. But knowing her brother was inevitably about to be carted off to another stint in rehab, a rescheduled show was probably off the table.

John gritted his teeth, his hands fisting at his sides. His eyes narrowed at Hank before landing on her again. "We'll finish this conversation when the show is over." He took off in a whoosh of aggravated after-shave.

Ella Mae let out a slow breath as the song's last note was played to deafening applause. And then she tensed when she distinctly heard her brother call her name into the microphone.

"*Peaches?* Yo, Peaches! Get on out here. I sat down, and I can't get up." He laughed as if making fun of himself.

A dagger of fear stabbed her in the heart as she peeked her head out to get a better look. Sure enough, her brother couldn't get his bearings, slipping and sliding in his boots as he tried to stand. Security was right in front of him on the arena floor, ready to catch him if he fell.

"Come on," she hollered to Hank.

He followed her onto the stage, his eyes wide at the spectacle of thousands of fans screaming in the auditorium. Coming from the other side, Willie joined them, and the threesome hoisted Travis to his feet, her brother laughing and immune to it all.

Bringing the microphone to his mouth again, his following bold statement left Ella Mae shaking in her boots.

"Friends, I'd like to introduce you to my award-winning, song-writing sister, Ella-Bo-Bella, and her sidekick, Hank Romeo."

He handed the mic off to her and took a step back, slapping his hands together haphazardly. His body was loose and languid as if he were feeling no pain.

"What are you doing?" she whispered tersely, holding the microphone low so the audience couldn't hear their conversation.

"I'm giving you and lover-boy here a chance to render a few so I can take a piss. Good idea, right?" He switched focus toward

Hank, his broad, toothy smile almost comical. "You'd like that, wouldn't you, buddy? Singing in front of all these folks?"

Ella looked at Hank, who'd turned white as a sheet. But maybe her brother was on to something. At least it would buy some time and keep the audience engaged for a spell before they figured out Travis was in no condition to perform and turned on him.

"Fine." She motioned two fingers toward a guitar tech who instantly rushed onto the stage carrying two acoustics. He handed one off to her and the other to Hank.

"Ella Mae, I don't know if this is such a good idea," Hank stuttered.

She could barely hear him from the excited noises coming from the appreciative crowd. "This is just like the Bluebird, only bigger."

Hank sheepishly slung the guitar strap over his head as another crew member whisked a standing microphone into place right in front of him.

Turning toward her brother, Ella Mae watched him grin and sway taking it all in. "Go take care of business, Travis," she shouted.

He threw his hand up in a peace sign. Calmly, Willie ushered him off stage as he waved goodbye to the crowd.

Eyeing Hank, she offered him a tentative nod and smiled. This could turn out to be a real shit show or the greatest performance of her life.

Chapter Twenty-Three

Hank

Every molecule in Hank's body buzzed, his eyes going wide following Ella Mae's lead. In his wildest dreams, he couldn't have predicted he'd be performing in front of thousands of people in the state-of-the-art arena venue. It was thrilling yet intimidating, filling him with a mix of adrenaline and fear. Between the crowd's roar and his thundering heart, he thought he might very well pass out from the rush.

Ella Mae clipped the microphone Travis had handed off into a chrome stand and started strumming her guitar with determined gusto. Hank immediately recognized the song and joined her playing, as did Travis's band. When it came time to sing, the audience filled the void as Travis was still off stage.

"Sing with them," Ella shouted with encouragement.

Hank's hands flubbed the chord for a millisecond as he cleared his throat before joining the audience in the sing-along. A wave of approval surged through the arena, Hank's vocals turned up a notch by the sound tech and reverberating throughout the space. Ella Mae authentically smiled wide for the first time all evening and nodded with glee, the rest of the band regaining their composure and having some fun right along with them. He knew she'd chosen an oldie but a goodie on purpose, a diversion to Travis's current inebriated state. When the song ended with a push of sound, it was as if everyone on stage breathed a huge sigh of relief.

"Y'all remembered that one, didn't you?" Ella Mae said into the microphone, evidence of pure joy donning her pretty face. "My brother and I wrote that song long ago, and thanks to all of you, it went all the way into the top ten."

Another surge of clapping and hollering hit Hank in the face as he watched Ella Mae command the stage. She was a natural, a born performer who made it look so easy. If only he could get his nerves to settle down.

She leaned toward him, away from the live mic, and shouted, "Let's do *Ride Cowboy Ride*. It's another oldie they're gonna love."

Hank nodded and immediately started the slow picking intro of the song, memories of the first time he and Ella sang together in their hotel room coming to mind. Closing his eyes, he concentrated on the words and tried to hit every nuance from Travis's album. When Ella Mae joined in with her harmony, he opened his eyes and stared at her. She was gorgeous under the bright spotlight, at ease in the curling swirls of theatrical fog magically drifting into the fly space. How did he get so lucky?

Ending the song in tandem with acoustics in sync with the band, the crowd was on their feet. He was flabbergasted when Ella Mae's voice hollered over the speakers, "Give it up for *Hank Bennett*!"

Hank took his hat off and pressed it against his chest, overcome with emotion. He dreamt of doing this his entire life—the feel of lightning running through his veins and a Friday night crowd in the palm of his hand. He was no longer riding five deep in a beat-up van, paying his dues in some no-name town, relying on tips in a sketchy bar. Nope. Fate had intervened, and she had a name: Ella Mae Miller. She brought him out of the shadows and into the light, and for the first time in his life, Hank felt like he was right where he was supposed to be.

"This next song is one we've been working on together. It's a Hank original, and I think y'all are going to love it." Ella Mae started strumming *Brotherly Love*, surprising him.

Hank gave her a look as if to say, "Are you sure about this?" to which she giggled and nodded aggressively. As he situated himself behind the microphone, ready to sing the first verse of his original song in front of thousands, he was interrupted by an inebriated Travis Miller sauntering out onto the stage. The crowd went nuts, screaming and shouting Travis's name. Hank stopped playing and respectfully hung back, the entire audience going into a two-beat chant, *Tra-vis*, *Tra-vis*, repeatedly.

His drunk country music idol slung an arm across Hank's shoulders and gave him a sloppy kiss on the cheek. His low,

BREATHLESS LOVE

insinuating voice was gruff in his ear. "You know I can't let you take over my show, Romeo. Your time will come." A guitar tech swiped the instrument from Hank's possession, another crew member readying Travis so he could resume his concert center stage.

By this time, Ella Mae was right next to her brother, pleading with him. "Let him do his original, Travis. Come on." She was not having it.

"No, it's okay," Hank reassured. "What we did was... amazing. Thanks for the opportunity, Travis." He put his hand out, and Travis went to shake it, but his momentum caused him to stumble into Hank instead.

"Easy does it," Hank muttered, helping the man regain his footing.

"Fuck," Travis said, pushing Hank away. "Don't mess with me, goddammit."

Ella Mae saw the entire exchange and bullied her way between them, gripping her brother by the arm. "Stop it, Travis. He was only trying to help you."

Travis swiped his hand across his mouth while giving Hank the evil eye. "You know what? I don't need your help, Romeo. I didn't want you here from the get-go. You think you're 'all that', but you ain't nothing."

"*Travis*!" Ella admonished.

"Come on, Ella Mae, let's give your brother back the stage so he can entertain his fans." Hank plastered a fake smile on his face, aware of the fans watching. He offered her his hand, anxious to escape Travis, who was a ticking time bomb. The band had started the fanfare of a popular hit, the music pulsing and building with each note.

"You're such a disappointment," Ella seethed as they passed her brother. Her words must've struck a nerve because he grabbed her by the arm and whipped her around, tearing into her with his cruel words.

"I'm the disappointment? What about you gallivanting your... your fucking prized pony around like y'all are the CMA Duo of the Year, huh? What about me?"

"*What?*"

Hank tried to diffuse the situation. "Come on, Travis, not in front of your fans—"

"Fuck you, Romeo," he interrupted, throwing his arm toward the wings. "Get the hell outta here. This is between me and my sister."

Willie made his presence known, coming up behind Travis and pressing a firm hand to his shoulder. "Simmer down, Travis. People paid good money to see your show, not to see you argue with Ella. Everybody's watching."

Obviously ticked off, Travis brusquely batted Willie's hand off him. "Well then, get these mother-fuckers off my stage so I can do my thing."

"What did you just call us?" Ella Mae stood her ground with her hands on her hips as the band continued to vamp.

BREATHLESS LOVE

"You heard me. *Mother. Fuckers.*" His harsh words held a mix of enunciated slurring as he got right into her face.

Hank watched the two siblings in a standoff, beads of nervous perspiration dribbling down his cheeks. He knew Travis wasn't in his right mind, but to blatantly disrespect his sister like this? He tried to bite his tongue, but he couldn't take it.

"Watch your mouth around your sister, Travis. She doesn't deserve to be talked to like that, especially after she just saved your ass."

"Oh, yeah?" Travis bristled.

"Come on, Hank, we don't need this bullshit." She started toward the wings, and Hank followed. Pausing, she deliberately spoke to her brother one last time, the daggers coming out of her eyes noticeable. "I'm heading back to Tennessee without you, Travis. I've had enough. Have a fantastic show."

"You'll be sorry someday. So long mother fuckers."

Hank wasn't sure what did it. Maybe it was the tone of Travis's voice or the foul language he used when referring to him and his sister. Maybe it was the fact the man didn't give a rat's ass about his fans watching the entire scene unfold, hundreds of camera phones recording every second. Whatever it was, he'd also had enough.

When Travis reached for Ella Mae again, something snapped inside him, and he protectively whirled around with a clenched fist, striking Travis in the mouth. The man fell flat on his ass with his boots high in the air, laughing hysterically.

Willie and Ella Mae sprung into action and helped Travis back to his wobbly feet before quickly ushering him off stage. The roar of the crowd was rowdy, the flashes of phone cameras filling the arena like lighters at a Garth Brooks concert. Travis's bodyguard, Mario, pounced, and forcefully escorted Hank offstage keeping a firm grip on his bicep. At the same time, Willie gave Travis the once-over, mumbling calming words to the man. Blood dribbled from Travis's split lip, his usually white smile smeared red. He ran the back of his hand across his mouth and spat on the ground.

"Oh, my God! Are you okay, Travis?" Ella fretted. Her pretty features contorted as she allowed Willie space to tend to the star. A stool appeared out of nowhere, and Willie gently eased Travis onto the seat and handed him a water bottle and a towel.

After taking a long pull from the bottle, Travis came up for air and looked right at Hank. "Wowza! I didn't think you had it in you, buddy."

Buddy? Why in the hell was Travis Miller calling him buddy again?

"I'm... I'm sorry, Travis. You shouldn't speak to a woman that way, especially your own sister," he stammered.

Ella Mae shifted her gaze to the floor and kept quiet. The way she clung to her inebriated brother made Hank edgy. Why wasn't she saying anything? Why wasn't she sticking up for him after he came to her defense?

The band continued to play as the audience grew louder with the chanting of Travis's name over and over again. The man either didn't care or was too shit-faced to oblige, happy to sit and simmer in his drunken la-la land. Willie whispered something into his ear, and he nodded, handing back the water bottle. Hank was pretty sure the liquid inside was vodka.

"Let him go, Mario," Willie said. "We don't want to press any charges tonight. Travis here is fine. It was all an unfortunate... misunderstanding, is all. He's good." Willie stood tall, his imposing figure making Hank cower even though he had just let him off the hook.

Mario stepped back, and Hank remained in the shadows watching Willie and Ella Mae fuss over the country music star. Ella smoothed back his hair and kissed him on the cheek, Travis eating up the attention like a spoiled child. When he finally stood and strode onto the stage, he glanced back at Hank. There was an evil gleam in his eye, and he knew then it was the beginning of the end for him and Ella Mae.

Hank could never compete with someone like Travis, whose world was big and full of things he couldn't even imagine. Drugs, alcohol, and women panting at his feet were the celebrity's kryptonite. Hank was just a small-town guy who scribbled songs in store-bought spiral notebooks filled with wide-ruled paper, a man who expected nothing less of himself, especially with how he was raised.

At least he realized something from this three-week jaunt on tour—his reality was *better* than Travis's. The man was a player and treated women, including his sister, with total disrespect. The last thing Hank wanted was for Ella Mae to think of him that way. He'd do it all over again and knock his country music idol on his ass, showing her the very definition of gallant behavior.

He'd been honest from the get-go, telling Ella Mae he was at a crossroads. She was the one who insisted he join the last three weeks of the tour so she could show him what life was like on the road—a firsthand experience like no other which included collaborating on music and keeping each other company. Well, he'd discovered much more than he bargained for while touring with a narcissistic addict. Everything had come to a head at what was probably his last Travis Miller concert ever.

But there was also one thing he hadn't anticipated—falling head over boots for Ella Mae.

"Hey," he started, coming up beside her. She flinched when he palmed her lower back and took a purposeful step away from him, crossing her arms against her bosom. Travis was already mid-song, oblivious to the world around him as he swayed to the rhythm in the bright spotlight.

"What happened out there?" he asked, leaning low and trying to catch her eye.

Ella Mae shook her head. "I can't do this with you right now."

"Pardon?"

"You heard me. I can't do this right now. You said it yourself. My brother... he needs me. It's my job."

Hank jerked his head to look out at Travis, who was doing a silly drunk dance during a musical bridge. "The man needs help, Ella Mae."

"I know. And I'm going to make sure he gets help. He just needs to get through this show."

"And then what? Huh? Are you going to glue yourself to his side to make sure he doesn't take any more drugs? Are you going to open every plastic bottle handed to him and test it to make sure it's really water and not vodka?" Gentle in his actions, he gripped her by the shoulders and turned her around, so she had to face him. "What about you?"

Confused, Ella shook herself loose from his grip. The forlorn expression on her face broke his heart. "This isn't about me."

"Exactly," Hank replied. "When you invited me to come on this tour with you and your brother, I thought I'd get a first-hand look at the behind-the-scenes workings of a legit tour. What I didn't anticipate was seeing how messed up your brother is. He uses you, Ella Mae, and you let him."

"I do not!"

"Yes, you do." He pointed aggressively at the stage bathed in light. "You belong out there in front of a live audience just as much as he does, and he knows it, too. Can't you see it? He's gaslighting you. You're isolated from everyone. He undermines your confidence and insists you stay close by to keep him held accountable. I'm calling bullshit on that. He's got all the power and manipulates you with his lies. He's controlling and uses you as his beck and call girl while the rest of the band and Willie bask in the light and know the truth."

"And what is the truth?" Ella Mae's eyes turned muddled with tears as she struggled to hold it together, his words obviously striking a chord.

Hank paused for a beat, unsure if he should tell her his revolutionary thoughts. But she deserved to have someone honest in her life, someone to hold back the curtain and expose the reality of her situation. Now was his only chance.

"He doesn't want you to succeed, Ella Mae. He's... jealous."

"Jealous? Of... *me*?" She threw her head back and laughed. "You don't know what you're talking about, Hank."

"It's so blatantly obvious. Didn't you see him out there shutting us down? He doesn't want the world to know how incredibly talented you are. He wants you to stay in the dark trenches writing hit songs for his brand. He wants you totally dependent on him. I mean, my God, you're sequestered in a tiny bunk on the bus, and you don't even have any friends on the road to hang out with. You live and breathe Travis Miller twenty-four-seven."

"I do, too, have friends."

"Who?"

Ella Mae paused. "All the guys in the band are my friends. Willie's my friend... or he was. Martina and her husband, who run the t-shirt shack, are my friends."

Hank shook his head. "That's not the kind of friendship I'm talking about, and you know it."

His expression softened as he reached out to swipe a big fat tear trailing down her cheek with the pad of his thumb.

"I know you're lonely. I know that's one of the reasons you befriended me back in Langston Falls. And for what it's worth, I'll always be your friend, and I'll always be here for you. But I want to know why you continue to allow Travis to do whatever the hell he wants whenever he wants? Aren't you tired of being used by him? Don't you have your own dreams?"

"You don't understand what we've been through," she whispered.

"Yes, I do. You've paid your dues time and time again. You don't owe the man anything. He doesn't see what I see. He's just ... hopelessly gazing at your brilliance, holding his breath until you wise up. I've seen you shine, Ella Mae. You're kind and compassionate. You're the most selfless person I've ever met in my entire life. You have so much more to offer the world than a few Travis Miller lyrics and melodies."

Ella Mae studied him hard, tears surging and sluicing freely down her face. Her mouth opened as if she were about to say something, but Willie picked that precise moment to invade their private conversation.

"He's deteriorating fast. Unfortunately, we're gonna have to shut this party down."

Chapter Twenty-Four
Ella Mae

Ella Mae numbly stared out the car window into the dark night, the headlights on the highway whizzing by in streaks of blinding high beams. Travis lay passed out in the backseat next to her, his body broken and pathetic, with his head resting in her lap. His lip was swollen where Hank had punched him, and his skin was pale and clammy. Stroking sweaty pieces of hair back from his face, she sat rigid in her seat, her role as caretaker coming to a head.

Was Hank right? Was Travis gaslighting her all these years, turning her into a beck-and-call girl? But he was her only family. He'd kept her out of foster care while she was still in high school, taking on the role of caregiver and provider when their parents died. She owed it to him to make sure he was okay, their role reversal a debt she was happy to pay. Right?

"We'll be there in about ten more minutes, darlin'," Willie announced from the front passenger seat.

Ella Mae nodded in the dark, unsure of how to even communicate with Willie anymore. Was he a friend or foe? One thing was for sure, she was well aware the man was an enabler regarding her brother. And now he wanted to swoop in and act like he'd saved the day by making arrangements to transfer Travis back to a rehab facility near his West Coast home in California. And even if she did want to press charges and have Willie arrested for supplying drugs to her brother, she couldn't because that would probably lead to Travis being arrested for possession. What a mess.

Closing her eyes, she leaned against the seatback and replayed her last moments with Hank. He'd watched helplessly from the wings as Willie, Mario, and some of the band practically carried her brother off stage, the audience booing loudly and John Fobas spewing all kinds of legal threats. The guys managed to get Travis into the back of a vehicle parked near the loading dock, their nearby empty tour bus throwing slanted shadows among the crew.

"*Ella Mae*," Hank had hollered before she opened the back door for her escape.

"I'll... I'll call you as soon as we land." She shrugged, not knowing what else to say under the circumstances.

He nodded and walked right up to her, his strong hands gripping the edges of his cowboy hat held at his stomach. "You're doing the right thing. He's your family. And family... is everything." His voice was deep, coated in warmth, his smile tipping up on one side of his mouth into something beautiful. It was a moment she wanted to stamp into her memory for the days and nights ahead when she knew she'd feel lost and miserable for what might have been.

Taking a deep breath, she held onto those precious seconds and jutted her chin into the air with bravado before offering him a timid wave goodbye.

"Take care of yourself," he waved back.

"You do the same," her voice warbled.

And then he was gone.

The car pulled onto the tarmac of a private runway at a small airport, a team of burly men assisting Travis onto a sleek jet accompanied by a doctor she was sure she'd met before. How Willie, John, or someone else from the record label made this happen in such a short amount of time and away from the lurking paparazzi and fans was beyond her.

Slinging her duffle bag over her shoulder, she carefully ascended the stairs to the plane and entered. Scoping the interior, she found a lush leather window seat near the front, away from the men and her brother, where she wearily planted herself for the long flight ahead.

"Can I get you anything?"

Ella Mae looked up into the kind eyes of a steward, his crisp navy uniform fitting his body like a glove. A stiff cocktail would surely take the edge off, but the mere thought of alcohol made her grimace, knowing her brother was in a precarious state. Shaking her head, she looked away.

"Not right now. Thank you."

The man gave her privacy, and she used the quiet minute to pilfer through her bag to find her phone. The device came to life when she pressed the screen, a picture of her and Hank filling the rectangular space. The photo was a random selfie taken on the day he'd made dinner at her farm. The sun was about to set over the sizzling horizon, the hues of orange and gold rays the perfect backdrop to their happy mood. Their heads were pressed together, their smiles rivaling the radiance of the sunset. They were like the summer in Tennessee, steamy and carefree, shining like the golden hour. But now she was alone again, a cold chill settling deep into her bones.

Shivering, she shook her head. God, if she had known Hank wouldn't be here anymore, she would've made those moments last a little longer. And it was her own damn fault for not giving him a proper goodbye.

Even though they hadn't been together for very long, she knew Hank was more than a friend or a lover. He was wind-chimes in the sticky summer heat, both of their boots propped up onto the front porch railings as they hummed the perfect pitch pinging the wind. He was homemade spaghetti with curls of parmesan cheese, the sauce thick and robust. He was six strings on an acoustic guitar rendering a love song. He was cedar and pine, his warmth enveloping her like a crackling fireside hug on a cool autumn day. Her relationship with him was the closest thing to a happily-ever-after she'd ever experienced. But she couldn't—she wouldn't risk that for a chance to see what they could be. That would mean giving up on her brother and choosing sides, right?

Gritting her teeth, she was well aware she showed up for everyone but herself. And she was tired, so very tired. Maybe it was time she made a hard decision between real love and life. Hank had filled the empty places during their three weeks together, slowly, carefully, with his boyish grin and chivalrous behavior.

Hank Bennett had brought her into the love light.

Her mood turned frantic, and she typed out a text message on her phone with fat fingers, anxious to reach out to him while they were still in the same zip code.

I'm sorry. Please forgive me and my brother.

She immediately frowned and pressed the backspace button, deleting her words. Travis didn't deserve to be a part of her apology text. Chewing on her thumbnail for a beat, she dug deep, the time she and Hank spent together flickering through her mind like an old film projector.

I'm not going to say goodbye to you, okay? For now, it's... goodnight.

Holding her breath, she fastened her seat belt as the jet engines roared to life. Staring at her phone, she was thrilled to see the little bubble with three dots come to life on the screen. Knowing Hank was about to text her back filled her with hope. But then the bubble disappeared, the lack of response filling her with dread. Had she majorly messed this up for them? Was it really over?

The captain's voice crackled through a speaker on the plane, his words monotone in Ella's ears, letting everyone know they were cleared for takeoff. And as the jet surged forward with power pressing her body into the supple leather seat with force, she was rewarded with a distinct ding from her phone. Peering at the one-word response on her lit-up screen induced a burst of happy tears.

Goodnight.

***

Ella Mae looked out the floor-to-ceiling window at the magnificent view of the Pacific Ocean, the water churning with dark waves coming ashore. Crossing her arms against her chest, she glanced at her wristwatch, concerned Travis was late for their first official visit since he'd been checked into the rehab center on that fateful night.

It had been one week since they arrived, seven days since she'd communicated with Hank Bennett. This wasn't by choice but because she needed to think some things through and wanted to ensure Travis was situated before she dropped a bomb on him. She'd had plenty of time during the week while she stayed in his Malibu beach house to ponder her next steps and was confident she was making the right decision.

Hank was right. She was tired of being used by her brother. Was she grateful he was there for her after their parents died, keeping her out of foster care? Damn straight. But she'd paid him back time and time again over the years. Decision made, she was ready to move on with her own dreams, but after she made sure Travis was in the clear. And she sincerely hoped part of those dreams included handsome country music artist Hank Bennett.

Her brother was in precarious health, hospitalized for the first few days to get the drugs and alcohol out of his system. It was touch and go for a few hours, but then, like always, he'd turned a corner. And, like always, she dutifully waited to see him, taking care of the mess he left behind while he underwent treatment.

The door squeaked, and Ella turned to see her brother enter the room. He was alone, his eyes bright with sobriety. There was more color in his complexion, and a thick scruff covered his cheeks. His hair was slicked back as if he'd recently showered, and his sheepish smile indicated he was sorry—like always.

"Hey," she said, keeping her distance.

"Hey."

Ella nodded toward a small table with two chairs in the corner, both of them sitting in silence. She wanted her brother to offer the first icebreaker.

The sound of the ocean seeped through the window's edges, the crashing waves reminding her of holding up a colossal conch shell to her ear when she was a child. Funny how the memories of past beach vacations when her parents were still alive always came to the forefront when she was on the West

Coast. Staring at her brother from across the table, she was reminded of the colorful Hawaiian shirts he used to wear back in those days. Travis emulated their father, who was his music idol, the two of them strumming guitars for anyone on the beach who would listen. Oh, how she wished they could go back in time and relive those precious moments as a family—uncomplicated and innocent, with nothing but love and music to fill their hearts.

Minutes passed, and she finally cleared her throat with irritation. "You're gonna come home to Nashville when you're done, right?"

Travis ran a hand through his shaggy hair, the hospital band around his wrist hard not to notice. "I don't know. Do you not want me to?"

"Of course I want you to." She forced a smile.

"Well, I thought I might stay in California for a while. You know... until things die down."

Ella Mae sighed and reached for his hands from across the table. "I just want you to be healthy and happy."

Travis nodded, averting his gaze. "I'm working on that. Listen, I'm, uh...." His expression contorted, and he sniffled, trying to keep his emotions at bay. But he couldn't and completely broke down, his sobs shredding her heart into pieces.

"I'm a dumb ass. And I'm so sorry." His voice was meek, his humble apology everything she'd wanted to hear.

Coming around the side of the table, she knelt before him, kissing his knuckles with reassurance. "It's okay. It's not your fault. It's the drugs and alcohol. It's not you. You have a disease."

"Yeah, but I humiliated you in front of thousands of people."

"No you didn't."

"I embarrassed you in front of Hank."

"Hank is your biggest fan. You know he loves you."

Travis slid to the floor and wrapped his arms around her, holding on for dear life. They rocked back and forth, the sound of the ocean white noise in the sterile environment.

"It's not your fault," she whispered repeatedly.

But a tiny little voice whispered in her head it was her brother's fault—just like her father's.

Chapter Twenty-Five

Hank

Hank walked along the rows and rows of Christmas trees on Bennett Farms with the sun setting behind the backdrop of the North Georgia Mountains. The late-summer air was still enough to hear how his boots crunched along the hard-packed ground scattered with pine straw. He spread his fingers wide and grazed the edges of the evergreen pine needles with gloved hands, inhaling the familiar scent of his childhood, feeling like he was the only person in the world.

But he wasn't. He had his entire family on the farm with him.

Since he bid Ella Mae goodnight over a text message, he hadn't heard a word from her for the better part of a week. But he understood their circumstances. The entertainment channels and newspapers were filled with grainy video footage and photos of Travis Miller's concert, capturing the man spiraling out of control in front of a sold-out audience. The hashtag "Hank Romeo" was trending for a few days, the media circus following him back to the hotel in St. Louis, where he laid low until he could get out of there unseen. Hank couldn't imagine what Ella and her brother were going through on the West Coast, the paparazzi camped near the rehab center while Travis recovered. He wished he could be there to protect her, be with her, and shelter her. To fulfill his promise, she would never be alone.

Now that he was back in Langston Falls, guarded by the private fenced-in acres of the family compound, he dove back into his former farm life before the Millers. Hank poured himself into the grueling outdoor work, the tour feeling like it happened a million years ago.

He was stressed knowing there was evidence in the world of him striking his country music idol when the man was not in his right mind. Who does that? The only thing on his mind at the time was protecting Ella Mae, the woman he was sure he was in love with.

The phone at Bennett Farms rang off the hook for the first forty-eight hours of his return, news media and nosey townspeople vying for the scoop. Hank's response was always, "no comment," his regretful actions a source of vexation in his mind. If only he could talk to Ella Mae about how to smooth things over with Travis and the fans. But she was in her own self-imposed sequestered bubble, offering no comments to anyone, including him.

Hank stopped among the Fraser firs and watched his oldest brother, Teddy, approach with a grin, indicating it was quitin' time.

"You about done out here?" he asked.

Hank nodded, swiping a gloved hand across his sweaty brow. "Yup."

"Good." Teddy cupped Hank's shoulder, and the two brothers ambled toward the big red barn. "The girls won't be home for supper. They're at a spa retreat in nearby Blue Ridge, celebrating Elyse's post-production with some of the female crew. We thought it'd be fun to have a boy's night while they're gone. You know, grill out at my place, kick back and relax after the hard week with a few burgers and beers? Whatdoyousay?"

Pulling off his work gloves, Hank thought Teddy's invitation sounded like a great idea, especially the part about the beer. Numbing his mind with a few tall ones was the perfect antidote to his stress.

"I'd love that."

After a much-needed shower and change of clothes, Hank hopped into Ted's Jeep, and they headed toward the Bennett/Morgan compound three miles down the road. The wind whipped Hank's hair wildly, the top of the Jeep taken off during the summertime. Barbed wire on fence posts whizzed by on either side of the backcountry roads lit up with the gorgeous afterglow of sunset, the vehicle's headlights guiding them to their destination.

Teddy and his wife, Robyn, lived in the cottage near the pond, the Tiffany-blue home with white shutters pristine from a recent paint job. A screened-in porch looked out over an open meadow and the water. Robyn's late grandmother's farmhouse, where Walt and his fiancé, Elyse, lived, was a tiny blip in the distance against the backdrop of the mountains.

Walt and James were already there and stood among a perimeter of tiki torches lit up to keep the mosquitoes at bay, the charcoal grill already smoldering for the cookout. With bottled beers in their grip, the two threw up their free hands in a wave as Jaxson and Delia cantered across the weathered boards of the dock with tails wagging and snouts panting. The big dogs stopped in the grass and violently shook and rolled, water flying everywhere from their recent dip in the pond.

"Hey, fellas. Thanks for setting up. Did you have trouble finding anything?" Ted asked.

"Nope. Everything was where you said it'd be," Walt replied. "I brought over condiments from the big house and picked up some more beer." He flipped open a nearby cooler and pulled out an iced-down bottle, handing it off to Hank, his biceps flexing against his tight tee. "How you doin', little bro?"

"Yeah. How are you?" James repeated. His expression among the tiki flames appeared concerned, marring his usually handsome face.

Hank took a long pull from the bottle and patted the wet dogs, who sniffed and licked his free hand in a greeting. "I'm good."

James eyed Teddy before taking a swig of his beer. "Well, let's have a seat, and you can fill us in while the charcoal gets nice and hot." The men pulled plastic outdoor chairs into a semi-circle and sat. The summer cicadas and bullfrogs offered a natural symphony of sound among the splashing of dogs back in the pond.

"By the way, Becky insisted I bring dessert she baked for us tonight. It's your favorite, Hank. Chocolate-chip cookie bars."

Hank sighed with gratitude. Leave it so his little sister, Becks, to try to cheer him up with her delicious treats. He tugged on his whiskered chin, the beard peppering his face patchy since he stopped shaving. Eyeing each of his brothers, he contemplated where to begin. He knew this little impromptu cookout was a means to get him to open up, away from their worried father, Roy. As much as he appreciated the brotherly gesture, he was unsure how to explain his feelings.

At the moment, he was indifferent, numb to the national spectacle he was a part of and the repercussions of his actions. His father was the one who told him about the social media backlash against Travis, fans siding with "Hank Romeo," and his gallant behavior protecting Ella Mae. Roy asked if he wanted to make an official statement to appease the curious crowd, which Hank refused. If he were to ever say anything publicly, he wanted it to be with Ella Mae by his side.

"You haven't said much since you got back from St. Louis. Why don't you tell us your version of what went down," Walt encouraged.

James frowned. "But only if you want to, okay? We're here for you. We want to help you get through this. But we don't know how to help if we don't know what happened."

Hank tilted back his beer and finished the bottle, biding some time.

"You want another?" Teddy asked.

"Yeah. Sure." Hank waited for his brother to produce a bottle from the cooler, thankful for the liquid courage. On instinct, he pulled the pocket watch from his jeans and flipped the lid open. His eyes scrolled the faces in the faded photo tucked inside. He did it when he was unsure or stressed, his mother's beautiful face calming his spirit.

"What do you have there? Is that a... pocket watch?" James asked, leaning forward to get a better view.

Walt snickered. "What are you, Hank, a railroad conductor from the 1800s?" His comment induced a bout of rowdy laughter from his brothers.

Ted handed off the beer to Hank and presented his open palm to take a closer look. "May I?"

"Sure." He passed the piece off and watched his brother's rugged face soften within seconds.

"I've always loved this photo." Ted handed the open watch to James.

Walt leaned closer to his brother, their dark heads pressed together, taking in the image of their family posed on the farm's front porch many years ago with their late-mother beaming among her brood. The tiki flames threw slants of orange light across their pensive faces as the big dogs finally shook and settled in the shadows.

"Did Dad give this to you?" Teddy asked. He sat down, leaned his elbows on his knees, and held his beer bottle between his hands.

Hank cleared his throat as James handed the watch back to him. Glancing at the photo a final time, he shut the hunter case of the antique and stuffed it safely into his pocket.

"Yes. Dad gave it to me before I left town for the tour. It belonged to Papaw Bennett."

"That's right!" James announced. "I remember seeing it on a shelf in dad's office."

"Leave it to dad to give you a parting gift. Did he go into one of his weepy speeches? Did he explain why he was giving it to you?" Walt asked.

All three of Hank's brothers looked at him, the curiosity in their expressions vivid. He leaned back in his chair and looked up into the twilight, the smattering of stars starting to brighten the dark sky.

"He said I take after Papaw—that I had big dreams just like him."

"You always have," James offered.

"He said I have wanderlust in my blood and told me the story about how Papaw took over Bennett Farms from his father."

"Tell us," Walt insisted.

"Well, y'all already know most of our family history. Papaw had plans for growing Christmas trees, but he didn't stop there. In his mid-70s, he started growing grapevines on the farm. Apparently, he dreamed of opening a winery but never lived to see it. Daddy said he likes to think Papaw's dream is better than he could have ever imagined because of how we've kept things going."

The four men turned silent for a few seconds, the pride on their expressions noticeable. Hank took another swig of beer, his father's words resonating with him deeply. "Dad said I remind him of Papaw because of my love for music and my desire to make something out of myself. He didn't try to stop me from leaving. In fact, he encouraged me to go. He said I have...." He stopped, a realization suddenly hitting him in the gut.

"You have what?" Walt asked, sitting on the edge of his seat.

Hank's heart seized with understanding, the hope in his being igniting like the charcoal briquettes in the grill. "He said I have what it takes."

"Well, duh. Of course you do. We all know that," Walt quipped.

Swallowing hard, Hank looked toward the dark water of the pond, his fingers rolling his lower lip.

"What's wrong, Hank-ster? Please tell us. You haven't been the same since you came home." Ted's voice was laced with worry.

"Yeah. I mean, we saw the video footage from the concert in St. Louis. Are you being threatened with a lawsuit? Do you need Robyn or Samantha to get involved?" James added.

Hank knew his brothers and father were worried about him. So were the ladies in the family. Since Robyn was a legit lawyer now, and Samantha was an officer of the law, he knew if he needed serious help, any of them would come to his aid. Heck, even his sister, Becky, had enough gumption to weasel him out of a tight spot. And Elyse, with her extensive background in the entertainment industry, might know of a public relations team who could help if need be.

But he wasn't worried about himself. No. His concerns had everything to do with a gorgeous country music songbird.

"I have what it takes," he repeated. Pressing his teeth into his bottom lip, he nodded with decision, the answer to his conundrum tucked among his father's parting words all along.

"So, you're gonna go back to Nashville and play music like you'd planned?" James asked.

Hank stood and squared his shoulders, feeling like a billion pounds had been lifted from his spirit. "Yes, I'm going back to Nashville. But I'm not going back for the music."

"Then why go?" Walt asked, rising to his feet. Ted and James stood too.

Hank looked at each of his brothers, grateful for their unconditional love.

"I'm going back because I have what it takes to love someone—exactly as they are."

Chapter Twenty-Six

Ella Mae

Ella Mae would do the same thing every time she came home from a tour, or in this case, a California rehab. Open all the windows airing out the stuffy rooms of her old farmhouse, filmy curtains billowing in the summer breeze. Place fresh, spindly flowers from her cutting garden in a clear vase on the entry table, the scent of gardenias permeating the rooms, thick like perfume. Croissants for breakfast slathered with real butter and Chuck's wife's homemade strawberry jam. Offer a big bone to Lucky to gnaw on as she sat on her front porch, taking in her brood of chickens hunting and pecking the ground while she drank a second or maybe a third cup of iced coffee amidst the calm pinging of wind chimes.

The repetition of "there's no place like home" from *The Wizard of Oz* ran over and over in her head, condensing the meaning of the word "home" into something else: all hers. But she'd added another tradition to her post-tour checklist, scrolling through her phone and pining over the images of Hank Bennett in the few photo ops they'd shared. She was holding him close, the sweet ache of missing him a sharp pain in her chest.

Shaking her head to clear her thoughts, she steadied herself with a deep breath. She wasn't sure why she hesitated to call him, and by now he probably thought she'd ghosted him. She just needed a little more time to distance herself from the chaos of Travis's tour, and then she'd be all in.

The last time she laid eyes on Hank was ten days ago, the craziness of their last night together nothing but a distant memory in the public eye. A PR Crisis Manager was hired, the same guy Hollywood superstar Brad Pitt had used during his Angelina scandal. Travis's public relations team finally offered the media and fans a statement, letting them know the country star was, in fact, recovering in a California rehab facility for an undetermined amount of time. This seemed to appease the masses, the avalanche of unfavorable news coverage coming to a halt as fans completely switched gears and expressed their well wishes for a speedy recovery. Fans were fickle like that, hating you one day and then expressing their undying devotion the next.

While in California, Ella Mae had a rehabilitation of her own. With boldness, she confronted her brother and finally expressed her desire to branch out independently. At first, he was despondent, begging her to reconsider and promising the sun and the moon. But Ella knew him too well, his selfish motives reminding her how many years she'd lost to accommodating his needs and not her own. Their sibling bond was the longest relationship she'd ever been in, and she owed it to herself to get down to the heart of the matter. He agreed to meet with her and a therapist. During those meetings, she reassured him that her focus moving forward did not include living without him in her life but with loving and healthy boundaries set between them.

Ella grappled with lingering resentments and squabbles throughout their sessions over her role as his sole songwriter and accountability partner. The therapist pointed out that the two of them already had so much to build on, and their good relationship as kids and teens before their parents died was a solid foundation in which to rebuild. They talked a lot and remembered what it was like before. Before fame and fortune. Before Travis's celebrity lifestyle involved drugs, alcohol, and women. Before their little family of four tragically became a family of two.

Ultimately, they agreed to hit the "reset button" on their relationship, her brother reluctantly setting her free to figure things out on her own.

Taking a deep cleansing breath of fresh air to clear the cobwebs of the past, Ella Mae stood to take her breakfast plate back inside. Lucky barked once, causing her to look over her shoulder with the screen door resting on her backside. Frowning, she didn't recognize the truck picking up dust on the dirt road traveling toward her house. Had a sleazy reporter deliberately bypassed her front gate and no trespassing sign on purpose? God, the lengths these people went to get a story.

Setting the plate down, she stood on the top step of her front porch and leaned her shoulder against the post crossing her arms. Her yellow tank top rose and fell in aggravated huffs as she readied herself to give whoever stepped out of the truck a piece of her mind. The hot sun produced a bright glare without her sunglasses, and she winced in the intense light, eyes focused on the vehicle.

The truck door opened, and a man wearing boots and a black cowboy hat exited, his face shaded by the rim. Her breath hitched, and even though she couldn't see his face outright, she knew that blue-jeaned amble anywhere.

"Hank?" Tucking her hair behind her ear, she stood tall, the fluttering of butterflies assaulting her tummy.

His pace slowed, and he reached down to pet Lucky who offered him a wildly wagging tail. Approaching the bottom stair, he was lazy in his actions and removed the hat from his head, his eyes hidden behind sunglasses as he looked up at her. Sweaty curls clung to the nape of his neck, and he held the hat to his chest. She watched him lick his lips.

"Are you done hibernating?" His question left her confused.

"I'm sorry. Hibernating?"

"Yes." He shifted on the pebbled path and removed the sunglasses. His eyes mapped her face, and she could practically feel the drag of his gaze shift downward over her bosom. Wouldn't you know it, she wasn't wearing a bra.

Hank offered a half-smile, his expression holding humor in his dark eyes. "The last thing we texted each other was 'goodnight.' You've been sleeping for a mighty long time, Ella Mae Miller. It's time to wake up."

A slight grin pulled at the edges of her mouth. "I got home from California last night."

"I know."

"Huh?"

"Willie told me."

"Willie? You've been talking to Willie this whole time?"

Hank ascended the porch stairs, each step agonizingly slow. Ella edged back as he stood before her, the sunlight a natural orb surrounding his manly glory. Breathless, her wide eyes roamed his stance, not caring about Willie or how Hank knew she was home or how a delicious heat naturally unfurled between her legs having him so near. The man drove all this way to see her, and she was finally face-to-face with him again.

"Yes. Willie reached out to me to ask if I needed any help navigating the media circus."

Ella Mae bowed her head in shame. She was the one who should've reached out to Hank, not Willie. But she was too wrapped up with her brother and his problems playing caregiver again like she always did. She imagined Hank floundering and wanted to kick herself for not coming to his aid.

"I'm sorry, Hank. You know it's been crazy."

"I know. And you needed space. I knew you'd come around eventually, but truth be told, I got tired of waiting."

By this time, he'd set his hat and glasses on the wide porch rail. His calloused fingers traced her cheeks and reverently cupped her chin. The stroking action of his thumb across the fullness of her lower lip caused her stomach to go haywire from his effortless affection. She swooned on her bare feet, the magnetic pull from her cowboy luring her closer to his handsome face. They were but a breadth apart, eyes thirstily drinking in the other. The air stilled, the sunbeams filtering through a fluffy cloud.

She arched an eyebrow. "Well then, I guess there's only one thing to say."

He pinned her with a playful look, his smile adorably lopsided. "And what do you want to say to me, darlin'?"

Ella Mae leaned in and whispered the words, "good morning," before pressing her lips to Hank's. He groaned and wrapped his arms around her in a tight squeeze, his heated breath rumbling against the shell of her ear.

"Good morning."

Hot lips pressed against her temple, his feather-like kisses making a trail down to her mouth. Their lips and tongues came alive, the simple greeting turning into a passionate longing plea. Her hands danced over his broad shoulders, her grip urging him forward as tears pricked her eyes. For Hank Bennett to make the first move and track her down was a play out of his chivalrous behavior handbook. And how wonderful they were on the same page, her plans to reach out to him on her first day home, something she'd been obsessed with for days. He must've read her mind because here he was in the flesh, driving several hours to welcome her with open arms. What kind of a man even does that? She knew what kind—the man she was in love with.

"I love you," she admitted in an exhale of breath. Her eyes blinked open, shining with tears behind an authentic smile.

Hank palmed her cheeks and tilted his head, looking back at her, his expressive dark eyes holding urgency as if he couldn't respond fast enough.

"I've loved you since the first morning I woke up with you in my arms. You snuck into my bed in that hotel room, remember?"

Ella Mae laughed loudly, her body loose and relaxed as if the weight of the world had been lifted from her shoulders.

"I've loved you since I first spotted you at the outdoor concert in Langston Falls when I was running the t-shirt shack for Martina and her husband. You looked so pitiful and lonely. And a little tipsy, I might add." She continued to hold him, studying him from this vantage point—his arms caging her in his embrace. Dark stubble shadowed his jaw but hardly took away from the look of pure love emanating from his gaze.

"I was absolutely libate-ed. Lonely? Maybe." He hesitated, swallowing hard. "But then you walked into my life. I was standing at a crossroads, and you pointed me in the exact direction I should go. Ella Mae...," he paused for a beat pushing his fingers through the sides of her hair like a comb. "With you by my side, I'll never be lonely again."

She understood because she, too, would never be lonely again. In the darkest night—in the biggest, loudest arena crowd—in the entire freakin' world and universe, she'd never have to search the crowds again.

Because having Hank Bennett in her life meant his face would be the only one she'd ever see.

Chapter Twenty-Seven

Hank

Hank leaned back in the generously sized claw-foot tub, arms and legs wrapped snuggly around Ella Mae's soft body. Candle flames flickered, hazy orange dots peppering the soapy remnants of bubbles on the water's surface. The powdery, romantic scent of lilac permeated the air, the heat from the water and her body causing tiny beads of sweat to glisten on his forehead. She shifted against him, tilting her head and finding the perfect resting crevice between his jaw and clavicle, fingers pruned and tangling with his.

"I want to meet your family," she said simply.

He imagined her face flushed from the steam of hot water—and their earlier love-making. They'd been inseparable since he arrived that morning, his muscles working overtime for hours, pleasing her in the king-sized bed. The deep bath was exactly what they needed, muscles easing and energy replete as they relaxed luxuriously, the woman he loved pressed naked against him.

"I'd love for you to meet my family," he replied with a gentle kiss against her temple.

Hank knew his brothers, sister, and father would welcome Ella Mae with open arms. Roy would undoubtedly be smitten by her southern accent and charm, offering one of his coveted bear hugs before anyone else. Teddy might get emotional and refer to him as Hank-ster, the childhood nickname full of youthful memories and promises they'd never grow up, let alone fall in love. His warm welcome would put Ella at ease among the brood of large men.

Walt would snicker and nod, light-hearted in the moment meeting the woman of Hank's dreams. And James would thrust his hand out in a proper greeting, showing off his manners in front of everyone. Becky would wait patiently for her turn, saving the best for last, her cheerful, sunny smile welcoming his female guest with sisterly love.

"I want to see where you grew up and worked. I want you to show me the loft where you wrote your first song."

Water lapped at the tub's edges as Ella Mae shifted in his arms, visions of stacked hay bales and old floorboards coming to mind. He could almost smell the ripeness and feel the texture in the loft, the hours he sat on the pliable hay scribbling into his wide-ruled notebooks a hazy image of dust and field particles in his mind.

"Can we go visit them soon?"

Hank kissed the lopsided messy bun on top of her head. "We can go whenever you want to, darlin'. I've got nowhere else to be."

The water sloshed and splashed over the porcelain curve of the bathtub. Hank remained languid, marveling at Ella Mae's soft, wet curves in the romantic candlelight. She leaned against the opposite side and faced him, her brow furrowed and her nipples pebbled.

Hank picked up one of her feet and started kneading her arch with his strong fingers. This induced a slow moan from her mouth, and she sank further into the tub, eyes rolling back in her pretty head.

"Does this feel good?" he asked with a sly smile. Pleasing Ella Mae was what he lived for.

"It always feels good with you."

Hank lifted her small foot and kissed the tips of her blue-painted toenails. He could get used to this. Bubble baths in the evening. Unbridled passion during the day. Slow, decadent mornings on a small farm in Tennessee shared with the woman he loved. But he knew there was more to it. They needed to make some plans.

"I have some money saved up," Hank stated, lowering her foot underneath the silky water. Her toes grazed his dick, making him flinch.

"Oh?"

"Yes. I'd like to record a few songs with you. I want to see how far we can take this thing." He stopped and ran a wet hand through his damp hair. "But only if we're on the same page. I don't want to record anything if we don't do it together."

Ella stared back at him, dark eyes emoting calm. "What do you mean exactly when you say 'we'?"

Hank's nostrils flared, and he nodded. "I want to create music with you, Ella Mae. I want us to record our songs, play them for people, and see how far we can go as a duo in this business."

She seemed to be tracking with him, nodding as he rattled off his agenda. "And what if we don't make it in this business? What if it doesn't pan out for us like it did for Travis? What happens then?"

Hank inhaled a deep breath. "Then I guess we call it quits."

Ella Mae recoiled with a grimace. "Call it quits?"

"In the music business." His voice rumbled with laughter.

"Oh," she nodded.

"I mean, we could still write songs. Become session players? The sky's the limit with our combined talents, don't you think? We don't have to be the next Johnny and June."

Her foot tapped his dick again, and he sat up straight, the touch of her hot skin awakening his desire. A splash of water tickled his face, and he blinked back at her. She kneeled in front of him in the water and wrapped her strong hands around his shaft, squeezing.

"Ella Mae...," he warned.

"So, if things don't pan out for us as performers in the music biz, we'll quit, but not quit us, right?" Her hands continued their erotic assault on his raging boner.

An insatiable craving rolled through him, spreading slow and sweet like hot syrup over a stack of buttery flapjacks. His breathing turned erratic, his palms pressed against the bottom of the tub in his rigid seat, feeling every squeeze and pull of her delicate fingers.

"I'll never quit you," he stuttered in an exhale of hot breath.

His eyes traced the flushed curve of her face, the mess of hair on top of her head twisted like a lopsided halo. This woman filled the vacant space in his heart with her kindness and unconditional love. Once upon a time, he was at a crossroads, and she was the one who pointed him in the right direction—toward her.

"I don't think I could ever quit you either." She continued to tug and pump his bulging cock.

His voice came out raw and aroused. "If you don't quit doing what you're doing with your hands, I'm gonna mess up this water real bad."

She offered him a naughty grin and didn't let up. The fracture low in his belly grew bigger and wider, the beginnings of an earthquake in his groin registering a seven on the Richter scale. In an instant, he stood, water sluicing off his body in large rivulets. He offered Ella Mae his hand and helped her out, bath water pooling on the drenched mat. He said nothing and watched in fascination as she kneeled before him like a goddess and took matters into her hands—and mouth. She sucked him hard, and he wavered in his stance, the intensity of her actions lighting up every last nerve ending in his body. His muscles trembled, his tension mounting as the delicious ache of release finally climaxed.

"*Ella*!" he hollered, seizing and grabbing her shoulders for stability. Even with eyes pressed tight, bright flashes blinded him, the release oh so satisfying as he gasped for a precious lungful of air.

His legs wobbled, and he crumpled to the floor on his knees, eye level with Ella Mae. She licked her lips, the aftermath of his orgasm glistening in the corners of her lush mouth. Running her fingers through the sides of his hair, her expression seemed pleased.

"So, we're in agreement then?" she asked.

Hank panted, sweat dribbling down his cheeks. He had no idea what she was talking about, his mind obliterated after her incredible performance. "Say again?"

"We can never quit each other."

His lips morphed into an adoring smile. "Never. I'm in this for the long haul."

She stared back at him for a beat before she shoved her hand out in the small space between them to shake his. Hank cocked his head and laughed. Grabbing her hand, he pulled her flush against his naked body, her wet bosom pressed against his chest.

"I'm yours, no matter what happens," he whispered into her ear.

"You sure about that?" her voice was laced with apprehension.

Pulling back from her, he held her head between his hands and nodded, the seriousness of their light-hearted conversation not lost on him. There was only one other man in her life: her tortured brother, Travis. But he couldn't give her what she needed. He was the one blood relative who continually disappointed her, eroding her self-esteem not only as a performer but as a person. She had no one else—no other family to call her own. Hank wanted her to be a part of *his* family, loved and adored by many with no strings attached.

With Hank, it wasn't about the music or their connection, the rampant desire percolating between them or their unfulfilled dreams. Their relationship needed to start with a promise—to be there for each other through it all, no matter what. He could've never imagined offering this kind of promise to anyone until Ella Mae entered his world.

"Don't you know by now I want to be your everything? Open your heart and let me be the things you are to me. Please."

Ella Mae smiled, eyes shining with unshed tears. "You are my everything, Hank. You're my hopes and our shared dreams. You're the most important person in my life. I... I don't know what I would do if I ever lost you."

"You'll never lose me, Ella Mae. And how exciting is it that we have the rest of our lives to explore our forever together, huh?"

She giggled, wrapping her arms around his neck. "Forever together," she repeated. "Sounds like the beginnings of the perfect country love song."

Chapter Twenty-Eight
Ella Mae

Lucky sat on Ella Mae's lap, his head out the rolled-down window of Hank's truck with tongue and tail wagging. The winding country roads against the backdrop of the majestic North Georgia Mountains were a sight to behold, the horizon elevated with blue-ish green peaks and valleys.

Glancing at Hank, her eyes traced his handsome profile, his hair tussled in the late summer wind whipping in through the open windows. As if sensing her gaze, his dark eyes flicked to hers, and he smiled.

"We're getting close. Are you excited?" He reached for her free hand, not wrapped around her dog, and squeezed.

"Very excited." This was an understatement.

To be free of Travis and his tour agreed with her, life as she knew it slowing way down to a pleasant putter. There was nothing on her agenda. Nothing pressing she had to finish, like revising the bridge of a song or coming up with an upbeat hook for her impatient brother. No angry music execs or over-zealous fans to deal with. Nothing to do but bask in the love light of Hank Bennett and meet his family. There'd be time for writing and recording a demo later, their extended stay at Bennett Farms a welcome respite after the chaos of Travis's unfortunate downfall.

Ella didn't know what to expect at Bennett Farms. The only version of the farm and family she was familiar with was from studying a tiny picture in Hank's pocket watch he carried close to his heart. She'd asked him to share more photos before they left Tennessee, but he insisted she take in the farm in real-time, up close and personal, guaranteeing her a magical experience.

Driving through the quaint downtown area of Langston Falls, she remembered when Hank gave her a quick tour on their way to the river the night they first met. Even then, she knew he was someone special, his calm and kind demeanor a breath of fresh air in her whirlwind touring life. They continued and passed several large farms, including one with a pasture of grazing horses beyond a swoop-style picket fence, the grasses starting to turn from vibrant green to golden in the late season.

"Almost there." Hank grinned. He pointed up ahead. "See the big arch?"

"Yes?"

"That's the farm's entrance."

Ella Mae's pulse ticked. She was anxious to finally meet Hank's family. Restless to meet the pivotal people in his life that made him the man she fell in love with.

The truck slowed, and the entrance of the homestead greeted her with heartwarming splendor, complete with sprawling fields, looming mountains, and a large home reminding her of her own back in Tennessee, only more substantial to accommodate the large brood. Hank drove under the curve of the custom, heavy-gauge steel letters spelling out "Bennett Farms." She noticed perfectly trimmed gardenia bushes dotted with withering white flowers, the scent intoxicating and sweet wafting into the truck. A few tall Georgia pines flanked the entry, the entrance stunning Ella with legitimate awe.

"Wow," she said, turning to look at Hank again. "This looks like a filming location for Yellowstone. You really grew up here?"

"Yep." A look of pride crossed his features as he turned the truck toward the main house on the hill. "This farm has been in my family for generations."

Ella Mae spotted two men on the huge wraparound front porch, their heads turning as Hank punched the gas and sped up the hill. Lucky woofed at the two Labradors bounding across the yard toward the vehicle, the Bennett dogs barking fervently.

"Tell me the dogs' names again?"

"The yellow lab is Delia, and the black lab is Jaxson. They're gonna love having Lucky around." His expression said it all—he was happy to be home.

Ella was transfixed, knowing the older man with salt and pepper hair coming toward them across the grassy knoll was none other than Hank's father, Roy Bennett. The other man, she assumed, was one of Hank's brothers. Which one? She wasn't sure as they all favored one another.

"Hi-ya, Dad!" Hank hollered, putting the truck in park.

Mr. Bennett grinned from ear to ear. "Welcome home, son." He approached the truck's passenger side and opened the door for Ella Mae. Lucky leaped from her arms, startling her.

"*Lucky!*" she hollered, concerned her scrappy dog appeared tiny compared to the Bennetts' large labs. The three animals held their own introductions, sniffing doggie butts and muzzles. Jaxson took off in a frisky run, Lucky happily following.

Roy laughed. "Looks like Lucky's made some new friends. How are you, darlin'?" He offered a hand to help her out of the truck.

"I'm fine, Mr. Bennett."

"Oh, now... Mr. Bennett is way too formal if you ask me. I think we can be on a first-name basis, don't you?"

Ella Mae couldn't help the slow smile unfurling from her lips, Roy Bennett completely putting her at ease. "Okay, Roy. I'm very pleased to finally meet you."

"I'm pleased to meet you, too." Mr. Bennett closed the gap between them, wrapping his arms around her in a firm hug. The tender gesture surprised Ella Mae, her voice turned raspy with emotion. It had been years since she'd received a hug from a father figure.

"Thank you."

The man was all ease, the fleeting scent of pine trees and masculine warmth a familiar combination. They lingered in the hug until Hank slapped a hand across his father's shoulder.

"Hey, Dad."

Roy turned his attention to his son and gave him a bear hug, Ella taking in the exchange with wide eyes. She was startled when the man she assumed was one of Hank's brothers palmed her shoulder.

"Oh!"

"I'm James Bennett. It's so nice to meet you."

"Nice to meet you, too, James."

The two politely shook hands as the three dogs sped by in a flurry of frisky fur and friendly barks. Ella Mae laughed. If this was any indication of how the next few weeks on the farm would be, she was certain she was in for a lot of fun.

"Becky's got your room ready for y'all, and she's been cooking up a storm since you told us you were coming home for a spell. I'm willing to bet she made all your favorites for tonight's supper," Roy said.

"Sounds good, Dad. Becky's the best."

Ella Mae felt Hank sling an arm across her shoulder and glanced his way. His joy was evident, and he winked at her with pleasure.

The foursome meandered into the home, the sprawling open concept with vaulted ceilings and a mammoth stone fireplace reminding her of a five-star hotel in Park City, Utah, but with cozy personal touches. The hearty scent of grilled meat permeated the air, and Ella noticed a woman in the kitchen beyond the living area, sure it was Hank's only sister, Becky Bennett.

As if on cue, Becky turned around and wiped her palms against her apron, her face lighting up with delight. "Hey, y'all! You're early."

A few wisps of golden hair escaped from her high ponytail, and she blew a puff of air, skirting them out of her vision. Hank had told Ella Rebecca was the youngest in the family, an "oops" baby coming into the world and blessing the brothers with a baby sister. Her big, brown eyes fixated on Ella Mae's as she slowly approached.

Ella held her breath, mesmerized by Hank's gorgeous little sister. Sure, she'd watched Becky before on her YouTube cooking show, *The Farmer's Daughter*, but the up-close, in-person version of the woman was stunning. She looked like a model for a Ralph Lauren advertisement.

"Hi, Becky. It's so nice to meet you in person. I'm a huge fan of *The Farmer's Daughter*," Ella Mae said, thrusting her hand out to shake Becky's.

"Oh, my," she giggled. "I'm the one who's a huge fan. Your songs on the radio are incredible."

"Thank you."

"I hope Hank, here, wasn't too much trouble out on the road with you. I know for a fact how messy he can get. We've shared a bathroom in this house forever."

Hank pulled Becky by the arm into his embrace, growling for all to hear. "Now, don't be telling Ella Mae all my dirty little secrets, okay? I'm a changed man, you'll see."

Ella took in the brother and sister exchange, her cheeks aching from smiling so hard.

"Hank, why don't you show Ella Mae around the farm? And I'll have some wine and appetizers ready for y'all when you get back," Becky suggested.

"Yes, and I can unload your things from the truck and get them upstairs, too," James added. "Sound good?"

"Sounds awesome."

"And I'm making one of your favorite meals tonight. Fajitas!"

Hank kissed Becky on the cheek. "Seriously, you're the best, Becks." He looked around at his family. "All of y'all are the best."

Roy took in the domestic scene with hands on his hips, pure bliss emanating from his weathered features. "Teddy and Walt are in the northeast Christmas tree field today with a few hired hands, so steer clear of that section if you're looking for some privacy."

Hank clasped his hand with Ella Mae's and squeezed. "Got it, Dad. We'll be back shortly."

The Bennett Farms vineyard in summer was a breathtaking experience. Standing in between the long trellises, Ella Mae could feel the heat radiating from the earth, the mixed smell of sweet fruit, pine, and green grasses wafting in the gentle breeze. Bees were hard at work, their vibrations harmonizing with the bird's melody. Satisfying rows of grapes and leaves were neatly lined up. Hank explained the fruit on the vine receiving heat and sun was an important contribution to the wine. He also told her how vital the cool mountain breezes and temperature drop at night were, as they allowed the grapes to ripen without stripping the acidity. She learned the days and nights of the beautiful lingering summer harmonized, creating the wine they'd eventually drink from their glass.

"Summertime in the vineyards is when the vines are full of life," he said. "See how the vibrant green leaves and the grape bunches appear and grow? That there is a sign of Véraison."

"Véraison? What's that?" Ella Mae asked.

"It's "berry softening," the point when the grape begins to ripen. It goes from hard to soft. Black grapes will turn red or purple, and the white varieties will become clear."

Ella stopped in her tracks, transfixed by Hank's vineyard knowledge. He laughed, repositioning his hat on his head.

"The grapes will swell and fill with water. Grape sugars then rise, and the acid in the grape drops. My brother, Walt, will start acting like an anxious father waiting for the harvest. And all of us will be hoping and praying there won't be any major storms and only good, steady weather for a couple of months."

"Wow. I had no idea about the depth of hard work that goes into maintaining a vineyard. It's fascinating."

Hank helped her up an embankment, the scent of pine bold and robust. When Ella Mae got her bearings and looked up, a blanket of evergreen surging up the mountain hills lay before her as far as the eye could see.

"Oh, my."

"I know, right?"

"Hank, this is impressive." She turned and looked him right in the eye. "What your family has done here is amazing."

"The Christmas trees are my favorite part of the farming business," he admitted. He stuffed his hands into his back pockets, making his biceps bulge from underneath his short-sleeved tee. "You should see this place in December when happy families come to pick out a tree. There's so much joy and anticipation, you know?"

She scrolled Hank's face, her mind playing back to the years when her little family hunted for the perfect holiday tree. Those were good times, for the most part. She needed to remind herself of the good times.

"I like to think about where our trees end up. Loaded with lights and ornaments and a big ol' bright star on top." Hank arched his neck, looking up at the tall Fraser fir right in front of them. "Presents stacked three deep underneath, little kids begging to open them. Maybe a toy train traveling in circles around the tree stand on a track?" He grinned, his pride apparent. "A little piece of Bennett Farms in other people's homes making their season bright."

Looping her arm through his, Ella Mae leaned against his shoulder, imagining the tree in front of them decked out in seasonal splendor. She could see it all so clearly, exactly the way Hank explained: the lights and ornaments. The star on the very top. Boxes and bags of presents artfully arranged underneath. She could even envision a tiny toy train trundling its way around the base of the Christmas tree, the entire setting picture-perfect.

"I want my next Christmas tree to be from Bennett Farms," she proclaimed.

Hank looked down at her in delighted surprise. "You do?"

"Yes. I sure hope you can deliver."

Hank laughed in his throat, the sound heartfelt and husky.

"For you, Ella Mae, I think that can be arranged."

Chapter Twenty-Nine

Hank

Hank woke up wrapped around Ella Mae, his heartbeat pressed against her back. Cocooned in their own little world in the familiar confines of his boyhood bedroom, he relished her closeness, thankful she fit right in with his family.

As they gathered around the dinner table the previous night, his father, sister, and brothers, with their significant others, which included Robyn, Elyse, and Samantha, made him proud. His jaw physically ached from smiling and laughing, the family meal the perfect start to what he hoped was a long respite from Ella Mae's troubled past with her brother. Travis was, after all, a global phenomenon. And how did one ever get a break from that? By traveling to Langston Falls and sequestering oneself beyond the arching entrance of Bennett Farms, that's how.

Stirring in his arms, Ella Mae sighed.

"Good morning," he whispered, kissing her on the cheek.

"Morning," she mumbled.

"Did you sleep well?"

"Like a rock. You know I get my best sleep in your arms."

Her comment made Hank chuckle, visions of the first night she snuck into his hotel bed coming to mind. It seemed like a lifetime ago.

"And this is the first time in years I haven't woken up lonely or sad," she admitted. "It's a relief to finally feel a part of something—of someone." She shifted to where they were nose to nose in the bed.

Hank watched her wipe her fingertips under her eyes, her natural beauty causing his chest to suddenly feel too small for his heart. She wore one of his faded tees, the same one he'd worn the other day. When she'd slipped it over her head the night before, she'd told him the shirt smelled like him, and he was never getting it back. Saying things like that only anchored him closer, the mere thought of ever losing her inducing a breathlessness he wasn't sure he could ever recover from.

"I hate thinking of you lonely and sad," he admitted. "But I know what you mean. I've been down that road, too—until you came along and pointed me in the right direction."

She gave him a look, a half-smile curled across her lips. There was a secret there, hidden in the blush of her cheeks. For weeks he'd imagined her walking with him through the vineyard and the rows and rows of Christmas trees, just the two of them. He wanted her to sit at his ancestor's dining room table and gab with his entire family, eat a home-cooked meal prepared by his little sister, and watch the dogs chase one another by the big red barn. He wanted her to see and feel the magic of Bennett Farms.

Lucky woofed from his sleeping position on the braided rug beside the bed as Ella Mae's cell phone buzzed. Her brow furrowed as she reached for it.

"That could only be one person texting this early in the morning," she grumbled.

"Who?" Hank asked. She turned the phone around so he could see the screen, Travis's name in bold lettering. "Is he okay?"

Ella Mae sat up among a bevy of pillows and concentrated on the message. "Mmmhmm. He must have insomnia. He says he misses me."

Hank sat up next to her and nodded. "Well, that's a good message, right? It could be worse."

"You got that right." She flung the sheet off her body and stood, bending low to pet her dog. "I'm going to hit the shower before breakfast. Do you mind letting Lucky out for me? I'm sure he'll be happy to see Jax and D again."

"I don't mind at all."

He watched her like a voyeur, her actions jumpy and quick as she grabbed her clothing and exited the room, her mood turned sour. Listening intently to the sound of water from across the hallway in the bathroom, he reached across the bed and flipped her phone over to get a better view of Travis's actual message. He knew full well he should've asked Ella Mae for permission to look at her personal property, but knowing Travis was in a precarious state of mind made him protective of her and what they had together. She was finally starting to relax, and they were making plans—so many plans.

Scrolling the words, he gritted his teeth.

Peaches, I miss you.

I'll never make a mistake again. I promise.

Please reconsider and write songs with me again.

Tour with me again.

Be my baby sister again.

Don't shut me out.

You're being too harsh and unfair.

I love you.

Hank knew it was Ella Mae's decision to distance herself from her narcissistic brother. But would he ever adjust his expectations of her? Probably not. Obviously, he wanted to return to a comfortable status quo within their sibling relationship. But Travis was in a vulnerable state and probably feeling out of control, not owning up to how his behavior hurt Ella. She needed to stay strong and not back down from her decision to live on her own terms. She already expressed her boundaries in an attempt to preserve her integrity. The only way to keep moving forward was to not back down. She needed to be consistent in her reactions every single time he reached out. She needed to show Travis how serious she was about her intentions. Only then would her consistency incentivize real change.

Hank grinned, reading Ella Mae's quick response. Atta girl.

I love you too.

Please don't interrupt me again while I'm on my vacay.

***

Dust particles floated in the beam of sunlight shining through the open barn loft door, the sweet and dusty scent of hay permeating the high space. Hank and Ella Mae sat cross-legged on bales stacked in the corner, their acoustic guitars resting on their thighs. A wide-ruled spiral notebook was opened, Ella scribbling a lyric with a pencil on the lines. Her neat and precise cursive writing induced a lazy smile from Hank's lips. Her eyes flicked to his, and she giggled.

"What?"

"Nothing," he replied.

Shifting to where she rested her forearms on the instrument, she tilted her head. "Seriously, why are you grinning at me like that?"

"Because you're pretty. And... and I love what we're doing here at this moment."

She nodded. "I love it, too. Thanks for showing me your special writing space. Even though it's dusty, hot as hell, and a little hard to get to while carrying a guitar, I love the primitive remoteness away from technology and distractions."

"You mean your cell phone?"

Ella Mae hung her head and sighed. "I'm sure you've noticed. Travis has been texting me non-stop today." Her eyes glimmered with the slightest hope when she looked up at him. "Maybe he's just having a bad day?"

Hank reached for her hand and squeezed. "Sure. It's just a bad day, that's all."

She stared at their hands entwined together, the space between her brows indenting with worry. "But what if it isn't? What if he continues to badger me because I set up boundaries between us?"

"You have to stay strong, Ella Mae. Don't give in."

"I know." She let go of him and shifted the guitar off her lap. "He always does this, Hank. He says he'll do better and give me space, but he never does. And then we end up right back where we started, Travis getting his way. I don't want that to happen again. I want him to give me space. God, he's so suffocating."

"Is he still in California?"

"Yes. He'll probably be there for a while. It's the best place for him, close to his therapist." She rolled her eyes. "I'm so sorry for putting a damper on our day. I promised myself I wouldn't let Travis mess with me, and that's exactly what I'm doing, isn't it?"

"Well, you could always put your phone on silent? Only answer him when it's convenient for you."

"I've already done that," she huffed. "But it's only going to make him try harder to get my attention. I wouldn't be surprised if he tracked me down in person, got on his hands and knees, and begged me to reconsider."

Hank frowned. "Well, let's hope it doesn't come to that. He may get another fist in the mouth or a strong lecture from my father."

Ella Mae's eyes went wide at his comment.

"I'm teasing... maybe." He laid his guitar on a hay bale and shifted closer to her, gripping her thigh with his hand. "This is going to take time. It's not something that'll happen overnight. And don't forget, I'm in this for the long haul. Whatever you need, I'm here for you."

She nodded and placed her hand over his. "Promise?"

"I promise."

Ella Mae hesitated and pressed her teeth into her lower lip.

"Is there more?" he asked.

She swallowed and looked him right in the eye. "He texted to let me know he's been working on a new verse and wants me to take a look at it. But it could be click-bait to get me to respond."

"A new verse? To a new song?"

"No. It's actually... your song."

"Mine?"

"Uhhuh. *Brotherly Love.*"

Hank stilled, his breath caught in his throat.

"I asked him if he's been hiding this from me since we played it together on the bus. He told me with all the time on his hands now, he can really sit down and think, you know? He said the lyrics kind of fell out of him one afternoon while he was pondering his life on the beach. It's the first time he's written anything in ages. He's always written his best stuff when sober, so maybe he's not bullshitting me."

"You sure about that?" Hank asked. There was no telling what lengths Travis Miller might take to get his way and have his sister back by his side.

"He said, and I quote," Ella Mae lifted her phone to peer at the screen.

Run this by Romeo.

I'm emailing you a verse I wrote for his song.

It's from a female perspective.

She looked up as if to gauge his reaction before she continued.

If y'all are going to be performing and recording together, you might as well make his song a duet.

It's a damn good song.

Hank cleared his throat, stunned by his country music idol's admission he'd written a good song. "Wow," he managed to say. "So he thinks my song is good after all."

"Do you want to take a look at it later? Or we can totally ignore him—"

"No," Hank interrupted. "I'd love to look at it later." His focus homed in on Ella Mae's concerned expression, suddenly thankful for a glimmer of hope in their situation.

"Ella, this is good. This shows me Travis is trying to make amends and move on. It sounds like he's coming around and is open to the idea we want to write and perform together. This is positive." He reached for her hand and laced his fingers through hers again.

"You think?"

Hank slowly exhaled in relief, knowing she was still on edge after everything they'd been through.

"I know."

Chapter Thirty
Ella Mae

The clip-clop rhythm of the chestnut horse beneath Ella Mae lulled her into a relaxed state, the tips of the mountains rising ahead of them eclipsed by a muggy summer haze. Hank had asked the family's long-time neighbor, Fred Wagoner, if he could borrow a couple of his horses and show her the countryside on horseback. She was thrilled when the man said yes, the ride something she looked forward to.

A cowboy hat hung low on her head and shaded her eyes, her breasts jiggling underneath her hot-pink tank in the undulating motion of the animal. Eyeing her handsome cowboy riding a black stallion a few feet over, she marveled at the slower pace of life since joining him in the North Georgia Mountains.

They decided to put their music on hold, their remaining days in Langston Falls spent exploring the area, venturing downtown, or fishing at Hank's favorite spot on the river. They hiked near the waterfalls, the freezing water deliciously invigorating after working up a sweat traversing the shaded trails over steep rocks and ravines. Driving ATVs on the Bennett Farm property, Ella discovered more beauty in the rolling vineyards and Christmas trees up close, the dogs cantering from behind, trying to keep up. They swam in the pond on Ted and Robyn's property and watched Elyse in action at a live shoot on a set location nearby, Hank's brother, Walt, beaming with pride. Ella Mae enjoyed coffee talk every morning with Roy and James and often helped Becky in the kitchen. The entire Bennett clan felt like family, and she was more than rested—she was grateful.

A picnic tucked inside a knapsack hung off the back of Hank's dark horse. The only important task for this day was to find the perfect spot to lazily lunch and enjoy each other's company. Nothing was pressing on their agenda, only enjoyment.

The way Hank sat in the well-worn leather saddle over the horse's back in his faded denim jeans replete with his hat and western boots induced a warm flush across her cheeks. He was a good, solid man. Dependable and capable in her time of need. And don't get her started on the way he serviced her body every night, his large hands roaming her curves as his hot mouth licked and kissed every crevice.

"Are you getting hungry?" he asked, eyeing her from underneath the edge of his wide-brimmed hat.

"Always."

Hank pointed at a large meadow where a lone, aged oak tree stood prominent among the faded grass. Ella looked out across the stretch of land, thinking the shade under the gnarled branches of the magnificent tree was the perfect spot for a romantic picnic.

"We could park it under the tree, but you should know that's where my ancestors are buried," Hank said.

Ella Mae glanced at him. "So it's your family's... cemetery?"

"Yes. It's where my mom is buried, too."

A cold shiver peppered her skin, and the heat of the day suddenly vanished. Her parents didn't have a traditional burial, their wishes granted when she and her brother, Travis, forlornly scattered their ashes in the Pacific Ocean.

"Will that be weird or spook you if we take a break here? I mean, we can move on and find another place if it makes you uncomfortable. It's really quite peaceful, though. And the shade from the tree is awesome. Teddy and Robyn got married under this tree last spring."

"It's not weird. I'm fine with it."

Ella Mae allowed the horse to continue the course toward the meadow before Hank brought his to a halt. Climbing off the saddle, he stepped off the graveled road onto the grass and guided the animal toward a rusted gate in the fence line, the hinges squeaking with age as he pulled the animal through.

"Easy does it," he said. He waited for her to go through the opening before closing the gate behind them.

Hank easily hiked his long leg back over his horse and tapped his heels against the animal's belly, inducing a trot. "Come on," he grinned.

Warm air skirted across her face, and dappled light showed through the branches of the mighty oak, highlighting the fading summer leaves. Ella Mae focused on the tree, the whooshing sound from the fluttering foliage comforting in her curious state. As they came closer, she noticed the Bennett family plot of headstones covered in lichen and moss. Hank's mother's stone wasn't hard to pick out, the white marble decorated with a wreath of wilted daisies. He must've noticed her focus and explained.

"Becks likes to come out here from time to time and create those wildflower halos in the summer. It was something she and my mom used to do together. They'd wear them around their necks and in their hair. It was their thing."

The thought made Ella Mae smile, her own longing for those innocent moments as a child with her mother coming at her full force. There was that summer when she and her mom collected seashells on the beach, gluing them to Popsicle sticks and making frames for their vacation photos. They also liked to randomly gather in the kitchen and bake cookies, dozens of oatmeal-raisin, snickerdoodle, chocolate chip, and Travis's favorite, peanut butter. Ella was a whiz at cookie baking, often reverting to the memorable task when she felt especially melancholy and missed her mom. It was always her mother she missed the most. Her dad, not so much.

A gust of air blew tendrils of her long hair back from her face as Hank helped her off the horse. She breathed in the lingering scent of summer, the woodsy musk of the outdoors and ancient farmland mysterious and primitive. Taking her hat off, her eyes traced the area where Hank's family was laid to rest, the beauty surrounding her evoking serenity in her spirit. The unmistakable desire to bake cookies came over her, the memory of her mother entwining with Hank's mom somewhere in the atmosphere symbolic in her fragile mind.

Hank made haste and tied the horses off at a convenient post hammered into the ground, giving the animals leeway to graze the patchy grass. As he untied a rolled-up blanket and the knapsack from the saddle, Ella Mae tenderly ran the tips of her fingers across the words etched into the stone of his mother's marker, "Beloved mother, wife, and friend."

"Hank?"

"Yeah?"

"I need to tell you something."

Hank approached with arms loaded, dropping the items onto the grass a reasonable distance from the tombstones. "What is it?"

Ella Mae set her hat down and busied herself unfurling the blanket so they could sit in the shade. "I haven't been totally honest with you."

Hank took off his hat and ran a hand through his sweaty curls, his lips pressed into a thin line as he lowered his muscular body to the fabric. "What haven't you been honest about?"

Ella inhaled a deep breath through her nose. "My mother and father."

Hank nodded and kept quiet, allowing her to take her time with her forthcoming confession.

"Remember when I told you my parents died in a car accident?"

"Yes."

"Well..." She paused, unsure how to tell him the God-awful truth.

He seemed to sense her anguish and scooted closer, peering into her face. His handsome features were soft and reassuring. "You know you can tell me anything, right?"

"I know," she struggled.

"But you don't have to if you don't want to—"

"No," she interrupted. "I want to. It's just... hard, that's all. Not many people know the truth."

Hank nodded and offered a weak smile. Ella looked up into the bright blue sky through the tree branches. Puffy clouds floated above them, and she was overcome with the need to come clean, especially in his mother's divine presence so near.

"My parents died in a car crash. That part is true. But I didn't tell you the other part."

"Go on," he encouraged, holding her hand.

"My father... he was an alcoholic and a drug abuser, just like Travis. My dad... my dad, was the one driving that day. He'd been drinking and lost control of the car. If my mother hadn't been with him, she'd still be alive. My father killed my mother," she said matter-of-factly.

Hank appeared stunned. Ella Mae sat stoic, her lack of tears reiterating how far she'd come. Through years of therapy, she'd been able to move on from the devastating loss, for the most part. But she rarely talked about her parent's demise with anyone other than her therapist or Travis. She chose to remember the good times, not the bad, the favorable memories of her parents getting her through the most challenging days.

Unfortunately, her mother was an enabler, always attempting to conceal her father's addiction from their friends and family. And she had a hard time setting personal boundaries, something Ella could relate to when it came to Travis's addiction. She knew exactly how her mother must've felt all those years being taken advantage of and used, her father freely engaging in substance abuse right in front of her and Travis as they grew up.

And wasn't Travis cut from the same cloth? Her brother was genetically predisposed to developing alcohol and drug addiction because of their father. And her damn dad didn't help matters, offering Travis alcohol when he was in high school, the two of them bonding over music and beer. Unless her brother continued with professional treatment in California, he faced the inevitable: a relapse, a DUI, or, God forbid, a repeat of her parent's deaths. She'd be damned if she allowed

Travis to continue his behavior around her, the boundaries she set up rock-solid. So she hoped.

With the truth exposed in the summer light, she hoped Hank understood Travis's precarious predicament.

"Wow," he muttered. "That's a lot. I had no idea."

"How could you? I told you my parents died in a car accident but withheld the horrid details. It's not something Travis and I freely go around talking about."

"I understand. And I'm so sorry for your tragic loss." Tucking an errant strand of hair behind her ear, he pressed his palm against her cheek. Ella Mae leaned into him, her eyes fixated on his.

"You're not alone in this thing with your brother."

"I know."

"You've done the right thing setting boundaries. I'm proud of you, Ella Mae."

She offered him a fractured smile, holding on to the possibility she could be stronger than her mother ever was.

"I'm proud of me, too."

Chapter Thirty-One

Hank

Hank leaned comfortably against the mighty oak with Ella Mae's head resting in his lap. Her eyes were closed as he continued stroking his fingertips across her temple into her hair.

God, she was beautiful. The way her long lashes fanned out across her skin and her rosebud lips parted ever so slightly. Her dark hair was soft, caressing the frame of her striking face, and her perfect brow relaxed in an afternoon cat nap. He was overcome with a strong feeling of gratitude, the air thick with heat and primal need, lust, and love. Between her gorgeous features laid prostrate in his lap and her earlier confession regarding her folks, he was feeling it all.

Remnants of their earlier picnic were strewn across the blanket, Hank's thoughts reverting to Travis's admission that he'd written a good song. He was anxious to return to Ella's home in Tennessee, where they'd open her brother's email and scan the verse he'd written specifically for Ella to sing. What could his country music idol have included in the verse? Heartbreak and sorrow were a given with what these two siblings had gone through together. Maybe life in the fast lane? Hotels? Fans? Ella picking up the pieces every single time Travis messed up?

He wondered if Travis was daft enough to think Ella Mae might eventually join him on another tour after everything they'd been through. She'd made her wishes crystal clear when it came to him. He hoped Travis would acquiesce and give her the space she desperately wanted. Selfishly, he wanted to fill the void her brother left behind.

"Mmmmm," Ella hummed, stirring in his lap.

"Hey, sleepy-head."

"Did I dose off?" She blinked back at him from her position, her eyes wide, looking up at him.

"You sure did. You were sawing logs and sounded like one of my brothers."

"I was not!" she laughed, sitting up.

Her hair was tousled, reminding Hank of a backup dancer in a rock and roll video. He grinned, tenderly palming her hair back into place. "I was teasing. You barely made a sound. You were the perfect angel sleeping in my lap."

He watched her eyes trace his face before moving lower to where her head rested moments ago.

"Uh-oh," he murmured. "What's going on in that pretty little head of yours?"

A sly smile unfurled from her lips as she batted her lashes at him. "Do you think anyone will stop by this place today? You mentioned Becky does from time to time."

"I doubt it. The boys are all working on the farm. Dad's gone into town, and Becky's recording an episode for her YouTube channel. Why?"

Ella Mae hoisted a leg over his thighs and straddled him. Pulling a hair tie from her wrist, she gathered her long hair into a ponytail and secured the elastic close to her scalp. Palming his cheeks, she leaned in and kissed him.

"Mmmm. Yummy," he hummed. "You, uh, want to go back to the farm and have a little afternoon delight?" He wiggled his eyebrows comically.

She shook her head, her ponytail swinging from side to side.

"You don't?" His grin faded.

"We don't have to go back to the farm. We can do it out here." She shifted off his lap and unzipped her blue jeans, jerking them down to her ankles.

Hank was stunned and stared up at her in astonishment. Running his hands down her bare legs, he skimmed his fingers across the damp lace of her panties.

"Touch me, Hank."

Dipping his fingers underneath the lace, he stroked her heated center, his penis coming to life and straining against his tight denim. "Does that feel good?"

"Yes," she hissed. Planting her booted feet wide, she leaned forward and pressed her hands against the tree trunk, her ass sticking out from behind her.

Hank exhaled a hot breath and scrambled to get out from under her, insisting she stay planted in her sexy position. "Don't move."

"Why? What have you got in mind, cowboy?" She looked over her shoulder at him, her salacious gaze smoldering, urging him faster.

Jerking his jeans downward from his commando disposition, he came up right behind her and pressed his thick cock against her wet folds. "I've got the right mind to take you from behind." He flicked his fingers against her swollen nub, her body jerking in response. "You're so ready." Inserting two fingers into her hot well, he stroked, her body writhing beneath him. If he didn't get inside her soon, he'd come all over her fine ass. Gripping her hips, he positioned himself at her primed opening and teased.

"Please, Hank," she begged.

He ran his fingertips lightly across her porcelain flesh before his open hand met her skin with a firm slap. She yelped, and he thrust inside her. The grip on her hip bones intensified as sweat poured from his face and dripped onto her hot-pink tee as he pushed himself harder and harder. The summer heat was unforgiving as it swirled around them.

Claiming her like this out in the open was erotic. Sexy. Forbidden. His world spun faster and faster, the dizzying temperature erupting like a volcano as he pounded her from behind.

Hank didn't know if it was the heat from Ella Mae's core, the hot summer sun peeking through the mighty oak's branches, or the idea of being caught out in the open by the ghosts of his ancestral past that made him see stars. On the cusp of orgasm, he yelled out her name and slammed into her with such force he thought he might pass out.

"*Hank*!" Ella shrieked.

His body quaked with release, hot, thick bursts pouring into her. Dragging his lips across her exposed neck underneath her ponytail, he heaved a deep breath.

"Holy shit," he uttered. With his arms wrapped around her middle, he pulled her to a standing position and hugged her from behind. "God, I love you, Ella Mae."

"I love you, too, Hank."

They stood there wrapped up in each other's arms savoring the moment. The lone caw of a crow echoed across the meadow, and a slight breeze tickled Hank's bare bottom. The pounding of his heart dissipated as they pulled up their jeans and gathered their belongings around the tree, sneaking loving looks from each other.

"Would Becky mind if I baked some cookies this afternoon?"

Hank tied off the blanket and knapsack to his saddle, his brow furrowed with curiosity. "She won't mind at all. Why do you want to bake cookies, Ella?"

Parking her hat on her head, she put her boot in the stirrup and hoisted her body onto the horse. "Being out here and seeing your mom's final resting place made me think of my mom. You said the flower halos were her and Becky's thing. Well, baking cookies was kind of our thing."

Hank smiled with understanding. "I think that'd be perfect."

On the graveled road, the two moved slowly on their horses toward Bennett Farms, laughing and talking about anything and everything. The sounds of a vehicle picking up gravel and dust behind them made Hank pause, and he pulled his horse to a stop. He didn't recognize the black truck and waited for the vehicle to pass. But it didn't. The truck came up right next to them.

Hank watched as the tinted driver's side window rolled down, and Willie's bearded face appeared.

"*Willie?*" Ella Mae questioned.

He offered a tentative smile and rested his forearm on the open window. "Hey, Ella Mae. Roy said I might find you out here."

"What do you want, Willie?" Hank asked, the reins in his hands pulled tautly.

"I need to talk to you, Ella. Are y'all headed back to the farm?"

Shaking her head, she became defiant. "No. Tell me right here, Willie. What's Travis done now?"

Willie put the truck in park. His expression was pained, the dark circles underneath his eyes a telling sign he was worried or upset about Travis's latest antics. Or maybe he was miffed he was the one who had to track her down again. "Please. Let's return to the farm where we can sit and talk."

"*No!*"

Hank jerked his head to look at Ella. The horse underneath her grunted and pawed the ground with its hoof.

"What'd he do now, Willie? Another DUI? Or maybe he got into a barroom brawl? Wait, I know what he did. He knocked up some trailer trash hussy and wants me to know he's going to be a father. I guess that means I'll be an auntie. Am I right?" Her tone was condescending, and her face was animated with an exaggerated, cartoonish grin.

Hank didn't like the sound of Ella's voice and quickly dismounted his horse. "Maybe Willie's right, Ella. Maybe we should meet back at the farm and have this conversation."

"Dammit, Willie. How dare you come and interrupt my vacation with Hank? Tell me right now, or don't tell me at all."

Hank anxiously turned to look at Willie for answers knowing Ella was being bold. The man's movements were slow as he exited the vehicle and lumbered closer to Hank.

"He's gone, Ella." His voice held an agonized whisper.

"Pardon?"

Hank looked from Willie to Ella Mae, his mouth gaping with the horrifying truth.

"He's gone."

"What do you mean he's gone? He left California? So, he's back in Nashville?"

"Ella—" Hank started. But she cut him off, moving her horse to the other side of the truck.

"No, Hank! This is between Willie and me." Staring down at the man with wide, watchful eyes, she asked him one last time, "Where is he?"

The big man's face contorted, and he choked on a stifled sob. "He's gone, Ella Mae! He's dead. They found him at his Malibu beach house. He overdosed on a pill laced with fentanyl."

Ella Mae's complexion went white, her dark eyes large staring back at Willie. Her lips trembled as she struggled with a response.

"You're... you're *lying*. This is just one of Travis's pranks to get me to go back on tour with him. You're lying, Willie. I don't believe you."

Willie shook his head and pressed his palms against the truck's hood for support. "I'm not lying about this, darlin'. I would *never* lie to you about something like this. I'm... I'm so, so sorry."

She looked back and forth between them as Hank slowly approached her horse with an outstretched hand. He was desperate to take the reins and get her off the animal and into his arms.

"Come on. Dismount your horse and let Willie take you back to the farm. You're going into shock, Ella, and I—"

Before he could finish his sentence, Ella Mae kicked the animal and took off. Hank went into protection mode and quickly mounted his horse to chase after her.

"*Meet us back at the farm*!" he yelled to Willie. By this time, the large man was openly sobbing and wiping at his face with a tattered bandanna.

Hank stood up in his stirrups, his lean body angled forward, allowing the horse beneath him to move at lightning speed. Ella was a tiny blip in the distance, her ponytail fluttering from behind. He'd passed her wayward cowboy hat a few yards back, discarded along the roadside.

"*Ella*!" he hollered. But she was in full flight response, instigated by the stressful news of her brother's death. She wasn't slowing down.

The powerful stallion easily gained on her, and soon, he galloped alongside her.

"Stop your horse, Ella," he pleaded. His heart broke as she wailed into the strong wind, her beautiful face contorted with absolute sorrow. She wasn't slowing down.

Knowing she wasn't in her right mind and in a dangerous situation, he wrapped the reins around the saddle horn and unhooked his boots from the stirrups. Shifting his weight, he swung one leg over the horse's neck and said a quick prayer, prepared to jump from his horse to hers. He and his brothers had practiced this daredevil stunt a time or two while growing up, but it was always performed after an immature adolescent bet, not during a fight or flight scenario.

Mustering all the strength he could manage, Hank grunted and flung himself through the air between the two animals, landing on the back of the chestnut horse. For a moment, he felt himself slip but managed to cling to Ella and bring himself into an upright position. Grabbing the reins from her hands, he pulled hard, and the horse finally came to a stop.

Adrenaline coursed through his body as he took in deep lungfuls of air, caging Ella Mae between his arms. She was limp in his embrace, succumbing to his gallant attempts at rescuing her, her cries fracturing his heart into a million pieces.

"I've got you," he huskily reminded. "You're safe, Ella. I've got you, and I'm never letting go."

Chapter Thirty-Two
Hank

The view from the back deck of the Bennett home was a feast of color, texture, and light. Evergreen Christmas tree fields. The poppy-red planks of the ancient barn. The smoky North Georgia Mountains on the horizon covered in lush forest hues. The renovated carriage house where his brother James resided. Row after row of twisting vines, striping the earth with vibrant greens and colorful orbs of fruit.

Hank took a deep breath, filling his lungs with the familiar scent of his ancestral land that defied description. He was heartbroken. Devastated. And the urge to run through the fields and weep for Travis and Ella Mae was genuine. He wanted to get lost in the vineyard and hide out for a few precious moments among the evergreen fields. He wanted to run hard across the scattered pine needle paths, pushing himself until his chest threatened to split. But he couldn't fall apart—not with Ella finally fast asleep in his bedroom upstairs. She needed him to be strong for what lay ahead.

Pressing the heel of his hand against his eyes, Hank willed himself to keep it together. Moving back and forth in a slow rhythm in one of the rocking chairs, he heard the screen door creak open and the subsequent click of canine nails on the weathered porch boards. Delia shoved her snout under Hank's hand and sat next to him as if sensing his melancholy mood.

"Hey, girl," his voice rumbled. He'd left Lucky upstairs snuggled against Ella in her bereaved sleep-deprived state.

James sat in the vacant rocking chair next to him. He held a mug of coffee, the scent of body wash from a recent shower surrounding him.

"You're up bright and early," he said.

Hank sighed. "Couldn't sleep."

"Understandable," James hummed. "You get some coffee?"

"Not yet."

The two brothers rocked in silence and watched the golden light of sunrise morph from subtle pinks and lavender to a bold orange creeping above the mountain peaks.

"I keep going over and over it in my head, Jimmy."

James lingered in a sip of coffee before he spoke. "Were there any warning signs?"

"Of course, there were warning signs. He was in a fucking rehab for weeks. He was an addict."

"I know that. But did they figure out where he got the fentanyl-laced pill from?"

Hank stilled the rocking chair. "No. He was alone in his Malibu beach house when he died. He could've gotten it from a friend, or maybe he bought it off the street? I don't know. It wasn't a prescribed medication he took regularly. Ella told me he used Xanax as a recreational drug. He loved the way it made him feel."

James nodded. "Samantha said counterfeit pills sold on the streets are being laced with fentanyl these days."

"What exactly is fentanyl?" Hank asked.

"It's a synthetic opioid. Sam said it's fifty times stronger than heroin and one hundred times stronger than morphine. Illegal drug manufacturers have been mixing their pills with fentanyl to give users a stronger high. Dealers can charge more money because it's more potent than a typical Xanax pill. The deadly combination of Xanax and fentanyl is causing countless deaths and overdoses across the country. It's an epidemic."

His brother stopped rocking and looked right at him. "I'm so sorry you have to deal with all of this, Hank. It's a fucking tragedy. We all know the man was your music idol. If you need anything, you just say the word. We're all here for you and for Ella Mae."

Hank's eyes stung with unshed tears, the lump formed in his throat the size of a wine barrel. "Thanks, bro. I appreciate it." Hank stood and pressed his hand against his brother's arm. "I think I will get some coffee and then shower. It's gonna be a long day."

"Hold up a second," James said, rising to his feet. The look on his face indicated the seriousness of his next words.

"You should be prepared. Everybody is going to want to talk about how Travis died. The news channels, social media, and magazines. You need to help Ella Mae remind the public this isn't about how Travis died. It's about his contribution to the country music world and to your world. I know his life mattered to you. And it mattered to Ella Mae. It mattered to a whole lot of folks who are going to be confused and heartbroken." Love emanated from his eyes as he pinned Hank with an empathetic stare.

His brother continued, his voiced scratched with emotion. "I once heard or read a quote from somewhere that really stuck with me. It went something like this: It's okay to shed tears for another person. It's not a sign of weakness. It's a sign of a pure heart."

Hank clenched his jaw, his brother's heartfelt pep-talk zapping him in the feels.

"Hank-ster, you have the purest heart of us all. Stay strong."

Hank nodded, his warbled words caught in his throat. "I'll try."

James opened his arms wide, the two brothers hugging as the first bright beam of sunlight appeared over the mountain tops, cracking open the morning sky.

"Thank you, Jimmy. I love you, bro."

"I love you, too, Hank-ster. You got this."

***

News of Travis's death stunned the world of country music and his fans. The minutes ticked slowly by on their trek back to Tennessee, Ella shell-shocked and quiet. She sat in the front seat of Hank's truck with Lucky in her lap and stared out the window, her movements slow and gentle as she stroked the animal's fur. Hank kept a sturdy grip on the steering wheel, staying silent to give her space. She'd talk when she was ready.

"I'm hungry," she announced a half hour later.

Hank's mood picked up, knowing Ella hadn't eaten much of anything since their picnic under the oak tree. He reached for her hand and squeezed.

"What's your hankering, darlin'? Anything you want."

Ella Mae stared out the front windshield and licked her lips. "The Loveless Café. It's off the beaten path on Highway 100, west of my place."

"I've heard of it. But isn't it a tourist destination? You sure you don't want me to whip something up for you in the privacy of your home?"

Shaking her head, Ella Mae sat up a little straighter and fished her phone out of her back pocket. "It'll be fine. I'll order for us online, and we can eat outside at one of the picnic tables so Lucky can join us."

"Cool."

She concentrated on the screen before turning toward him. "Travis and I used to make our bus driver, Lenny, stop if we were in the area. We'd order enough food to feed an army and feast for days. I highly recommend the fried chicken. It was always his favorite." The love light in her eyes gleamed and made Hank smile.

"Then fried chicken it is."

The iconic neon roadside sign welcomed them to the Nashville landmark, Hank parking his truck near the old homestead. The house and fourteen-room 1950s motel had been converted to a restaurant and quaint shops for tourists. There was also a huge modernized barn on site used for corporate events and weddings.

Hank helped Ella Mae out of the vehicle, and she set Lucky down. The animal immediately pulled the leash taut, coaxing her toward a grassy area.

"I'll get Lucky taken care of while you pick up our order over there," she pointed. "And I'll meet you in the area with all the picnic tables, okay?"

"Sounds good."

Hank ambled through the parking lot and noticed a large family playing a rousing game of cornhole in the shade. Tipping his cowboy hat at the crew, he smiled, glad to be doing something semi-normal with Ella Mae. He knew it was the calm before the storm. At least she'd have a full belly moving forward.

By the time he picked up two large sacks filled to the brim, his stomach rumbled with anticipation. The succulent Southern food aromas were intense, and he knew he was in for a treat.

Ella Mae squealed with pleasure from her seat at a picnic table when she saw him approach, her eyes shaded by a pair of sunglasses and appearing incognito. Hank set the bags down and pulled two Styrofoam cups and straws off a cardboard carrier.

"Here you go," he said, passing one off to her.

She shoved the straw into the plastic lid and took a huge gulp. "Mmmm. Sweet tea is the nectar of the gods," she playfully announced.

Hank took a sip of his and agreed. "Damn, girl. This is good."

"You ain't seen nothing yet." She grinned.

They noshed on country fried chicken, the dark meat tender and juicy. Ella flicked a few bites toward Lucky, the dog happily indulging. Turnip greens, the famous Loveless biscuits, macaroni and cheese, fried green tomatoes, and marinated cucumbers and onions rounded out their meal, Ella Mae ravenously eating from every container. But it was the last course that really sent Hank into a food coma—banana pudding with house-made vanilla wafers.

"Ugh," he lamented, rubbing his bloated belly after their feast.

Ella Mae seemed to take it all in stride and used her index finger to swipe the last bit of pudding, leaving the container completely empty. "Good, right?"

"Oh, my God. We're coming back, but only once or twice a year, or else I'll end up as big as a house."

Her giggle was heartfelt. "I'm glad you liked it. This was Travis's favorite place. He loved the food here. I thought it'd be... fitting to enjoy one of his favorite meals." She looked around as if thinking back to those times she visited with her brother. Her expression was soft, the earlier signs of despair practically vanished. She started to clean up their picnic area.

"Hold on, Ella Mae," Hank insisted. Leaning across the table, he gripped both of her hands, his focus pinpointed on her beautiful face. "Let's linger here a bit longer. We can play a game of cornhole. Maybe peruse the gift shops and act like tourists. We could take a fun picture in the face-in-hole photo board in front of the famous neon sign."

She cocked her head and smiled. "I think I'd like that. As long as Lucky's in the photo." The dog's ears perked at the sound of his name as if anticipating another scrap of fried chicken.

Hank squeezed her hands, knowing time was a luxury before the inevitable preparations regarding her brother's memorial service and the onslaught of emotions and fatigue that would come with it. A few uninterrupted hours of mindless pleasure and maybe a second helping of banana pudding to-go was absolutely something he could give her.

"Of course, Lucky will be in the picture. He's family. And... family sticks together, right?"

He wasn't sure if the word "family" did it, but Ella opened up to him like a spring flower in full bloom. It was as though she'd finally made her peace with Travis.

"While you were getting our food, some kid over there at the other picnic table started randomly singing one of Travis's hit songs." She swiped the sunglasses off her face and pointed toward a large family gathered together.

"At first, I was angry and wanted him to stop. But as I listened to him sing, something changed inside me." Unshed tears glimmered in her wide eyes as she stared back at him.

"What changed?"

"I realized... it wasn't all for nothing. Travis made an impact on people. He mattered to them. His music mattered."

"Of course it did."

Ella Mae sighed. "You should know I spoke with some of the label execs before we left Langston Falls. They're already making the arrangements for a public memorial service, with my blessing, of course. They're even thinking about having it televised."

"Televised? Wow. And you're good with that?"

She nodded. "I know it's not going to be easy saying goodbye to Travis in front of millions of people. But I know it's what he would've wanted. For myself. For his fans. For you."

"Me?"

A tiny teardrop dribbled down her face as she stared back at him. She reached for his hands again, anchoring herself, and squeezed.

"I need you, Hank, now more than ever. I know you're grieving, too. But... but I need you to help me say goodbye."

Chapter Thirty-Three

Ella Mae

Friends and fans alike came together and celebrated the life and music of Ella Mae's brother, Travis Miller. The televised event took place at Nashville's Ryman Auditorium. The full influence of their collaborative songs and his recordings were felt by numerous country music stars who dropped in to perform or offer a remembrance of the singer who died at the age of thirty-two.

Ella was numb as she stood on hallowed ground in the "Mother Church" of country music. Looking out into the twenty-three-hundred-seat venue of refurbished, century-old, wrap-around church pews, her skin prickled with goosebumps. The entire Bennett family sat on the front row, there for her and Hank every step of the way. Swallowing a lump of emotion, she looked up into the bright lights, awestruck by the legacy and history of the place. She could feel the essence of her brother, who had made his historic Grand Ole Opry debut years ago, and was humbled. Never in a million years did she ever imagine herself performing in this place and saying goodbye to him in front of millions of his fans with Hank by her side.

Hank's acoustic guitar hung around his neck as he rested his right arm on the instrument's body. When the cue was made by the television crew to start, he cleared his throat and removed his cowboy hat from his head, holding it over his heart. His introduction of her brother—his country music idol—moved her, his steady voice reverberating in the great hall with warmth and clarity.

"We are here tonight," he paused, choking up, "to honor an icon who left country music way better than he found it. It's been my honor knowing Travis Miller, and I will always give him full credit for introducing me to his lovely and talented sister, Miss Ella Mae Miller." He swung his arm toward her in the introduction as polite applause ensued.

Ella swallowed, her first words in front of the crowd heartfelt. "Thank you for being here. Thank you from the bottom of my heart."

Feeling Hank's devoted presence next to her, she continued. "Tonight is a celebration of my brother's life. I can't put into words how devastated I am. I miss him so much, but we will *always* have his music, and it will never die."

She picked up Travis's beloved Martin guitar from a stand and slung the strap over her head. Strumming the intro to one of their earlier hits, she continued to speak with a strength she didn't realize she had.

"Travis was my only family. And when it's family, you forgive them. When it's family, you accept them because there is no other choice. When it's family, they're like a reflection of the worst and the best in you. I've always tried to do my best when it came to my brother, but if you knew Travis at all, y'all know he was always putting me to the test."

The audience chuckled, the honest statement adding some levity to the somber occasion. "And now? Well..., now it's up to God to handle the rest."

She counted off the beat to the first song, Travis's longtime band falling into the rhythm. An unexpected, thunderous eruption of applause swelled in the famous auditorium as she looked up into the heavens and started to sing.

For the next hour, the music became the star of the show—music she and her brother created as a means to carry on after her parents died all those years ago. She imagined her brother in heaven, strumming his guitar alongside their musician father, both men wearing outrageous Hawaiian shirts and grinning from ear to ear as their beloved mother clapped along. The vision gave her peace, and she held on to it, realizing she'd come full circle.

Countless songs written by Ella and Travis were performed, the heartfelt tributes from guest country artists fitting for a man who paved the way for so many of them. But she saved the best for last—the final song Travis ever worked on.

A hush fell over the audience as Ella watched Hank's hands pick and strum the guitar effortlessly in the hauntingly beautiful melody he'd created. This was the moment she had feared, the emotional climax performing for her dearly loved brother. Hank's voice echoed throughout the building as he sang, the atmosphere serious and heavy with the weight of grief. The vulnerability and transparency he evoked were precious at that moment. This is what made her love him with everything she had. This was a man who never held back from his emotions. He was real and sensitive, and creative. He was her song, his melody harmonizing with hers and pumping her with new life.

With eyes pressed shut, flashbacks of when she opened Travis's last email came to mind. It was the final correspondence she ever had with her brother, the added verse to Hank's song, *Brotherly Love*, attached to the message and shaking her to her core. She knew this song was good from when Hank first played it for her on the tour bus. And now? Now, this song was going to be a number-one hit, the royalties alone catapulting Hank Bennett into another income bracket. It was as if Travis knew exactly what he was doing in his last days—preparing her for this next stage in her life with Hank by her side.

But it wasn't just the added song lyrics that left her in awe. It was Travis's final words typed at the end of the email, his sentiment filling her with absolute love and forgiveness:

Peaches, it was always you I wanted to be like when I grew up, not dad.

Hank's powerful song was the final selection in the memorial service. Feeling the swell of emotions surge through her, Ella Mae took a deep breath of air, prepared to sing her verse penned by her brother. She sang of Travis's bright light going out too soon and how they never got the chance to say goodbye. And when the band quieted down for the closing acapella chorus, her and Hank's harmonious voices rang out inside the Ryman with love—so much love.

I wish I'd known

How our world would change without you.

I wish you'd known

The way we really felt about you.

Our love was home

And now we're moving on without you

This ole song we wrote about you is all we'll hold.

I wish I'd known.

I wish you'd known.

And now you're... home.

Ella Mae tilted her head skyward and smiled, knowing Travis would've been proud of her. Hank threw his arm across her shoulders, and they bowed to a heartfelt standing ovation. His voice was barely audible when he whispered, "I love you," in her ear.

With tears of relief streaming down her face, she nodded, the weight of this somber day finally off her shoulders.

"I love you, too."

***

For two weeks after the memorial service, Ella Mae made the rounds appearing on morning shows and interviewing with country radio and even popular magazines. She was adamant she carry the narrative of her brother's death. Hank was by her side every step of the way like he promised, his presence a lifeline in the aftermath of her grief.

"I don't want Travis's demise to be part of the gossip nation," she told a host on *Good Morning America*.

"Everyone close to Travis knew about his struggles with addiction. And he was dearly loved by his peers. But the severity of his addiction was more powerful than any amount of adulation from his fans or even me. No matter how often he entered rehab, he couldn't kick it. Addiction is savage, the level of catastrophe going on inside his mind preventing him from any real change."

One interviewer asked her about the rumors of a potential upcoming tour to honor her brother. She was already in talks with label execs, a tour giving her a sense of purpose and a way for her to move on and heal.

"Yes. We've decided to do a tour." Her admission lit up social media, eliciting an overwhelmingly positive response from the fans. She was, after all, co-creator of most of Travis's hit songs, so it wasn't far-fetched.

"Travis would've wanted me to continue, and I will, with my partner, Hank Bennett. There are so many wonderful songs to sing and play, music that Travis became known for."

"I'm hoping these performances will be therapeutic for not only me but for audiences, too. I want to give the people who have grown up on this music and love it so much the opportunity to grieve and celebrate with us. We'll have Travis's original band working with us, too. And I'm so happy to announce Hank Bennett's song, *Brotherly Love*, has gone viral, so I'm sure audiences will be thrilled to hear it live."

Hank beamed from the wings of the television studio.

The interviewer asked, "Speaking of songs, *Brotherly Love* was originally written by Hank Bennett, who wrote about his own brother's struggles, correct?"

"Yes, that's correct. While Hank was with us during the last few weeks of Travis's tour, we worked on his song together. Travis loved it and tweaked a verse for me to sing."

"So, Hank gave you his blessing for his song to turn into a duet?"

Ella Mae glanced at Hank again in the shadows, thankful the world considered them a duo.

"Yes. The song is definitely a duet. As a matter of fact, we've been in the recording studio putting the final touches on the single that'll hit country radio soon. And we're planning on writing more songs we can play and sing together for a full album. We hope the fans will appreciate our efforts in continuing Travis's legacy with some new material added to the mix."

"Well, as an award-winning songwriter, you certainly have what it takes to continue a long and successful career with your talents," the interviewer said.

Thankful for the praise, Ella Mae nodded and wrung her hands together in her lap. "The fans don't need to worry. Even in Travis's death, I plan to work hard on his behalf. And with Hank Bennett by my side, the sky's the limit. Mark my words, y'all will love him and his talents very much."

An adoring smile tipped Hank's lips up into something beautiful. She wanted to stamp the image of her cowboy into her soul for the nights when she might feel lonely and sad for her late brother. Taking in a deep breath, she smiled back at him.

The future belonged to them, their belief in the country music dreams they shared culminating into the perfect pairing. A duo. A twosome. Two people coming together and creating beautiful music together. Music filled with powerful love.

And it was Hank's love that would give her the strength she needed to move on into the next chapter of their lives.

Three Months Later

Hank

Hank Bennett was nervous. Well, nervous was an understatement. He was downright petrified.

Pacing the backstage area in his shiny new boots, he listened to the crowd assembled in the arena. The space buzzed with an undercurrent of excited Travis Miller fans, Hank and Ella Mae's first official show of their three-week tour headlining together, something he'd only dreamed of. He was vaguely aware this was one of John Fobas's venues, the big wig pulling out all the stops for a successful opening night.

Glancing stage left, Hank noticed Willie in the wings giving last-minute instructions to the monitor tech. The big man was dressed up for the occasion with a bolo tie surrounding his neck, and his long hair pulled back into a ponytail. Travis's former road manager was brought on board to help them navigate the new tour, and he was glad Ella and Willie had made their peace with each other. Ella Mae said it best. Willie and the band would always be a part of their music family. And family forgives family.

"Hey, Hank. You look as nervous as a cat on a hot tin roof. Do you need anything?" John Fobas came out of the shadows and slapped him on the back.

"No, sir. I'm fine. Just fine."

John nodded, his signature black suit pressed perfectly. "Three weeks of sold-out shows," he beamed. "Everyone at ASM Global is thrilled y'all decided to partner with us. Whatever you need, just ask. I want to make sure my favorite clients stay happy." He winked enthusiastically.

Hank exhaled a half-laugh, unaccustomed to being the center of attention. "I appreciate it very much."

"Well, good luck tonight in your first show. Enjoy every second."

"Oh, I will. Thanks."

John walked off with a definitive pep in his step, a far cry from the last time they were backstage together when Travis was drunk off his ass. But Hank wasn't going to dwell on those painful memories anymore. Tonight was all about Ella Mae and her amazing gift to his fans.

Hank was happy to be along for the ride, grateful for the opportunity, the accolades, and the financial blessings pouring in from his song, *Brotherly Love*. His dreams of country music fame had come true thanks to Ella. Through her connections, she got his song on country radio, and he vowed to spend the rest of his life thanking her. And continuing to be her personal cabana boy, of course.

But he still had another dream in mind, one that hadn't come to fruition—yet.

The musicians meandered onto the stage, and Hank slipped his acoustic guitar over his head. A guitar tech wired him up as he waited patiently for Ella Mae to get into place. His entire world went into slow motion when she came around the corner.

Hank studied her silently as she approached him, trying to memorize every detail: Her bright smile that rivaled the hot lights. The swaying leather fringe of her custom-made vest that matched her cowboy boots. Thick curls hanging over her shoulders beneath her hat. Her cherry-glossed lips glinting in the illuminated space. She looked like a famous country music star, and he was floored.

Standing beside him, she thanked the guitar tech, who quickly got her situated with her instrument and wireless pack.

"You ready, cowboy?" she asked. There wasn't a hint of nerves in her voice, her professional demeanor apparent by how she treated the crew with her kindness.

Hank couldn't stop staring at her as the band started a low vamp, his heart galloping wildly to the beat. He was at a loss for words, and when he didn't answer her, the space between her brow creased, and she reached for him.

"You okay?"

Hank swallowed and quickly nodded, his voice vaporizing in his throat.

An announcer's booming baritone rumbled over the speakers introducing them. "*Please welcome to the stage, Ella Mae Miller and Hank Bennett!*"

It didn't matter they'd practiced their entrance for months back at a rehearsal studio in Nashville. It didn't matter they were working with seasoned professionals in a freakin' sold-out ASM arena. It didn't matter that he was a farmer's son whose song he originally wrote about his brother had been catapulted into the top ten on country music radio one month after Travis's emotional memorial service at the Ryman. Hank was still stunned speechless, standing there backstage with the love of his life by his side, the two of them about to embark on an adventure of a lifetime.

But his feet wouldn't budge.

Willie appeared from around the corner and ushered them forward. "It's time, kiddos. Knock their boots off!"

Hank shook his head vehemently and held up his palm. "Can you please... give us one more minute?"

Willie looked at Ella Mae, who nodded. Jerking his head toward the loitering crew, he said, "Come on, fellas. Let's give them some space."

The team dispersed, and the band continued to vamp. By this time, the crowd was clapping along to the beat, the immense sound echoing loudly in Hank's ears.

"You got this, Hank," Ella Mae reassured. God, she was gorgeous.

"I know... I just have something I want to ask you before we start this thing."

"Okay?" Her big brown eyes danced with delight. Delight and adoration and precious months of love and sorrow, twisting and twining together like the grapevines back home at his family's winery. Everything they'd been through together. Everything they were going to be together in the future.

"When I first met you, I told you I was at a crossroads. And then you invited me to go on tour with you. You said that after three weeks on the road, if I still felt like I was at a crossroads, you would've failed me. But darlin', I knew after three *days* what I wanted." He paused and touched her silky hair falling over one shoulder.

"I want you, Ella Mae. This isn't about the music or the money, the fame, or the performing. I want *you*. Only you."

She demurely dipped her head, her cheeks blushing with a rosy hue. "You already have me, cowboy."

Hank was sure she could see the outline of his heart thumping through the fabric of his custom-made shirt that matched hers. Slinging his guitar behind his shoulder, he gathered her hands in front of her instrument.

"I love you," he announced.

"I love you, too, Hank. Very much."

"I want you to remember this night and the significance of it forever."

"I promise you, I will. We've been working hard for this."

"No. Not because we've worked hard. And not because Travis's fans are waiting to hear the music. Not because you're finally in the spotlight where you belong. And not because I'm so fucking proud of you and what you've accomplished." His nostrils flared with a deep air intake, the words finally flowing.

"I want you to remember this night because I want to ask you something important, and I need an answer before we walk out there—"

"Hank...," she interrupted, squeezing his hands.

He awkwardly repositioned himself to one knee and looked up at her, his beautiful future towering above.

"Marry me. Let's tell the world together tonight that our duo is official. Marry me and fulfill the biggest dream I've ever had in my life."

Ella Mae slung her guitar behind her and mimicked his posture on the stage floor. The smile she offered him was a rare one. It was a smile she reserved only for him, the one that made him feel like he was soaring and falling at the same time.

"I thought you'd never ask."

Hank grabbed her by the cheeks and pulled her forward into a searing kiss, her love and life pouring into him.

When they came up for air, they were laughing and crying simultaneously as he awkwardly retrieved a diamond engagement ring from his front denim pocket and slipped it on her finger. He'd been carrying the ring around for a week, the diamond burning a hole in his jeans. But he had never found the perfect moment to give it to her until now.

"Oh, Hank!" she exclaimed, admiring the glinting diamond among her splayed fingers.

Helping her to her feet, he kissed her bejeweled hand. "I want to wake up with you in my arms every single morning. I want to write love songs on the front porch. I want to cook spaghetti for you and eat fried chicken and banana pudding at the Loveless Café. And I want—I want to hold your hand every day. I want to be your husband. So is that a yes? Do you want to be my wife?"

"Duo partner, too?"

Her smile made his heart beat double time. "Always my duo partner, darlin'."

"Yes," she said. "I would love to be your wife."

Excited, he ushered her toward the wall of sound and bright lights, anxious to dive into their future together.

"Come on, future wife-ie. Let's do this."

"Ooh, I like the sound of that," she laughed. "Sounds like the beginnings of another new song."

"Our song," he announced.

And as they walked out in front of the masses hand in hand, Hank victoriously lifted their arms into the air to the boisterous roar of the crowd. They were the embodiment of a country love song, honest and sincere. And together, they shared their realness as a duo, a real human experience of true love and loss for the entire world to see.

THE END

Thank you!

Want a glimpse of the Bennett family in earlier years?

Check out this bonus scene but be warned. You're going to need tissues. Click here!

(https://claims.prolificworks.com/free/c0S5ZqbW)

Thank you so much for reading ***Breathless Love!*** I hope you love Hank and Ella Mae as much as I do.

The next book in **The Bennetts of Langston Falls** series continues with Becky's story in ***RECKLESS LOVE***. She's the baby sister in the family who falls for the enemy.

Order ***RECKLESS LOVE*** now so you don't miss it!

And to find out about new books and if I'm singing in a town near you, sign up for my newsletter:

www.kgfletcherauthor.com/contact.htm

Thanks again for reading Hank and Ella Mae's story! Now, turn the page for a look at **Book Four**...

Reckless Love
The Bennetts of Langston Falls ~ Book 4

She's fiercely protected by her four older brothers. He's the arch-enemy of the family. Can the two navigate the pitfalls of forbidden love?

Becky Bennett is a YouTube sensation. Her cooking show, *The Farmer's Daughter*, is a hit, and her role on the family farm is something she's proud of. But being an online success and the queen of Bennett Farms hasn't always been her goal. She'd much rather be working in her garden wearing big floppy hats and overalls, daydreaming about having a little house to call her own. Tired and moody, Becky ponders her lot in life and blames her unforgiving heart on her nemesis, Glen Kirby.

But never in her wildest dreams did she expect to develop feelings for him.

He's more humble in his sobriety, easy to talk to, and has the best intentions when it comes to her family. There's something special about the brawny lumberjack of a man she's known her entire life. But Becky knows her family will never approve and does her best to hide her desire for a man she can't have—a man who almost killed her brother.

When their secret pining is exposed, Becky hightails it out of town, with Glen following closely behind. These two frenemies can't fight their feelings anymore, and his respectful chivalry pays off in a night of extraordinary passion. Every moment with him is stamped on her memory. Every second, every touch, every word. Theirs is a love that was never supposed to happen—and when it does, a dark secret is revealed that could destroy them all.

Is Becky strong enough to fight for her own happily ever after? Or will everything she holds near and dear to her heart implode into a serving of heartache?

Playlist

The Bennetts of Langston Falls

Here are a few favorite songs that inspired my writing for this series. You can download the playlist on Spotify **HERE**

What My World Spins Around - Jordan Davis

I'll Never Love Again – Lady Gaga & Bradley Cooper

Somebody - Justin Bieber

Doin This – Luke Combs

Till You Can't - Cody Johnson

Son of a Sinner – Jelly Roll

Don't Wanna Write This Song – Brett Young

Can't Help Falling in Love - Elvis

American Honey - Lady A

Half of my Hometown – Kelsea Ballerini

Mountain Music - Alabama

Golden Hour – JVKE

Leave Before You Love Me - Jonas bros

Just a Kiss - Lady A

Never Till Now - Ashley Cooke & Brett Young

The Furthest Thing - Maren Morris

Forever For a Little While - Russell Dickerson

I Believe - Jonas Brothers

Want it Again - Thomas Rhett

XO – John Mayer

For more music, books, theater, & to find out if I'm performing in a city near you, check out my website:

www.kgfletcherauthor.com

BONUS ~ ORIGINAL SONG!

Check out the

Original Song featured in:

Breathless Love

The Bennetts of Langston Falls, Book 3

"Brotherly Love"

COMING SOON TO SPOTIFIY

OR

LISTEN ON MY WEBSITE: https://www.kgfletcher-author.com/audiovideo.html

Acknowledgments

As always, I must thank my incredible husband and sons who are my biggest supporters and put up with this Mama constantly working and stressing over deadlines. To my Insta-author friends for sharing the love and letting me know, I'm not alone in this journey as an indie-author. To the best beta readers on the planet, Ladd, Blair, and Craig, thank you for putting up with me talking nonstop about the Bennett Family and how much I love them. Craig, when you sent me that text saying this was the best book I'd ever written, I sobbed. To my Atlanta bestie, Anne, for introducing me to Linville Falls (the inspiration for Langston Falls) and accompanying me on that EPIC book research trip where we met ninety-one year old Jack Wiseman, the patriarch of the Linville Falls Winery. I can't wait to go back again this summer with physical books in tow so we can take ALL the pretty pictures!

HUGE shout-out to my son, Hutch, who helped me pen the original song, *Brotherly Love*. Y'all, we wrote this song in two hours on Christmas Day while the rest of the frat-house watched football. And then we recorded it in his studio in

Atlanta. What a joy it is to watch my boy thrive with music in his life. Hutch, you are a ROCK STAR!

Special thanks to Vicky Burkholder, my long-time editor and friend for making this story shine. And to Gigi Blume, my incredible cover artist at Once Upon a Cover. You are and always will be my author bestie. Thank you for talking me off the ledge.

For my awesome team of ARC readers and all the fantastic bloggers who came on board with this series - THANK YOU for loving romance books as much as I do. Your gorgeous posts and teasers make my heart sing!

For my critique partner, Carrie, who always has my back and makes the best cocktails on our writing retreats. And to all of my readers, thank you for your support. You have no idea how much your kind comments on social media, and your private messages mean to me. I'm so glad we are kindred spirits and can escape into the wonderful world of books. The consistent reviews you've posted on Goodreads, BookBub and Amazon are virtual hugs I will cherish forever.

I hope you will continue the Bennett Family's journey in Book Four of the series, *Reckless Love*. Get ready for Becky's forbidden love story!

xoxo

Kelly

About Kelly Genelle

Dubbed, "The Singing Author," KG Fletcher lives in her very own frat house in Atlanta, GA with her husband Ladd and three sons.

As a singer/songwriter she became a recipient of the "Airplay International Award" for "Best New Artist" showcasing original songs at The Bluebird Café in Nashville, TN. She earned her BFA in theater at Valdosta State University, and has traveled the world professionally as a singer/actress.

KG currently gets to play rock star as a backup singer in the National Tour, "Remember When Rock Was Young – the Elton John Tribute," www.almosteltonjohn.com She is also a summer artist-in-residence at her alma mater performing roles in musicals for the Peach State Summer Theatre program, her favorite roles to date being Donna in *Mamma Mia!*, and Marmee in *Little Women the Musical.* During lockdown and all through the pandemic, KG got creative using a bedroom closet and used her BFA to full advantage narrating and producing the first four books in her Reigning Hearts Series. (Now available on Audible.) She plans on narrating and producing ALL of her stories!

KG is a hopeless romantic. When she's not on the road singing, she's probably at home day dreaming about her swoony book boyfriends, or arranging a yummy charcuterie board while sipping red wine and listening to Frank Sinatra.

KG loves to interact with readers on social media and share about her writing and singing journey. She is also a conference speaker sharing social media basics, and how music can enhance a writer's experience. For more info about tour/conference dates (and FREE concert tickets), go to https://www.kgfletcherauthor.com/contact.htm

Books By KG Fletcher

The Bennetts of Langston Falls Series

Faultless Love (Teddy)

Shameless Love (Walt)

Breathless Love (Hank)

Reckless Love (Rebecca)

Fearless Love (James)

The Stardust Duet

*Love's Refrain

(*2022 Maggie Award of Excellence)

Love's Reverie

Reigning Hearts Series

(Now available in AUDIO and in a BOX SET!)

Run to the Sea (friends-to-lovers beach romance)

Stars Fall From the Sky (small-town-second-chance)

A Sun So Bright (billionaire-heiress-enemies-to-lovers)

I'll See You Again (Scottish-rock star-opposites-attract)

A Cold Creek Christmas (a single-dad holiday novella)

Southern Promises Series

(Now available in a BOX SET!)

Georgia Clay (friends-to-lovers)

Georgia On My Mind (opposites-attract)

*Georgia Pine (second-chance)

(*2019 Maggie Award of Excellence Finalist*)

__Single Titles__

Unexpected (millionaire-romantic-suspense)

Love Song (friends-to-lovers rock & roll suspense)

The Nearness of You (British-celebrity-love-at-first-sight)

www.kgfletcherauthor.com

Hang Out with KG!

f
facebook.com/kgfletcherauthor/

BB
bookbub.com/profile/kg-fletcher

g
goodreads.com/author/show/16175390.K_G_Fletcher

instagram.com/kellyf9393/

tiktok.com/@kgfletcherauthor/

https://twitter.com/kgfletcher3

pinterest.com/kfletcher3

http://www.youtube.com/channel/UCxD4r0_mOYWWiVmlT_JSSdg

amazon.com/K-G-Fletcher/e/B01MECVIJ1?ref=sr_ntt_srch_lnk_1&qid=1661799285&sr=1-1

You can also sign up for my **NEWSLETTER** and receive exclusive content, bonus scenes, and comp tickets to shows!

BUT WAIT, THERE'S MORE!

Can't get enough romance?

How about my **FREE** yummy, bite-sized short story, **SWEET THING**:

Life after the breakup was peachy, but unexpected forbidden fruit made her crave more.

Click here for SWEET THING

(or go to my website: www.kgfletcherauthor.com)

Praise For KG!

"I can't put into words what it is about this author's writing that draws me in & doesn't let go, literally till the end." ~ Goodreads Reviewer

"Well-written stories with simply addictive storylines. KG Fletcher's characters are relatable & lovable, sweet & sexy." ~ Blushing Book Reviews

"Beautifully written, expertly crafted & so, so romantic." ~ USA Today Bestselling Author, GiGi Blume

"I don't know how she does it, but she always manages to tug at my heart strings. Hard." ~ Amazon Reviewer

#lovealwayswins

Made in the USA
Columbia, SC
27 April 2023